HIGH
JOVE HO

"In all of the H
I've been very taken with the loving renderings of
colorful small-town people doing small-town things
and bringing 5 STAR and GOLD 5 STAR rank-
ings to the readers. This series should be selling off
the bookshelves within hours! Never have I given a
series an overall review, but I feel this one, thus far,
deserves it! Continue the excellent choices in au-
thors and editors! It's working for this reviewer!"
—*Heartland Critiques*

We at Jove Books are thrilled by the enthusiastic critical
acclaim that the Homespun Romances are receiving. We
would like to thank you, the readers and fans of this wonderful series, for making it the success that it is. It is our
pleasure to bring you the highest quality of romance writing in these breathtaking tales of love and family in the
heartland of America.

And now, sit back and enjoy this delightful new Homespun Romance . . .

CAROLINE'S PROMISE
by Deborah Wood

Praise for *Maggie's Pride*:

"*Maggie's Pride* will thrill readers of romance."
—*Salem Statesman Journal*

"A wonderfully warm story!"
—*The Literary Times*

"Sure to warm the cockles of your heart."
—*Romantic Times*

Titles by Deborah Wood
(who also writes as Deborah Lawrence)

GENTLE HEARTS

SUMMER'S GIFT

HEART'S SONG

MAGGIE'S PRIDE

HUMBLE PIE

THE HAT BOX

CAROLINE'S PROMISE

Caroline's Promise

Deborah Wood

J

JOVE BOOKS, NEW YORK

CAROLINE'S PROMISE

A Jove Book / published by arrangement with
the author

PRINTING HISTORY
Jove edition / December 1997

The Putnam Berkley World Wide Web site address is
http://www.berkley.com

ISBN: 0-515-12193-2

A JOVE BOOK®
Jove Books are published by The Berkley Publishing Group,
a member of Penguin Putnam Inc.,
200 Madison Avenue, New York, New York 10016.
JOVE and the "J" design are trademarks
belonging to Jove Publications, Inc.

PRINTED IN THE UNITED STATES OF AMERICA

10 9 8 7 6 5 4 3 2 1

For the Birthday Club—
Betty Crumpler, Dawn Bredimus, Eve Della Ville,
Georgia Danna, Laurie Barnhill, Maralyn Gerdes,
Margaret Miller, Paulette Isham, Shirley Zerman,
and Susan Barnes—Lincoln City's finest

And a special thanks to Tucker
for his unique inspiration

1

THE STORM HAD finally moved on. Caroline Dobbs opened all the windows in her house and tied back the drapes in the parlor. The sunlight was almost blinding after the latest cloudburst that had lasted for days and devastated the Willamette Valley. As she emptied the bucket of rainwater that had leaked through her roof overnight, her cat, Tucker, darted outside. He came to a sliding halt at the edge of the lower step with his thick black tail high in the air, eyed the water-soaked yard, and gave a shrill cry.

She returned to the kitchen and freshened the pot of tea for her houseguest, Mrs. Williams. Two days before, the poor woman had been rescued from the flooding Willamette River above the falls and brought to Caroline's because her house was on high ground and because the men hoped she could nurse Mrs. Williams. She was in the family way and her husband hadn't been found yet.

Caroline had tried to keep her guest's spirits up, but it was becoming more difficult with each passing day. She had lost Mr. Dobbs just before her twenty-fourth birthday, almost two and a half years ago, and knew if Mr. Williams had drowned, it would be difficult for his wife to recover from the loss. Caroline had just set the teapot on the tray when there was a knock at the front door.

The moment she opened the door and saw the man, her hopes soared. He had to be Mr. Williams looking for his wife. He was different from what she had imagined, but she almost hugged him. "May I help you?" He was a powerful man, she thought, noticing the way his shirt barely fit his large frame.

He pulled his hat off and smiled. "Are you Mrs. Dobbs?"

His hat had covered dark brown wavy hair, and Caroline quickly imagined Mrs. Williams's baby with dark eyes and hair. "I am. Are you Mr. Williams?" He stood on the top step and was still a head taller than she.

"No, ma'am." Her disappointment struck a familiar chord, one that still angered him, even after five years. However, her character wasn't his concern and had nothing to do with why he was there. "I'm Daniel Grey. Mr. Bennett said you needed some repairs on your house." The valley was flooded, Oregon City waterlogged, and she looked as fresh and pretty as if it were a summer day. Her reddish-brown hair swept back from her sparkling hazel eyes and her dark red dress did a good job of showing off her fine figure. The sign out front said she was a dressmaker, and Bennett mentioned that she was a widow. Daniel didn't think she would remain one for long, but his judgment wasn't all that good. He'd thought his wife was faithful, until he discovered otherwise.

Gilbert had told her he knew a man who he believed would do the needed repairs, but he had neglected to forewarn her about the visit. Mr. Grey had a prominent chin and a pleasant voice, though a bit gruff. She caught herself staring at his full lower lip and glanced away. Knowing how particular Gilbert could be, she was certain Mr. Grey must be a decent man. She stepped back and held the door wide open. "Please, come inside."

"My boots are caked with mud. I better not. Mr. Bennett said your roof leaked."

"Yes, in several places, and the windows on the south wall leaked, too."

He leaned around the corner and peered past her into the parlor. There was a nice upholstered sofa, small tables, a sturdy armchair, and a caned rocker—mahogany—finished with deep crowning, curved armrests, and scalloped edge. On one side of the fireplace was a window, and water stains discolored the wall. "That side got the brunt of the wind and rain the last six weeks. Is there another room behind that one?"

She nodded. "Two, I'm afraid." Her bedroom was just beyond the parlor and the sewing room, where Mrs. Williams was settled, at the back corner of the house. However Caroline couldn't allow him to barge in on her without any warning.

"After I check the windows on that south side, I'll get my ladder and take a look at the roof."

"Thank you, Mr. Grey." She watched until he had walked around the outside of the house toward her room, then hurried back to the sewing room with the tea tray.

Mrs. Williams met her at the door. "Mrs. Dobbs, there's a man outside the window," she whispered.

"It's all right. That's Mr. Grey, and I hope he'll be able to repair the leaky roof and windows." Caroline saw him pass by again, returning to the front of the house. "Now that you feel like getting up, you don't have to stay in there. Would you like to have tea in the parlor?" Mrs. Williams was wearing the only clothes she possessed—the clothes she wore the night she and her husband tried to cross the Willamette—a high-waisted, faded green calico dress. The circles under her blue eyes grew darker each day. Caroline had braided the woman's dark hair, and it hung down her back as if it were a weighted pendulum.

Mrs. Williams braced the small of her back with one hand and lightly rubbed her swollen abdomen with the other. "Thank you. I would enjoy that. I'm sorry to be such a bother," she said, following Caroline down the hall, "puttin' you out of your sewin' room. An' you shouldn't wait on me like this. You're spoilin' me."

"You're no trouble. I enjoy your company." Caroline set the tray down on the marble-top table and smiled. "By the way you're carrying that little one, your time must be close."

"I calculated it'd be about midmonth." Mrs. Williams groaned and arched her back. "It feels like he's rowin' a boat. At least he's healthy. The others weren't nearly this strong. Maybe this one will survive," she said with a sob. Tears sprang to her eyes, and she clamped her teeth down on her lips.

Caroline quickly moved to Mrs. Williams's side and put her arm around her. "Don't fret over him. The way that babe's kicking, he's good and strong." Every woman who had ever carried a babe in her womb knew the fear Mrs. Williams was feeling, but Caroline didn't want her dwelling on it. "He's a big one, you'll see." The woman was overly large, and Caroline couldn't help wondering if her calculations were wrong. Babies weren't born on time, she thought. Trains and stagecoaches didn't stay on schedule; why should a baby's birth be any different?

Mrs. Williams gave a weak nod. "That's why Mr. Williams was so set on crossin' the river. After most of Lynn City washed away in the flood, he believed we'd be safer over here. An' close to a doctor if the baby was birthed sickly." Her eyes were awash in tears, but she kept lightly rubbing her extended abdomen.

Caroline understood her grief. Each day she waited for word about Mr. Williams, but she was hesitant to mention him to his wife. "All the towns along the Williamette have lost buildings. My good friend, Maggie Foster, lost her stern-wheeler." Mr. Grey's heavy footsteps on the roof gave her a start. She looked up and hoped he wouldn't fall.

"I couldn't believe what the current carried downriver." Mrs. Williams picked up the cup of tea, glanced at the ceiling, and slowly paced the length of the parlor. "I'm sure I saw an outhouse go by us in the water."

"Would you like to step outside? A spring day couldn't be nicer. The fresh air and sunshine would be good for you." And if it's her time, Caroline thought, walking would help ease the pain a bit. At least she believed it had helped her.

Mrs. Williams paused in front of the stone fireplace and sipped the tea. "I'd like to go out for a while. I thought I heard the waterfalls last night. It is far from here? I'd like to see it."

"It's down the hill. But it might be too much for you right now." Caroline drank some of her tea. She was relieved Mrs. Williams felt better. This was the first time since she arrived that she had the strength or interest to leave the sewing room. If she stayed a few more days, she might regain her energy and the birthing would be easier on her. The noise from the roof stopped. Caroline excused herself and went outside to speak with Mr. Grey.

Daniel lowered the ladder and started toward his wagon with it. Bennett had suggested that this repair work was important, but Daniel didn't think a leaky roof compared with a missing roof or walls. The ground was so water-logged in areas that many buildings had shifted on their foundation and were listing; others had to be razed. Even

Governor Abernethy's old brick store had fallen last night, so it was difficult for Daniel to understand the urgency with Mrs. Dobbs's job. When he passed the front corner of her house, she was standing in her front yard looking as bright as the day.

She didn't feel encouraged by the expression on his face and tried to remember how much money she had put away for emergencies. Dressmaking earned her enough money to live simply without having to remarry, but, with half the town being flooded out, she knew she wouldn't have much work, if any, for a long time. "How bad is it? Can you mend the leaks?"

He walked by her and put the ladder in the back of his wagon. Her windows needed repairing and the roof had at least two large leaks, but he was already committed to rebuilding part of Peterson's Dry Goods store. He brushed off his hands on his trousers as he turned to her. "The sashes have split corners and the molding needs to be replaced on one window." From the look on her face, he figured she didn't really understand what he'd said, but she didn't need to; he did.

She stared at him. He seemed cross with her, and she wasn't too happy with him, either. "You don't appear to be interested in doing the work. If not, why did you bother to check my windows and roof? What did Mr. Bennett say to you?"

So, he thought, there was more to the lady than a nice face, becoming shape, and pleasing voice. "Bennett made it clear the damage to your house needed to be attended to before my other work." He shrugged. "I expected to find a missing wall or foundation problems—major damage."

"I see," she said, insulted by Gilbert's overbearing inter-ference. "Did he tell you who would be paying you?"

"Not exactly." Daniel shifted his weight from one leg to the other. "He did tell me to report back to him."

"You needn't bother, Mr. Grey. I am responsible for my own debts. No one else is. If you don't want to do the work, I understand. But would you be kind enough to show me the damage to the windows and point out the problem with the roof before you leave?" Tucker ran around the corner of the house and planted himself at her side.

Daniel didn't want to know what was going on between her and Bennett, but his money was on her. Daniel glanced at the cat's defensive pose and decided it must be a male. "I'd be glad to, Mrs. Dobbs." He walked with her to the south side of her house. "This is the window sash," he said, pointing to the corner of the boards framing the window. "See how the two pieces of wood have come apart?"

She nodded and looked at each of the corners. No wonder the water poured into the house. Her husband had taken care of the upkeep, and she really hadn't given any thought to the maintenance. "Can they be fixed? Or will I have to have the glass put into new frames? If I didn't enjoy looking out so much, I'd have them walled over."

He chuckled. "It isn't that bad. A fairly easy job." He motioned to the front of the house and returned to the wagon with her. "You don't want to get on the roof, do you?"

His expression remained somber, but the glint in his brown eyes betrayed his teasing. She glanced down at her wine-colored day dress. "I'm not attired for climbing ladders today. Maybe some other time." He was still watching her, and she turned her attention to the roof.

He followed her lead, knowing he shouldn't treat her any different from Bennett or Peterson. "If you look at each of the shingles, you might be able to see that some are lifting up. And a lot of them are split. The roof's going to be more costly to repair than the windows."

As she stared at the roof, she silently counted the pieces that looked different. "How much are shingles?"

He glanced sideways at her, but her gaze was fixed on the roof. "At least half will have to be replaced. They might be as much as a dollar forty or fifty cents. It takes time to remove the old ones and replace them. Most of the cost will be in the labor."

The shingles sounded quite reasonable to her. If only she'd been a tomboy and weren't afraid to climb up to the roof, she would figure out how to do the repairs herself. He clearly wasn't interested in doing the work, but with so much flood damage in town, she couldn't blame him. "I appreciate your coming by, Mr. Grey." She met his gaze and felt a wave of disappointment. He seemed to be an honest man and probably did good work. "I'll be sure to tell Mr. Bennett what you've explained to me."

He'd expected her to ask him what he'd charge to do the work, but she didn't. Was she too proud? Didn't she have the money? Or was it him? "If you don't know any other carpenters, I could give you some names." If she had, why would Bennett have nearly insisted he estimate the work? Daniel wondered.

"That—" won't be necessary, she almost said, but stopped herself in time. She didn't know another carpenter or fix-it man, and she couldn't ask her neighbors for help. One of her neighbors was Mr. Noyle, a quiet gentle man, who wrote Oregon pioneer stories, lived on one side, and on the other was Mrs. Kinney, an elderly woman. Gilbert, Caroline thought, would be more trouble than help with his imposing ways. "I suppose most able-bodied men have already been hired."

"Even the sluggards are now helping out."

She grinned. "Do you know of anyone who needs the work and can do it?"

"I'd have to ask around. If the weather holds, it'll give you more time."

"And if it doesn't?" This was the rainy season, as if they hadn't already had enough to last another two months or more. She brushed at her skirt and glanced at the house. "You must be busy, and I have a houseguest. Good-bye, Mr. Grey."

When she started for the front door without a backward glance, he called, "Mrs. Dobbs—" though he wasn't sure why. Maybe it was her stubborn pride, maybe it was because his second opinion of her was higher than the first, or maybe it was because she didn't flirt and try to coax him, but it didn't make any difference. "Do you have something against me doing the work?"

Had she heard him right? She turned to him at the top step. "I didn't think you wanted the job." He wasn't a strikingly handsome man, but he had nice eyes and mouth, and a direct gaze. She liked that.

"If you don't mind my putting in a few hours each evening, I can do it." He figured he'd have it finished in a week at most, especially with his son, Ethan, helping him.

"What would you charge?"

"The work isn't as hard as some. A dollar sixty for a ten-hour day is a fair wage. I'd charge you by the hour, sixteen cents." He usually got a dollar seventy-five a day, but he didn't think she'd appreciate getting a "widow's special" rate.

"How many evenings do you think it will take you?"

"Four with my son helping me."

That's twelve hours, she calculated, a dollar ninety-two for each, plus the shingles and whatever else he would need. And it might take him longer than four days, she realized. However, the repairs must be made, and she did have money tucked away for such an emergency.

He watched her thinking. She had a nice wood-frame house, but it needed some work besides the south windows and roof. Being a widow, he thought, the expenses might be an imposition for her. "Ethan, my boy, is thirteen and only an apprentice. He gets seventy-five cents for a full day."

She remembered when she was ten and she had sewn for old Mrs. Frobisher after school and on weekends. It didn't matter how difficult the hems, seams, or fancy stitches were, she received five cents for five hours' work. "That doesn't sound fair. If he works as hard as you, his wages should be the same."

Daniel shook his head. "Don't you tell him that. He's an apprentice, just learning the craft."

For whatever reason, he had changed his mind, and she wasn't about to ask why. A ripple of relief washed over her. "When can you start, Mr. Grey?"

"I'll see about the shingles. With most of the mills and warehouses flooded out, they're in short supply. But we'll be here tomorrow evening." She smiled, a beautiful sight, and he was glad he'd relented.

"That will be fine. Thank you." She stepped inside and glanced back at Mr. Grey. There was something about him that intrigued her. He wasn't anything like Gilbert Bennett, and that was to Mr. Grey's credit. She didn't close the door until he had ridden away. She thought tomorrow would be a perfect day to begin the repairs. By then Mrs. Williams should be feeling even better and hopefully wouldn't be bothered by the noise.

That evening Caroline served hearty beef stew and biscuits for supper in the dining room. She sat across the table from Mrs. Williams. Tucker lay at Caroline's feet. The drapes were drawn and the table was set as if for a small dinner party. Usually she didn't bother with the amenities. "We can start making a few night dresses for your baby. I didn't want to mention it before, but your things are probably scattered downriver for miles and your baby's going to need a few things to start with."

Mrs. Williams nodded and rested her fork on the plate. She glanced in Caroline's direction without quite looking into her eyes. "I saved the dresses, nappies, and slips from the other babies and made more. Caps and socks, too." Tears streamed down her cheeks. "M . . . Mr. Williams was makin' a real nice cradle. We lost the old one on the trail through the Blue Mountains. He—" Mrs. Williams covered her face with her hands and gave in to the tears.

After the first night Mrs. Williams hadn't talked about her husband, and Caroline had been reluctant to also. The poor woman had lost her home and her belongings, but she clung to her hope with a desperation born in suffering. They both feared Mr. Williams had drowned, and neither wanted to voice that belief. When the baby came, at least Mrs. Williams would have their child to love and to help ease the loneliness. Caroline buttered a biscuit and wished Mrs. Williams would eat.

Mrs. Williams dried her tears with the napkin, then speared a piece of carrot with the fork. "I know I shouldn't be afraid or have bad thoughts. They might scar the baby or make him slow-witted, but I dearly miss Mr. Williams."

"Of course you do, and I don't believe what you think can harm your baby. I've known women who weren't very charitable or Christian in their manner or speech, and they delivered healthy babies." Caroline gave her an encouraging smile. "I'm sure yours will be beautiful and smart and strong."

Mrs. Williams muffled a groan and straightened her back. "I declare, he's not goin' to wait much longer."

Caroline watched Mrs. Williams's belly. The baby's movements were easy to see beneath the taut dress she wore. "He is a busy little fellow. You can eat standing up if you'd be more comfortable. He might be a bit cramped when you sit down."

Mrs. Williams braced her hands on the table and slowly got to her feet. "Oh, this does feel better."

Caroline dawdled over her meal, giving Mrs. Williams time to finish eating. As Caroline continued watching her, she realized she'd better not put off cutting out a few nappies, soakers—that held the nappie in place—and a couple of gowns. She lost her first baby early in the pregnancy and her second one a month before her time. Later, she gave away the baby clothes she had made, except the special gown she'd embroidered with honeysuckle around the neck and hem.

Suddenly Mrs. Williams cried out and bent over.

Tucker darted into the kitchen. Caroline sprang to her feet and ran to Mrs. Williams's side. "That was a strong one."

"Ugh—" Mrs. Williams gasped. "I think he means to be born tonight." She looked into Caroline's eyes. "You will help me, won't you?"

"I won't leave you, but I can send for Dr. Lindley if you want me to." Caroline wrapped her arm around Mrs. Williams's shoulder to steady her. "Or Mrs. Riggs—she's delivered babies here for years."

"You've helped birth babies, haven't you, Mrs. Dobbs?" Mrs. Williams watched Caroline.

"Yes, a few times." Caroline didn't want to mention her own miscarriages, not now, when Mrs. Williams was already worried.

"Then I don't see no need for a doctor or midwife. Women've been birthin' babies and, when it's the good Lord's will, they do just fine. This isn't my first."

Caroline nodded, understanding that Mrs. Williams had

put her fate in the Almighty's hands, as so many women did during pregnancy and especially the birthing. "Won't you call me Caroline? It sounds friendlier, and Mrs. Dobbs seems so formal under the circumstances."

"I wish you'd call me Addie." She started to smile, but her expression turned to one of surprise. She stared down at her belly as liquid ran down her legs and puddled on the floor.

"I'll get some towels and you can change into clean clothes." Caroline hurried down the hall to her bedroom ahead of Addie. There was no mistaking the pains. She hadn't eaten more than a few bites at each meal in the last two days and her struggle to survive in the river, when the row boat overturned, had taken its toll on her. Her baby was coming early.

As Caroline dashed into her sewing room where Addie was, she sent up a prayer for both of them. She hadn't thought she would be called on to help with the birth of a child.

2

$\mathscr{A}$DDIE'S PAINS HAD stopped for a while, and the women were taking advantage of the lull. Caroline unrolled the bolt of white flannel on the worktable and cut three pieces from the length. She cut each section in half, added them to the stack and unrolled another length of fabric. Twenty nappies and soakers would be enough to start with, and she decided she'd better cut out the nightdresses next. As she worked at the table, her skirts swayed. Tucker grabbed the hem of her skirt with one white paw and rubbed the material over his face.

Addie watched him. "Why's your cat doin' that? I've never seen anythin' like it."

Glancing down at the cat, Caroline grinned. "I'm not sure. He's always done it, and I don't mind as long as he doesn't clean his face on my clothes after he eats."

Addie grinned, then straightened up, drew in a deep breath and let it out slowly. "I'm goin' to help while I can." She stepped over to the worktable and picked up one of the flannel squares. "This's so soft." She rubbed the material on her cheek. "I don't know how I'm goin' to repay you."

"Don't you worry. You've got enough to think about right now." Caroline started cutting out the small nightdress. It would be a loose-fitting gown with a drawstring neck, so size wasn't terribly important. She cut a facing for the neckline and set it with the gown.

Addie refolded the nappie and picked up the little dress Caroline set down. "I wish there was time to embroider rosettes 'round the neck."

"We can add flowers later. But first the gown needs seams." Caroline found her large spool of white thread and set it on the end table by the small scissors. There was so much to do. The baby would need dresses, slips, and shirts. She wanted to line the small caps with flannel so they would be soft and warm.

Addie pulled a needle out of the pincushion, unwound and cut a length of thread from the spool, and sat down on the side of the narrow bed. She looked up at Caroline. "I can't allow you to do all the work, and I need somethin' to keep my hands busy."

"Then I'll work on another one." Caroline knew she couldn't replace all of the baby's lost clothes in a few hours. It would take another week or more to make enough to keep the child in dry clothing without having to wash every day. Tucker stood on his back legs at the side of the bed and swiped his paw at the thread dangling from Addie's hand. Caroline shooed him out of the room and cut two more small dresses. Addie stiffened with another pain. Caroline set one gown aside to finish later. It was going to be a long night. She sat down on her small chair and looked over at the seam Addie was tying off. "You have a good touch with the needle. That dress will be lovely."

"Not as—" Addie stared at the gown, then cut the extra thread. "It'll be nice. And this fabric is softer than what I had. When did you slip out and buy it?"

"I keep a bolt or two on hand for nightgowns and petticoats." Caroline turned the dress over and started on the second seam. "It's been a long time since I've made such small gowns." While she hemmed the neck facing and attached it to the neck, they worked in silence. By the time she began hemming one sleeve, she realized Addie hadn't had another pain in some time. "How do you feel?"

"Better—" Addie glanced down, frowned, felt her lower abdomen with her hand and looked at Caroline. "I believe the pains've stopped."

Caroline continued plying her needle. "They'll start again. That baby *will* be born." She gave her a smile she hoped was reassuring. "Maybe you'll have time to embroider a rosette or two on that dress after all."

Tucker ran into the room and let out a piercing cry the instant before a knock sounded at the front door, then he darted back to the parlor. Caroline grinned. "He's almost as good at guarding the house as our old goose back home. Please excuse me a moment."

When she answered the door the little brass bell overhead rang out. She was hardly aware of it anymore, but now it was jarring. She reached overhead, slipped the bell off of its hook, and set it on the shelf over the coat pegs.

"Aren't you going to invite me inside?"

Gilbert Bennett was standing on her stoop smoothing the brim of his round-topped soft felt black hat.

"Gilbert, yes, of course." No one could ever fault his appearance, and tonight was no different. His straight-cut dark gray trousers and brown overcoat fit perfectly. She stepped back, opening the door for him. "May I take your coat?"

Gilbert walked into the parlor and glanced at the cat. "That won't be necessary, Caroline. I can't stay."

She closed the door and joined him. "Won't you sit down?" Tucker stood at her side eyeing her guest, and she tried not to smile. He never had taken to Gilbert.

As if he hadn't heard her, Gilbert gave her a scrutinizing

gaze. "You're looking a bit peaked. I hope you aren't working late again."

She didn't have the patience for one of his gloved sermons on how she should run her business, and changed the subject. "Thank you for sending Mr. Grey over to check the storm damage. He seemed to know what he was talking about."

"He also came by the bank this afternoon and informed me that he would commence work tomorrow evening."

"Yes. He told me." She sat down on her caned rocking chair. Tucker sat nearby swishing his tail. "But why did he report back to you?" Before Gilbert received a sizable inheritance and purchased the two River's Banks last summer, he hadn't been quite so highfalutin. Of course he had only been a third vice president at the bank. But she had overlooked his haughtiness until he embarrassed her two weeks ago at a dinner given by Maggie and her friend Sam Adams. Since then, Caroline had seen him at the Thanksgiving dinner and again when he stopped by to check on her and left after hearing about Addie.

Gilbert paced from the end of the sofa to the fireplace and back. "I asked Grey to give me a detailed report of the damage and an estimate on the cost of the needed repairs." He motioned to her with a wave of his hand. "A widow in your position would be easy prey for an unscrupulous person."

She stared at him. Had he thought of her as a poor widow woman for the five months he had been seeing her? If he had slapped her, she couldn't have felt his stinging insult more. "If you didn't trust him, why did you send him over here?"

As if she were a disrespectful child, he gave her a reprimanding look. "We'll discuss this later, Caroline, after you've rested—and feel more amenable to my counsel." He started for the front door.

She couldn't recall the last time she had allowed her temper free rein, but she felt her guard slipping as she gave in to her vexation with him. "You overbearing, pompous jackass," she called, hurrying after him.

When he yanked the door open, she caught it before it hit the wall. "Don't come by here again unless you can be more attentive and respectful."

He stiffened and looked over his shoulder at her. "I might suggest you take your own advice."

As he continued down the walk to his shiny black buggy, she closed the door. The bell. She got the footstool from the kitchen and took down the little brass bell, feeling amazingly pleased she'd at last spoken her mind. Maggie didn't care for him, and she had been so right.

Tucker meowed and swished his black tail. Caroline chuckled as she followed him down the hall to the sewing room. "I'm sorry I was so long."

Addie looked up from her sewing. "I hope your gentleman caller didn't leave on my account." Addie leaned sideways and petted Tucker's back.

"No." Caroline laughed. "Mr. Bennett and I had a . . . difference of opinion." Since Addie seemed to be feeling all right, Caroline sewed for a while longer. She finished the little dress and a shirt by the time she poked her needle back into the pincushion. Addie had added six tiny yellow rosebuds to the gown she had completed, and looked tired. "Those flowers are lovely."

"Thank you." Addie yawned, then folded the small night dress with care.

"I think we've done enough for tonight. You'll need your rest." And so will I, Caroline thought. "Can I get you anything before I retire?" She added more wood to the small woodstove. "Will you be warm enough?"

"Fine. Don't you worry. When this baby decides to get born, I'll call out."

"All right. I'll leave my door open. Don't hesitate to call me."

Addie folded the gown and laid it on the worktable. "I don't know what I would've done without your help. Thank you, Caroline. I'll see you in the mornin'."

"Sleep well." Caroline stopped in the kitchen, set two kettles of water over the banked fire on the stove, and went to her room.

After she opened the window, she changed into her night clothes, left her robe at the foot of the bed, her slippers on the floor, and slid under the covers. Babies seemed to favor being born in the wee hours, and she wanted to be rested for the event. When Tucker jumped on the bed and curled up at her feet, she smiled drowsily and fell asleep.

Caroline came awake slowly the next morning. It took several moments for her to realize she had slept through the night. She slipped into her robe, tended her ablutions, let Tucker outside, and went to the kitchen.

Addie turned to the doorway. "Mornin'," she said, reaching for the teapot. "You look as surprised as I feel." She poured tea into a china cup and handed it to Caroline. "I thought for sure I'd be carryin' this baby in my arms by now."

"Thank you." Caroline sipped the hot drink. "You're cheerful this morning. Feeling okay?" Addie was wearing the same green dress. She looked worn down and the circles under her eyes had grown darker. Caroline tried not to stare, but she was deeply worried about her.

Addie grazed both hands over her enlarged abdomen.

"He's been thrashin' his arms and legs all night." She shook her head. "I surely wish he'd find his way out."

Caroline did, too. "You're certain it's a boy?" She had known women had the knack to tell if an unborn babe was a boy or girl, but she didn't. It would be nice for Addie if she was right about this one.

"If it's a girl, she's a rowdy one." Addie shuffled around the kitchen. "I hemmed the soakers and half the nappies."

"Goodness, you've been busy. I was leaving that until I finished the dresses. Didn't you get any rest?" Addie kept moving around restlessly, and Caroline prayed it was a good sign. But until the pains returned, she would have to continue sewing necessities for the baby.

"A little," Addie said, arching her back, "but I couldn't get comfy."

Time seemed to creep by. While Addie paced or tried to find a comfortable position on her bed, Caroline prepared the cord dressings and ironed them. After she cut out more dresses, two caps and flannel to line them, shirts, skirts, nappies, and soakers, she made ties for the soakers. It seemed like a lot of clothes, but she knew these would only last the baby a day or two. Neither of them was very hungry at midday, but she heated some chicken soup, and Addie drank a cup of the broth. Near suppertime Caroline's back and fingers were stiff, and Addie's pains still hadn't returned.

Caroline stood up and arched her back. "I'm hungry. Will you try to eat something?"

Addie braced her lower back with both hands. "If you let me help."

Caroline added the finished shirt to the growing stack of baby clothes. "I have a chunk of beef roast left over," she said, walking down the hall to the kitchen pantry. "How does hash and poached eggs sound?"

Addie shuffled along behind. "Good. I'll make soda biscuits."

Caroline handed her an apron and grinned. "It'll cover part of you."

Addie slipped the neck band over her head and looked down. "Am I bigger 'n I was a couple days ago? This dress even feels different."

Caroline watched fascinated by the ripples swaying the apron. "I'd say he's doing somersaults." She had become used to cooking only for herself and living alone, and she was surprised by how well they worked together. While Addie started the biscuits, Caroline put potatoes on to boil, cut up an onion, and used the mincing knife on the roast. When the potatoes were tender, she set them out to cool.

Addie shoved her hands into the large bowl and finished mixing the biscuit dough. "I should a made bread today. I didn't do anythin'."

"Not if you don't count sewing." Caroline smiled and sympathized with her. "The waiting is the hardest part."

"On the farm there was always somethin' that needed doin'." Addie finished kneading the dough and rinsed her hands in a bowl of water. "I'd like to get outside for a spell. Want to go with me?"

"Be glad to." Caroline hung her apron up and set the potatoes near an open window.

"I'll get my shawl."

"When Addie returned, Caroline walked outside with her. It was sunny and the few high clouds didn't threaten rain. A breeze ruffled her hair. It felt good after being inside all day. They meandered around to the back of the house. The view of the Willamette River and the horseshoe-shaped falls was splendid. It had been a beautiful sight before the flood. However, now little remained of Lynn City, across the river, and the area of Oregon City along the river was digging out of the mud. The thought of Addie struggling in the surging waters of the upper river sent a chill down Caroline's spine.

"I've never seen the river from this high up." Addie shivered. "There's still a lot of rubble in the water. We shouldn't've tried to cross in the dark, but Mr. Williams said we wouldn't o' lost the others if a doctor could'a seen 'em after they was birthed. He put a lot'a store in Dr. Lindley savin' this . . . baby." She wiped her eyes with one corner of her shawl and drew in a deep breath.

Caroline put her arm around Addie's shoulders. "He must have been very worried."

Addie nodded.

Giving Addie time to compose herself, Caroline watched the churning water in the basin. There was still so much rubble below the falls and along the riverbank. From what she had seen, she was afraid too many people shared Addie's loss.

Addie stared downriver, in the direction of Milwaukee and Portland. "I hope someone's found my valise and can use the baby things."

"Someone probably has." Caroline couldn't help wondering how far the valise had traveled. It could be washed up on the bank somewhere or, she realized, be halfway to the Columbia River. She took Addie's arm, and they wandered back to the front of the house. As they came to the walkway, a wagon pulled up with two men in it. When she recognized Mr. Grey, Caroline's heart quickened. He hadn't forgotten. She glanced at the roof and smiled.

Daniel jumped down from the wagon and looked at his son, Ethan. "We only have an hour or two of light left. Don't lag behind." Daniel tipped his hat to Mrs. Dobbs. Bennett had given him the idea that she was more to him than just a client of his bank, but it was strange to think of her on his arm. He struck Daniel as the type of man who didn't know how to be happy, but he had the feeling she did.

However, the woman standing at Mrs. Dobbs's side reminded him of how his wife, Emmaline, had looked just before Ethan was born. Refusing to give the woman he'd married more than a passing thought, Daniel motioned his son to join him. "Evenin', Mrs. Dobbs. This's my son, Ethan. Ethan, this is Mrs. Dobbs and . . . her friend."

Caroline held out her hand and shook the boy's. She had expected a child, then she remembered his father saying the boy was thirteen. He was gangly and nearly as tall as his father with the same wavy hair a few shades lighter. He also had his father's direct gaze. "I'm happy to meet you, Ethan." A good-looking boy, she thought, turning to Addie.

After the introductions were complete, Daniel glanced at Mrs. Dobbs. "It's going to be noisy." He didn't believe it would ruffle her, but he was concerned about her friend. He didn't want to be responsible for upsetting a woman in her condition.

She looked at Addie. "Will the noise bother you?"

Addie shook her head.

"It will be all right, Mr. Grey. Not having to set buckets around the house when it rains will be well worth a little racket."

He motioned to his son. "We'd better get busy."

Addie waited until he had walked away. "I'll finish the biscuits. Will they be stayin' for supper?"

"No. It'll just be the two of us." Caroline saw Mr. Grey ruffle his son's hair and smiled. Then she glanced at Addie; her desolate expression was an unmistakable reminder that Mr. Williams was still missing and may never know his son. As they walked back to the house, Tucker came from behind the hydrangea bush and ran inside ahead of them.

The first time Caroline heard Mr. Grey's distinct footsteps

thud across the roof, she wondered if he would fall through the ceiling. The cat yowled and bristled his fur.

Addie rolled out the dough and cut the biscuits. She set them out and filled two pans. "These're ready for the oven. I think I'll lay down a while." She paused in the doorway. "Would you hand me the big knife? Might as well put it under the bed now. Might forget later."

Caroline handed her the largest knife she had. Some believed a knife under the bed would cut the birthing pains. "I'll see how you feel when supper's ready." Addie's face was grayish and her gait ungainly. Maybe the knife would give her needed courage and strength.

Sending up a silent prayer that Addie's travail would soon be over, Caroline added water to the kettles heating on the stove. After she set the pan of hash on the fire, she put the biscuits into the oven, fed the cat, and went to check on Addie.

She was bracing her arms, grimacing as she leaned over the worktable.

"Why didn't you call me?" Caroline quickly moved to her side. She looked even more drawn than a few minutes earlier.

Addie sagged, resting her weight on her arms. "They're only now gettin' worse."

"That seemed stronger than the ones last evening." Caroline dampened the facecloth in the basin and wiped Addie's brow.

"That felt good, but you better go eat supper. I got some work ahead of me." Another pain gripped Addie, and she groaned.

Caroline placed her hand on Addie's lower back and felt the muscles tighten. "Breathe. You don't want to swoon." Caroline heard Mr. Grey's heavier footfalls overhead. It would be dark before long. If she needed to ask his son to fetch the midwife, she would have to do it soon. "I wish you'd let me send for Mrs. Riggs for help. I've heard nothing but glowing praise of her knowledge and experience with birthing. At least three husbands in town swear she's saved their lives."

"And what about their babes? Mr. Williams wanted the doctor, not me." Addie shook her head. "I trust you, Caroline. I don't want no strangers pokin' 'round me down there. Now go on. I'll be at this a while."

Caroline ate supper, stored the remains of the meal in her cold cellar, and washed the dishes. Tucker kept her company, and she knew he didn't understand the peculiar goings-on. And each time she looked in on Addie, Addie was in pain or praying and gave the feeling she wanted to be alone. When it was nearly too dark outside for Mr. Grey to work, Caroline went out to see to him.

"Don't forget the tools," Daniel called to his son as he carried the ladder back to the wagon. He wanted to speak to Mrs. Dobbs, but he was surprised when she came over to him. "Ma'am." He glanced at the house. "Is everything all right? I thought I heard your friend cry out."

Caroline gave him a hesitant nod. His voice was calm, and he sounded genuinely concerned. His presence was comforting, but she couldn't burden him with her worries.

She looked a little uneasy. A few of her friend's cries had unsettled him, too. "Want me to fetch the granny midwife? Won't be any trouble." He motioned for his son to get in the wagon and waited for her answer.

She took consolation in his offer, but she had to reject it. "Thank you. I appreciate your kindness, but we'll be fine." At the sound of a buggy she glanced over Mr. Grey's shoulder and saw Mr. Jenkins wave as he and his family passed by. "I'm surprised you're working on Sunday."

He shrugged. "With all the storm damage in town, I couldn't rightly rest—Sabbath or not."

"No, of course not." She didn't attend services regularly and hadn't thought about it until she'd noticed the Jenkins family returning home from the evening services. "How did the work go on the roof?"

"Good. We replaced all the shingles we removed tonight. In a couple of days I'll be able to get here earlier. I'll have to cut a hole in the roof and replace the sheathing under one section of the shingles. But I'll do the repairs so you won't be left with any holes in your roof overnight."

She smiled, grateful for his consideration. "I'd better get back. Will you return tomorrow evening?" She was anxious to have the leaks sealed. And the sooner the better, now that there would be a new baby in the house.

"I'll be here for an hour or so. All depends on how the warehouse job goes." He tapped the brim of his hat. "Evenin,' ma'am."

"And you, Mr. Grey." She returned to the house feeling bolstered by their short conversation.

He was a good-hearted man, which was reassuring. Addie moaned, and Caroline wondered what kind of man Mr. Williams was. She kept busy sewing for a couple hours after Mr. Grey left, until the disturbing moans grew too loud to be ignored. She dashed back to the sewing room and found Addie squatting on the floor beside the bed. Caroline closed the door and added more wood to the small woodstove.

Addie's legs began trembling. She gasped. "He's finally comin'."

Caroline bathed Addie's flushed face and neck. "Can you push?"

"I got to. Can't help it now." Addie squeezed Caroline's fingers in a viselike grip. "Sit with me, please. I need to talk . . . while there's time." She let go of Caroline's hand and grabbed the edge of the mattress.

Caroline pulled her small rod-back chair over to the bed and started rubbing Addie's back as another pain gripped her. It came faster and lasted longer than the others. Addie jammed her fist in her mouth and doubled up. Caroline wiped her face again, wishing she could do more to ease the pain. "Do you want some laudanum? I have a vial."

At length Addie lowered her hand from her mouth and shook her head. "I been sick all day. Won't be much longer." She grasped Caroline's hand again. "I'm not gonna get through this, but my boy will. And I want you to bring him up."

Caroline understood. Most women, afraid they wouldn't live through childbirth, put their lives in order in case they didn't survive. What did take her aback was being asked to raise the child. It was the second time she had been asked to raise an orphaned child within two months.

Her dear friend Maggie had been trying to find a home for her nephew, Jeremiah. Caroline had turned her down, which in the end, worked out for the best. Maggie seemed to be taking to motherhood, and Caroline couldn't have been happier for her. And she couldn't possibly keep this baby, either. While she was married, she had spent many a night praying that she would be blessed with a child, but she was in no position to start a family now.

Addie suffered another pain and clutched the mattress until it passed. "I don't need a will since we lost everythin'. An' we don't have no kinfolk left."

"You don't have a cousin or maybe an aunt who would welcome your son? I could care for him until they came. You don't know me, Addie. Surely you'll want him with his own people." Caroline scrambled to say something to help put her mind at ease. "Besides, you'll be here to see that he's brought up the way you would like. I think any woman who has given birth feared death at one time or another." Oh, Lord, she prayed Addie's fear was the usual, and not because she truly was too weak to endure the strain of childbirth.

Addie shook her head. "This isn't the same thin'. It just feels different than my other pregnancies, an' I lived longer than my mama and sisters. But it's okay. I'll rest easy knowin' you're raisin' my youngun. I'll see Mr. Williams and Mama and Papa." Yet another pain racked her. When it passed, she tugged at her braid. "I want you to cut it off. For the boy. It's all I got for him to remember me by." She screamed, then gasped, "Hurry," through clenched teeth.

Caroline grabbed the shears, held the braid of dark hair in her left hand and worked the shears through the coil until it was free. She quickly found a piece of narrow yellow satin ribbon, tied it around the hair and held it up for her to see. "That's nice, Addie. He'll treasure it."

Tears filled Addie's eyes. "Ain't that just like you to make it real purdy." The pains started again.

Caroline set the braid on the worktable. She had gathered string, extra sheets, linen cloths, and a small dish of lard, the navel dressing she prepared the day before. All was on the table along with the shears. Everything was there and water was simmering on the stove. Had she forgotten anything? In between Addie's pains, Caroline poured warm water in the washbasin, spread a piece of oilcloth on the bed, and covered it with a folded sheet. She glanced around and suddenly realized she'd forgotten to make up a bed for the baby.

Addie lost her balance, slipped sideways, and landed on one hip on the floor. "I gotta lay down." With Caroline's help, Addie climbed onto the narrow bed and rolled onto her back with her knees raised and apart.

While Addie struggled with a punishing cramp, Caroline quickly emptied one of the drawers from her dresser, lined it with a towel, and folded a second for the bottom.

Addie screamed, "He's comin'!"

Caroline rolled her sleeves up and grabbed the hem of Addie's dress. "Mrs. Riggs can help birth babies under a sheet or cover, but I can't. I need to lift your skirt so I can see what I'm doing."

"Go on. Do whatever—"

Caroline pushed the hem of Addie's dress to her raised knees. Addie was pushing, and the child was coming. "The ordeal's about over, Addie. I can see the babe's head. Dark hair—like yours."

Addie grunted and flung her arms out. She clutched one arm of the little chair next to the bed, squeezed and cried out. Her knuckles turned white. She groaned, bearing down.

"Hold on, Addie," Caroline said in a gentle voice. As soon as she supported the small head, the baby opened its mouth and cried.

"Is . . . he all right?"

One shoulder appeared, then the other and a tiny hand. "Oh, perfect so far." Suddenly the babe's bottom slipped out into her waiting hand. He was much smaller than she'd expected but perfectly formed. "It's a boy!" He wailed and his face turned red. She grinned. "A fine boy." A beautiful boy with dark lashes. She wiped his face with a linen cloth and smiled at him. He blinked and slowly opened his eyes. The moment she looked into those eyes, she felt an overwhelming surge of love and wonder she hadn't expected.

"Thank the Lord," Addie said. "Put him on my belly. I ain't got the strength to hold him." She unbuttoned her bodice and yanked her chemise up, exposing her breasts.

Caroline placed the tiny body on his mother's abdomen.

While she tied one piece of string on the cord a finger's width above his belly, the baby rooted for his mother's breast. After she knotted a second string a couple of inches from the first, she used the shears and cut the cord.

"Don't forget to tie the rest of the cord around my leg. Don't want it sucked back up inside." Addie groaned and guided the baby to her nipple.

Doing as she was asked, Caroline tied the cord around Addie's thigh. Next she wrapped two diapers over the baby to keep him warm. She rinsed her hands off and gently pressed the flat of her hands on Addie's abdomen in a rolling motion. "This may help."

"Nothin's ever born without sufferin', an' he was worth it an' more."

"A few more cramps, and the pains will ease up." And you can rest, Caroline thought. "I'll get warm water to bathe him."

Addie raised her son's hand with one finger, bent her head, and kissed his little fist. "We'll be fine, won't we, son?"

Caroline went into the kitchen and stood in front of the dry sink. The birth of a child always amazed her, but it had been a long time since she had helped with one. The first time she had witnessed the miracle, it had terrified her. Several years later Mr. Dobbs eased those fears, but she was never able to give him the child they wanted so badly. Now, she thought, I'd better set to the work at hand.

She rinsed out the washbasin and refilled the pitcher with warm water. She also started a pot of tea brewing and set a small pan with the last of the chicken soup on the stove to heat for Addie. She had survived the birth, but she needed nourishment to build up her strength and nurse her baby. It took Caroline two trips to carry everything back to the sewing room. She added more wood to the fire and stepped over to the bed.

"Take him—" Addie grabbed the edge of the mattress with her free hand. "Never had such bad after-pains."

"Nursing usually brings them on." While Addie suffered with cramps, Caroline washed and dried the baby boy, then dressed his navel with lard and bound him with the linen strips. He seemed to have finer features than his mother but his fingers were blunt and strong. She put a shirt on him and one of the night dresses, then a little cap on his head and wrapped him in a square of flannel. She kissed his soft brow and laid him in the makeshift bed, a dresser drawer.

Addie cried out, and Caroline began massaging her again, from the waist downward. Another cramp seized Addie. When it ended, Caroline continued. Suddenly she felt something hard in Addie's lower belly.

Addie screamed.

Caroline felt the movement again. *Another babe?* She lifted Addie's skirt. "Do twins run in your family?" Before Addie could answer, Caroline saw the top of the baby's head. No wonder the boy was so small. "It *is* another babe—" For an instant she feared this one wasn't coming out, but as she stared, she realized it was moving very slowly. Too slowly.

"I can't . . ." Addie panted, trying to push. "You have . . . to help. . . . Can't . . . push . . ."

Praying for knowledge she didn't possess, Caroline tried to ease the shoulders out, but Addie didn't have the strength to push. She and the child would die if Caroline didn't act quickly. After drying her damp forehead on her upper arm, she spread her hands on Addie's abdomen and gently beared down, trying to aid the birth. She counted to ten, released the pressure, counted again and pressed. Slowly the babe's shoulders came free and the tiny body slid onto Caroline's hand. "It's a girl! Addie, you have twins!"

The baby was bluish-gray and didn't make a sound. Acting quickly, she placed the baby on its side and vigorously rubbed her little body. The baby girl didn't respond. Frightened, and desperate that the child live, Caroline laid the baby over one hand and firmly patted its back with her other hand.

The first cry was weak. Hoping to make it easier for the baby to breathe, she put her finger in the baby's mouth to open it. No wonder the poor little angel couldn't breathe, she thought, removing the phlegm.

After a few whimpers the baby gave out a louder cry. Caroline hadn't been aware that she had been weeping until tears blurred her vision. "She's fine, Addie." She dashed the tears from her eyes. "You have *two* beautiful babies," she said, laying the babe on Addie's belly.

"Two . . ." Addie let out a long sigh. "It's truly a blessin'." She ran her fingers over the baby girl's dark hair. ". . . Never figured on that. You're gonna have your hands full."

3

*A*FTER PUTTING A linen cloth over Addie's private parts and lowering her skirt, Caroline cut the cord and dressed it in the same manner as before and wrapped the baby girl in a square of flannel. Addie was weaker than her baby girl, and Caroline prayed the afterbirth would be expelled soon. "You must be parched. Would you drink a little tea?"

"I'll . . . try."

Caroline moved the baby to her mother's side and helped Addie with the tea. Then she put the babe to her mother's breast and supported both mother and child with her arm. When the baby seemed to tire of nursing, Caroline bathed her, while Addie rested.

Once the baby girl was settled in the drawer with her brother, Caroline turned her attention to Addie. "Are the cramps any stronger?" The babies' faint fussing was the sweetest music to her ears. They were alive and both were a healthy color now.

Addie barely shook her head. "Can't do it. Have you got ergot? The doctor back home gave it to start the cramps." She rubbed her hands over her belly. "Sure could use some now. Gotta get the rest of the cord 'n' all out."

"I'll singe a feather and grind some peppercorns. Sneezing may be enough to get you through this." Addie was right, Caroline thought, and too weak to pass the afterbirth without help. If the birthing wasn't completed . . . but it would be. She'd see to it. She found the ostrich plumes and set one on the worktable.

"You can't use that!" Addie sat up and leaned on one elbow. "Just an old bird feather'll be fine. Doesn't Tucker catch birds?"

"It will have to do. There isn't time to look for another. I'll be right back." Caroline set the drawer on the floor beside the bed and hurried down the hall. She had no idea what time it was and realized she should at least know if it was past midnight. The parlor clock showed 10:27. She would always remember this night. After she'd ground the peppercorns, she carried the items back to the sewing room. When the door opened, Addie was lying on her side watching her babies.

"They're so pretty, I can hardly believe they are mine." Addie ran the tip of one finger over the baby girl's cheek. "There's nothin' so soft as a baby's skin."

"Have you thought about names for them?" Caroline moved to the side of the bed.

"Robert Farris Williams, Jr.—" Addie drew a quavering breath and quickly added, "Olivia Caroline Williams, after my beloved mother and you, for helpin' her breathe."

Caroline's throat tightened and tears filled her eyes. "Thank you, Addie. I'm flattered, but I didn't do anything a midwife couldn't've done better." At that moment her heart felt as if it might burst with love for the babies and their mother.

"I saw what you did. She wasn't breathin'. Her sister never drew a breath." Addie sank back on the bed. "Now let's see if those'll work."

Caroline held the ground pepper under Addie's nose. If

she sneezed hard enough, it might bring on the cramps necessary to deliver the afterbirth. If that didn't work, Caroline would have to give her a concoction to make her retch.

Addie inhaled deeply, sneezed once and again. She turned her head away and sneezed several times. "Try the feather."

Caroline cut the long stretch plume in half and held the top piece over the flame of the lamp until it was well singed, then she brushed it under Addie's nose. She began having a sneezing and coughing fit. Caroline dampened the facecloth and laid it across Addie's forehead. She grew pale and weaker as the pains continued.

Seemingly endless minutes later, the exhausting ordeal was over. Caroline packed a clean linen cloth into Addie's private parts and laid a second one to cover the area. "After I bury this, we'll get you into a clean nightgown."

Addie nodded. "I'll just rest so's I can nurse those babies of mine in a while."

Caroline carried the cloth-covered afterbirth out to the backyard. Tucker ran around to the side yard, and she was relieved. She didn't really need his help. The full moon cast enough light for her to locate the shovel and a suitable spot to dig. She started digging by the low salal hedge. The ground was soft, and she dug a deep hole. When she finished, she hurried back to the house.

Because Addie barely had the strength to roll over on the bed, let alone lift one of the babies, Caroline slept on a pallet on the sewing room floor. A couple of hours later one of the twins stirred. Caroline awoke immediately.

Addie moaned softly.

Caroline built up the fire in the woodstove and lighted the lamp before she checked on the twins. Olivia was working her lips, as if trying to suck on something, and becoming more frustrated by the moment. "Good morning, sweetie," Caroline whispered, cradling the baby in the crook of her arm. "We'll let your mama sleep a little longer while I change your nappie." She kissed the baby's forehead. As she changed her, she spoke softly. "You and Robert have made your mama so happy." She kissed the bottoms of the baby's tiny feet. "Me, too."

"Caroline?" Addie licked her lips and opened her eyes slowly.

"Olivia's hungry. I'll brew tea for us." Caroline laid the baby on the bed by Addie. "I need to change the cloths."

Addie nodded. "Feels like my innards are leakin' out."

Caroline raised Addie's skirt. The back of it was soaked with blood. So was the bed. Caroline struggled to keep her composure. It wasn't easy. "I forgot to get a bucket for the linens. I'll be right back."

She walked out of the room as if she were not overly concerned. However, once she'd closed the door, she ran to get the water bucket. She filled it with fresh cold water from the well out back, picked up an old bucket, and returned to the sewing room. "I'll help you change, but first I want to stop the bleeding."

After settling Addie on her side, Caroline handed her a glass of water and put Olivia to Addie's breast. The dark circles under Addie's eyes were larger and her face had a grayish tinge. Caroline dropped the blood-soaked cloths in the old bucket. She dipped a clean linen cloth in the icy water and wrung it out. "This'll be cold," she warned Addie just before packing the cold cloth into her private parts.

Addie gave a start, but her attention never left her daughter.

Caroline had helped do this before. The cold cloths were to stop the flooding, but she knew it didn't always save the mother's life. As soon as the cloths turned red, she replaced them with fresh cold ones.

Addie smiled at the baby. "We'll be okay." She watched her daughter nursing. "Hi, Livvie. That was your grannie's name, an' she's surely smilin' down on you now."

Caroline continued to apply fresh icy cloths to Addie. She repeated this many times before she noticed any improvement. Addie had fallen asleep and Olivia—Livvie—was still nursing.

When Caroline found Addie awake, she returned with a tray. "I brought biscuits and jam, in case I can urge you to eat a few bites." She set the tray on the worktable and held Livvie a couple minutes, rubbing her back. When she was settled in the drawer by her brother, Caroline checked Addie and changed the cloths. The flooding had slowed to what seemed normal, and Caroline sent up a prayer of thanks.

She helped Addie roll to her right side. Robert began to stir, and Caroline was grateful he had waited to awaken. It would be too much to hope they would always take turns so easily. She set Addie's tea and the biscuits on the seat of the little chair within her reach.

Addie looked at the teacup on its saucer and the matching plate, and she burst into tears.

"What's wrong?" Holding Robert against her breast, Caroline gently rubbed his back. It wasn't much larger than Caroline's hand.

Addie shook her head. "You're lookin' after me so good, like I was kin." She brushed the corner of the blanket over her eyes and picked up the teacup.

"Oh, pshaw. You would've done the same for me." Robert's eyes opened, and Caroline murmured, "You're a bright-eyed one for so early in the morning." It wouldn't be light for another three or four hours, but there wasn't any difference between day and night for babies.

"I'll be ever grateful I was brought to your house." Addie picked a biscuit and broke it in half.

Giving her a chance to eat, Caroline changed Robert's nappie. After making such a loud entrance into the world, he had been surprisingly quiet since his birth. She didn't believe he could see much of anything, but he was trying. Before she rewrapped his blanket around him, she kissed his knees.

Having taken only one bite out of the half biscuit, Addie set it back on the plate and sank back down on the pillow. As she watched Caroline, she murmured, "Lord, give her strength to match her love."

Caroline turned around and placed Robert at his mother's side. "I'm sorry, I didn't hear what you said."

"Just prayin'." Addie settled her son at her breast. "They're both so small. I hope they won't be sickly."

"They look fine to me. And their appetites seem to be good as well." Caroline refilled Addie's cup before she noticed the hardly touched biscuit. "Won't you try to eat a little more?"

"That bite didn't sit too well, but I'll sip on the tea." Addie picked up the cup and raised it to her lips. She had just set the cup down, when she grabbed her stomach and groaned.

"Another cramp?" Addie nodded, and Caroline felt an icy trickle of dread slide down her spine. "You've been through so much, it's not surprising. I'll fix milk-toast for breakfast." Caroline spooned a dab of jam on the other half biscuit and took a bite, desperate to act as if nothing untoward were wrong. But she felt sick at heart. It was as if Addie's fears were grounded.

Addie finished her tea and gazed down at her son. Tears suddenly filled her eyes and spilled down her cheeks. "Your papa'd be so proud." She ran one finger down his cheek.

"I remember Grannie Wates railin' at Mama cause she wouldn't put a corset on my sister, Baby Sadie." She looked at Caroline. "Mama was right. Sadie was the happiest little girl. I don't want these two trussed up like Grannie." Addie sighed and closed her eyes. "She died in her blamed corset."

"I won't bind them." Caroline agreed with her, but she wasn't ready to give up hope for Addie. Mr. Moss had promised to get word about Addie to Dr. Lindley, but he hadn't been by. Caroline wasn't willing to let her slip away without a fight. She would drag Dr. Lindley to the house if necessary.

It was eight o'clock Monday morning when Addie and the twins were once again settled. Caroline put on her cape and gloves and dashed out of the house. Dr. Lindley's office was in his house, in the north end of town. Fortunately the streets were drying, and she didn't have to wade through mud. Her pace was brisk. She greeted and waved to neighbors and acquaintances she passed, but there wasn't time to stop. She covered the last block at a run and didn't slow until she started up the doctor's walkway.

She had almost reached the front door when it opened, and he rushed out. "Dr. Lindley—" she blurted, a little short of breath, "I'm Caroline Dobbs. Are you on your way to see Mrs. Williams?"

He paused with his brows drawn together. "Williams?"

"She was near her time when Mr. Williams tried to cross the Willamette after Lynn City washed out. Mr. Moss helped pull her out of the river and brought her to my house. I don't believe Mr. Williams has been found yet."

Dr. Lindley shook his head. "Sad, sad situation that. As I recall, now, she wasn't injured and didn't want me to help her with the birthing of the child." He pulled his pocket watch out, shook his head, and poked it back into his vest pocket. "You'll have to excuse me, Mrs. Dobbs. There was a wagon accident on Abernethy Creek Road." He started down the walk toward his buggy.

"*Please*, Doctor, I've run halfway here," she said, dashing after him. "I need some ergot. Mrs. Williams was flooding and is terribly weak from her ordeal. I don't know what else to do. Won't you see her for yourself?"

He stopped at the buggy and faced her. "And the child? Did it live?"

Caroline smiled. "Twins. Boy and girl. They're doing fine. But if you don't see their mother, I'm afraid they will never know her." She stepped up to the buggy. "I don't live far from here. You could tell me what to do until you can return." She held his gaze, determined to have her way. At last he gave her a curt nod, and she grabbed her skirts, not ready to be left behind.

"Twins—" He shook his head and tossed his bag in the boot. He handed her up into his buggy. "Where do you live?"

"High Street, near Fourth." She sat back and the horse took off down the street, as if he were used to going full tilt on a moment's notice.

"Tell me about the birth. Was it difficult?"

During the short ride, Caroline recounted the first pains that started and stopped, the births, Addie's increasing weakness, and lastly the flooding Caroline had discovered in the early hours that morning.

"Is she still in pain?"

"She wasn't at first, but it started up again earlier this morning." When he turned onto High, she pointed out her house, and he stopped at her walk. She didn't wait for his assistance but quickly stepped out of the buggy, led the way inside and directly to the sewing room. Addie's eyes were glazed. Not a fever, Caroline prayed.

After a cursory glance at Addie, Dr. Lindley took a careful look at each of the twins, then turned his attention to their mother.

Caroline put her cape and gloves in her room and went back to Addie. "It's all right, Addie. He's Dr. Lindley. I asked him to look at you."

"The babes . . ." Addie licked her lips.

"Are sleeping. Don't worry, they're fine." She seemed to be slipping from their grasp. Caroline lifted the hem of Addie's skirt. Her flooding had started up again. "Doctor, the bleeding is heavier than a couple hours ago."

"Please get a glass of water." He withdrew a bottle from his bag.

Groaning, Addie crushed the blanket in her hands and drew her knees up. "It ain't . . . good, is it?"

He stared at her and shook his head. "This will help with the pain." He looked over at the twins and back to Mrs. Williams. "Have you made arrangements with Mrs. Dobbs to contact your family?"

"My family's gone, but Mrs. Dobbs agreed to raise the babies for me. She's a good woman. I don't want no one else raisin' up my younguns." She grabbed his hand. "You be her witness."

"If that's what you want, of course I will." He patted her hand, then pried her fingers loose. "You should have Mrs. Dobbs write down your wishes so you can sign it."

Addie nodded.

Caroline brought a small tray with water, a teaspoon, and a dish of blackberry jam to sweeten her mouth after the medication. After he mixed the remedy, Addie choked it down. Caroline added wood to the woodstove, as if that would help cure Addie's ills, she thought.

Dr. Lindley closed his bag. "I need to speak to you in the parlor, Mrs. Dobbs."

"Yes, of course." Caroline dampened the facecloth and placed it on Addie's forehead. "I won't be long." She followed him into the parlor. His grim expression confirmed her worst fear, and she braced herself to hear the words.

Dr. Lindley looked directly into her eyes. "I won't beat around the bush. She knows she hasn't got long and said she had her affairs in order. Do you understand what you've agreed to do? Hand-raising those babies won't be easy and that'll only be the beginning."

Tears sprang to her eyes, again, and she put her hand over her mouth until she composed herself. "I helped birth those babies. I won't give them up. I've promised her, and myself. I only wish I knew Mrs. Williams better. They'll want to know about her."

"You're a very brave woman, Mrs. Dobbs." He turned to leave and hesitated. "Ask her and write it all down. It may be a help for both of you."

"Thank you, Doctor." She walked him out to his buggy. "How long? Is there anything I can do for her?"

"I left laudanum on the table. Start with twenty drops in water as often as she needs it, and you'll need to increase the amount to keep her comfortable. Sometimes it takes eighty to ninety drops." He shook his head. "That's all anyone can do. I'm sorry, but she probably won't live through the night. I'll alert the undertaker, Mr. Fogarty. You have help, don't you, Mrs. Dobbs?"

She shook her head. "Mrs. Williams didn't want me to send for Mrs. Riggs."

"Too bad. You need someone, specially with twins." He set his bag on the floor of the buggy and sat on the seat.

"I'll need a few things from the dry goods. If you see any of the Penny family, would you tell them I could use Martha's help?" Martha wasn't the Penny's oldest girl, but she was the most levelheaded. Caroline knew she could trust her to run errands and return in a timely manner.

He picked up the reins. "I'll stop by their farm. Good day, ma'am."

"Oh, Doctor, how much do I owe you?"

"Nothing, Mrs. Dobbs. I should have come by before now, not that it would've done any good."

"Thank you." She dashed back into the house, got her writing paper, pen, and inkwell, and carried them into the sewing room. They had so much to do, and she meant to learn as much about Addie as her strength would allow.

As Caroline tied the soaker over Robert's nappy, he waved his arms around. Oh, he and his sister, who was asleep, were going to keep her busy—and be the light of her life. She finished and wrapped him in the blanket. Addie was resting peacefully, so Caroline carried him out to the parlor. Mr. Dobbs had surprised her with the caned rocking chair after she told him he would be a father. She had harbored a good measure of guilt when her babies hadn't lived. If Addie's fate could be changed, Caroline thought, she would gladly give her the chair.

The house was quiet. Even Tucker was resting, on the sofa, and watched the baby as if he didn't trust him. It didn't take Robert long to fall asleep with the gentle rocking motion, but Caroline continued holding him. It was a peaceful moment, one she knew couldn't last too long. She glanced at the clock, surprised it was only half-past ten. She hadn't slept much between three and six A.M., and she was feeling it now.

A knock sounded at the door. Tucker jumped to the front windowsill. With Robert cradled in one arm, she answered the door. It was Martha Penny. "Please, come in. I'm so glad you could help." At fourteen years old, Martha had youthful energy, sun-kissed cheeks, a rosy mouth, and wisdom beyond her years that showed in her dark eyes. Today her black hair hung in a thick braid down her back.

Martha stepped inside and peered at the baby. "He's pretty. Dr. Lindley told us about the babies. I never seen two babes birthed at once."

"I haven't known many twins myself." Caroline walked back to the parlor and sat in the rocker, motioning for Martha to be seated, too. "I've made a list of what I need from the dry goods store. We'll need fresh sweet milk. I'll give you the large pail."

"Oh," Martha said, jumping to her feet. "Mama said you probably needed milk and sent some along. When I saw the baby, I plain forgot it." She dashed to the door. "Said to tell you it's from the our youngest milch cow. Her milk's real sweet." She opened the door and brought the two-handled milk can inside. "I'll set it in the kitchen."

"Your mother is a dear. Please thank her for me." Caroline carried the baby as she retrieved the list from her corner desk, crossed out the milk entry, and handed it to Martha. "Ainsworth and Dierdorff should have every-thing—if they're open for business. The most important are the sucking bottles and India rubber nipples. I hope they have them. I'd like to have two of each."

Martha nodded. "Mama said if you needed dresses and nappies, you could use hers. She packed 'em away after Ritchie grew out of 'em." She smiled at Robert. "I don't think she wants any more babies."

After seven, Caroline thought, I wouldn't either. "She has a nice family." And has done her duty by all. Caroline took a few coins from the chipped cup and handed them to Martha. "Take this in case you need to purchase the bottles where I don't have an account."

Martha wrapped the coins in her hanky and shoved it to

the bottom of her shirt pocket. "I won't dally, Mrs. Dobbs."

After she left, Caroline went back to the sewing room and put Robert down in the makeshift bed. Addie was restless. Caroline smoothed the hair back from Addie's eyes and returned to the kitchen. There hadn't been time to think about eating until then, and Caroline realized she was indeed hungry. She made milk toast and took a tray with two servings to the sewing room.

Addie stared at the drawer. "They okay?"

"Fine. How about you?" Caroline set the tray on the chair by the bed. "I'm hungry. Will you try a bite or two?"

"You've been busy." Addie reached for the spoon, but her hand shook so badly she couldn't feed herself.

"Let me help." Caroline dipped the spoon into the warm buttery milk and fed her a piece of toast.

"Mmm. I know it's good, but it don't taste like it should. Must be the laudanum." Addie moved to lay on her side. "When you're done, I'll tell some more to write down for the babies. I better sign that letter you wrote for me, too."

"All right." Caroline dipped the pen in the inkwell and held the plain pine desk box for Addie.

Addie clamped her lips together and signed her name with care. "There. It's legal. You're the babies' mama now." She handed the pen to Caroline and sank back on the pillow."

Caroline put the letter in the box and took out a clean piece of paper, determined not to shed the tears gathering in her eyes and to sound more hopeful than she felt. "Where did you grow up, Addie?" She picked up one bowl and spooned a bite into her mouth.

"Clay County, Missoura. Papa had a livery and raised a few horses. All of us helped out." Addie smiled. "I used t'sneak out and ride the ol' mare early in the mornin'. The grassland and hillocks were so green in the spring. I used to think the whole world must be like that."

Caroline grinned as she recorded Addie's recollections. "Who do you take after? Your father or mother?" Caroline wanted to ask what the children would, when they were old enough.

"Papa said I looked like Mama, but I don't know. She was delicate like. He was a middlin' sort of man. If I'd a been a boy, I'd be his image. Mama said he had the Devil's own smile."

Caroline moved the empty bowl aside, poured more tea for both of them and began writing. When the account was caught up, she asked what she was most curious about. "Who do Robert and Olivia resemble?"

Addie smiled. "Livvie looks like Mr. Williams's mama, Eunice, 'specially round the mouth. Robert, now he's bright-eyed. He'll be the spittin' image of . . . my grandpa . . . Wilbur." She moaned and wrapped her arms around her midsection.

"You need more laudanum," Caroline said, reaching for the bottle.

"Wait—I gotta nurse the babies first." Addie picked up the teacup, held it with both hands, and drank. "Feels like the tea went straight to my tits, but they don't feel full."

"I have fresh milk with cream on top. They won't go hungry." Caroline got her hairbrush and brushed out Addie's hair, while trying to think what the twins might want to ask in a few years. "What is your favorite season?"

"Springtime, 'cause we could go barefoot, and winter 'cause my heavy cloak always had a big soft fur collar. Papa gave us our choice of the winter pelts." Addie clamped her lips together, grimaced, and pulled the covers up to her chin. "It's gettin' c-cold. Are the b-babies warm 'nough?"

Caroline checked each of the twins' cheeks with the back

of her hand. "They feel fine, but I'll build the fire up for you." She wanted to keep her talking, thinking about better times, as if that would put off the inevitable.

She asked more questions and recorded the answers, the memories. The babies didn't wake up, and by the time Addie finally agreed to take her dose of laudanum, she was in such pain that Caroline had to more than double the amount of drops before Addie found any relief from the agony.

Martha returned shortly after dinnertime. "Most of the stores're still mucky from the flood. I did find two bottles, but no one had any of those nipples on the ends of the rubber tubes. Mr. Dierdorff sent a pair of leather gloves, said the fingers'd work fine with a tiny hole in the end."

"Yes," Caroline said, smiling, "they will do nicely." She was grateful for the two sucking bottles and Mr. Dierdorff's kindness. She thanked her and offered to make her a petticoat in exchange for her help after school a couple times a week for a while. Martha left happy with their arrangement, and Caroline set to work. Robert and Livvie would probably wake up hungry very soon.

Caroline set the water pitcher by the sink. She spooned part of the thick layer of cream from the top of the milk into the pitcher, added milk, a little molasses, and stirred until it was well mixed. She remembered someone saying, "It should be on the sweet side." She tasted it and hoped the twins would like it better than she did. After covering the pitcher with a clean cloth, she put it and the milk can in the cold cellar. Lastly, she washed the sucking bottles and the fingers she had cut off of the leather gloves.

Before long, Robert and Livvie were hungry. Addie was sleeping restlessly, and Caroline didn't think it wise for her to try to nurse them. After adding an equal part of heated water to the milk mixture to warm and dilute it, she fed the babies with the sucking bottles. She felt very relieved when they accepted not only the leather fingers but the sweet milk and dozed peacefully afterward. She worked on more dresses, nappies, and shirts in the sewing room to be near Addie.

Late that afternoon Addie roused from the laudanum-induced sleep. "Caroline—" she said in a hoarse whisper.

"Yes," Caroline said, putting a gentle hand on Addie's shoulder. "I'm here." Rubbing her eyes, she seemed to be fighting the effects of the opiate. Caroline wiped Addie's face with the dampened facecloth.

Addie grasped Caroline's wrist. "Promise—you'll raise my babies—don't let no one take 'em. . . . Prom—"

Her eyes rolled back, and Caroline wasn't certain if she heard a low sigh or not. "Addie—" She prayed Addie had collapsed and tried to rouse her. A chill slid down Caroline's back. Addie had passed on. She was out of pain and at peace. Tears flowed down Caroline's cheeks as she kissed her forehead. "I promise."

As she bathed Addie's face, Caroline heard Mr. Grey on the roof. His heavy footfalls were comforting, reassuring. Life goes on.

Robert and Livvie needed her, and she realized, she needed them, too.

4

THE PLEASANT CINNAMON aroma drifted around the parlor from the kettle over the fire in the fireplace. Daniel stepped back from Mrs. Dobbs and the coffin. It was just a simple pine box, but she had draped a nice piece of green cloth the length of the wooden box and added a pillow before he laid out Mrs. Williams.

He was glad his first impression of Mrs. Dobbs had been wrong. She was a gentle, kindhearted woman—if only his wife had been more like Mrs. Dobbs. "Are you sure you don't want me to get Mr. Bennett? You shouldn't be alone."

"Thank you for offering, but please, don't, Mr. Grey. You've already done so much." She had asked him to tell Mr. Fogarty, the undertaker, that she needed his services, but Mr. Grey said he had made a few coffins for other flood victims and had one more in his shop. He not only set it in her parlor, he had moved Addie for her. Caroline crumbled a handful of mint leaves over Addie's skirt, hoping that and the cinnamon would freshen the room.

"Mrs. Dobbs," he said softly, "can I help with anything else?"

"You have done so much already. I'll be fine, thank you." She gave a tentative smile, then tenderly brushed Addie's hair.

"If Mr. Fogarty can't bury her tomorrow for you, I'll see to it, Mrs. Dobbs."

"I appreciate all you have done. Mr. Fogarty should be expecting to hear about Mrs. Williams." Caroline set the brush down and looked into Mr. Grey's gentle brown eyes. Later, once Addie had been laid to rest, she would find a way to repay his kindness.

Daniel glanced outside and saw Ethan standing by the wagon. The boy had done his part that day, doing a man's work. "I'll go by Mr. Fogarty's directly. See you in the morning, ma'am." She looked so tired, and with those two babies, he didn't think she would get much rest.

Caroline sank down on her rocker, closed her eyes, and set the chair in motion. Any time now the twins will awaken wet and hungry, she thought. Tucker pulled on her skirt and meowed. "I know I should add hot water to the babies' milk to warm it up." She sat up and scratched behind his ear. His ears perked forward and he darted to the window.

She had just leaned back in the chair and there was a knock on the door. When she answered it, she found her dear friend grinning at her. "Hello, Maggie. Come on inside." Sam Adams and Jeremiah—Maggie's recently orphaned nephew—were there, too.

"Guess what, Mrs. Dobbs," Jeremiah asked, hurrying to Caroline's side. "We got *married* yesterday! They're my ma and pa now!"

"Jeremiah, that's wonderful!" Caroline beamed at each of them. "Congratulations, Maggie, Sam." Tears of joy sprang to her eyes, and she dashed them away with her knuckles. "I'm so happy for you."

Sam smiled at his wife. "So am I."

Caroline hugged Maggie, saying, "Sam's a fortunate man. Were you married here in town?"

"We rode over to Clackamas and had a quiet ceremony

late yesterday afternoon. You had your hands full with Mrs. Williams and with so many people cleaning up after the flood, that seemed best."

Sam grinned. "You were there in spirit. She wore that pretty dress you made for her."

"This is indeed a grand compliment." Caroline laughed lovingly. "I used to wonder what it would take to get you out of those trousers you used to wear under your skirt."

Maggie eyed her. Caroline's thick reddish-brown hair was always loosely coiled and looked as if she'd just done it up, until now. "What's happened here? Your sign isn't out, and I've never seen you in such a state. Why didn't you send someone for me?"

Sam put his hand on Maggie's arm and nodded toward the parlor. He was as surprised and concerned by Caroline's harried appearance as Maggie. He thought about fetching Bennett, but quickly discarded that notion. The man was self-centered and about as useful as a wart.

Maggie lowered her arms and looked into the other room. "Mrs. Williams?"

"Addie didn't regain her strength," Caroline said, and closed the door. "Let's sit in the dining room." She went over to where Jeremiah was petting her cat. "He's happy to see you."

Jeremiah grinned at her. "I'm glad. But we're goin' to Sam's . . . Pa's ranch. It's far away, and I won't visit Tucker for a real long time."

"Oh, I didn't know." She smiled at him. "You can play with him all you want before you leave. Are you taking Cap with you?"

"Uh-huh." Jeremiah tickled the cat's nose with its tail. "He goes everywhere with us. He's waitin' out front now."

"He's a good dog." Caroline paused in the dining room on

the way to the kitchen. "Please, have a seat. It won't take me a minute to get a pot of tea ready."

"I'll help you." Maggie gave Sam's hand a squeeze. "Be right back."

"Take your time. She looks like she needs your company. If Jeremiah get restless, we'll go outside."

She pressed a quick kiss to his cheek, whispered, "Thanks for being so understanding," and went into the kitchen. "I wish I'd known, Caroline. When did Mrs. Williams pass away?"

"This afternoon. Mr. Grey said he would see that she'll be buried in the morning." Caroline poured hot water into the teapot.

Maggie thought a moment. "Who's Mr. Grey? I thought Mr. Fogarty was the undertaker."

"He is. Mr. Grey's repairing my roof and windows. He also makes coffins."

Maggie noticed the color returning to her friend's cheeks. Whoever Mr. Grey was, she was grateful he was helping Caroline. "Are you all right?"

"Yes. So are the twins." Caroline smiled at her.

"She gave birth? Two? Are they all right?"

"Robert and Livvie—small but healthy as can be. Oh, Maggie, they are so sweet. Wait till you see—" Caroline gave her a wide-eyed look. "I almost forgot. I need to get their milk ready." She went to the cold cellar and got the pitcher of sweet milk.

Maggie knew Caroline had longed for children of her own, and she noticed that her friend's eyes positively glowed when she talked about the babies. "No wonder you're weary." Maggie set the cups and saucers out. "Have you heard any more about Mr. Williams?"

Caroline poured some of the sweet milk into a pan and added a small amount of hot water. "Not yet."

"Did Mrs. Williams say where she was from? Tell you how to get in touch with her family?"

"From what she told me, there isn't anyone." Caroline set the two sucking bottles on the table. "She wanted me to raise the twins." She looked at Maggie. "I promised her I would."

Maggie went around the worktable and gave Caroline a hug. "No one could love them any more than you. I *know* that. What can I do to help?"

"Would you and Sam be their godparents?" Caroline hadn't had time to think of it before, but it was right. If anything happened to her, they would love the children. There was no one she trusted more than Maggie.

"I'm honored, Caroline, but we're leaving day after tomorrow. The roads are finally dry enough to get through. We can't wait any longer. . . ."

"Oh. I didn't know the stages were running again."

"They aren't. Too many bridges were washed out, but Sam bought a wagon and team. Captain Larkin said he'd take us upriver. If we can get to Corvallis, we're hoping the Long Tom Road will be clear."

"Maybe I can have Reverend Vincent christen the twins tomorrow afternoon." Caroline stirred the pan of milk. "Would that be all right with you?"

"Yes, tomorrow would be fine."

"The morning would be even better." Caroline held one of the sucking bottles in her hand. "I believe Addie would rest peacefully knowing her babies had been christened. Yes, I'll have to speak to him this evening." She glanced at the bottle and set it down.

Maggie set the teapot on the tray and picked it up. "Tea's ready. Let's tell Sam."

Caroline nodded. "If he objects to my idea, I'll understand." She followed Maggie into the dining room.

Maggie poured the tea. She had just handed Caroline a cup when she heard a faint cry.

"What's that?" Jeremiah went to the hall leading back to the bedroom. "Do you have another kitty, Mrs. Dobbs?"

Sam looked from Caroline to Maggie. Both of them looked as pleased as could be—about something. "I don't think it's a cat, Jeremiah."

"Excuse me." Caroline left to check on the twins. Sam seemed more amused than upset, thank goodness.

"No—" Maggie glanced at Caroline as she hurried down the hall. "Jeremiah, please come in here and sit down. I'll be right back."

Caroline picked up Robert and laid him on her worktable to change him. She was tying the clean soaker ties when Maggie came into the sewing room. "This is Robert. Livvie is still asleep."

Maggie stepped over to the table and gazed from Robert into the drawer. "No, she isn't. She's looking around. Both are beautiful and so alike." Maggie marveled at the infants and at the same time was grateful Jeremiah had come to her when he was six years old. She'd never taken care of such a small baby, but Caroline didn't appear to have any trouble.

Caroline finished dressing Robert and wrapped him in a blanket. "Would you hold him while I tend Livvie?" She placed the babe in Maggie's waiting arms and picked up Livvie.

Maggie cradled him in one arm. "He's precious." She grazed his soft cheek with the back of her finger. She didn't think she had ever held a day-old baby, and began to understand why women tended to fuss over them so.

"They both are." Caroline kissed the baby's tummy and tied the soaker strings. "Martha Penny is going to help me for a while." She pulled the clean dress down over Livvie's legs and picked up another blanket.

"Mind if I take him out to show Sam and Jeremiah?" Maggie kissed the baby's forehead and gently rocked him.

Caroline grinned at her. "Go on. We'll be out soon as I change their bedding."

She laughed to herself. Maggie, who knew she was one of the best riverboat pilots on the Willamette River, thought she could never be a mother, but appeared perfectly content holding Robert. Caroline wrapped the baby in a blanket and carried her out to the dining room.

Sam heard Caroline and looked up. She had a second baby in her arms. He leveled his gaze on his wife. "Is this what you didn't tell me?"

She laughed. "Caroline asked if we would be their godparents." His surprised expression had mirrored her first thoughts. She looked at Robert and realized the idea of having a baby wasn't as frightening now as it would've been three months earlier.

Jeremiah peered at the baby. "Will I be a god . . . brother?"

Caroline grinned. "I think they would like that." She looked at Sam, unsure if he would agree or not. "I know this's sudden."

Whew, he thought, he hadn't seen that coming. He was an attorney, though he hadn't practiced recently, but he couldn't ignore the implied legal responsibility they would be shouldering. On the other hand, Caroline was his wife's closest friend, and her feelings were evident. "I would be honored, and I believe you already know how Maggie feels."

Caroline smiled at him. "Thank you, Sam."

Robert whimpered, and Maggie rocked him. "I think he wants supper. Caroline, Sam can hold Livvie while you fill the bottles."

"It's almost time for supper," Caroline said, glancing from Sam to Maggie. "I hope you'll stay."

Jeremiah looked at Sam. "Can we, Pa? I'll hold the baby."

Sam shook his head. "Not now, son."

Maggie grinned at Caroline. "Just try and get rid of us." Maggie held Robert down for Jeremiah to see. "I want to help take care of these angels. Next time we see them, they'll be running around."

When Caroline put the baby in his arms, he couldn't believe how little it weighed. It felt as if he were holding only a bundled-up blanket.

After Caroline left to fill the bottles, Maggie spoke to Sam. "She wants Reverend Vincent to baptize the twins in the morning. Would you call on him tonight and make the arrangements?"

He regarded the baby—what a wonder it was—and then gazed at his wife. They had much to look forward to in the coming years. "Be glad to."

Caroline tucked Robert in by his sister and spoke softly to Maggie. "I'm glad you wanted to spend the night, but I am surprised Sam was so understanding." She added two more pieces of wood to the stove in the sewing room and picked up the infant dress she had started.

"He knows I'll miss you." Maggie turned down the lamp wick and followed Caroline out to the parlor. "Once Sam gets the house built, you'll have to come visit us."

"That would be nice, but I don't believe I'll be taking any trips until Livvie and Robert can walk at my side." Caroline refilled their teacups and sat down on the sofa with Maggie.

"Thank you." Maggie took a small sip of the hot tea. "I don't want to pry, Caroline, but will you be able to manage with two babies?" Up until two days ago, she had struggled against taking on the responsibility of Jeremiah, and he was much easier to care for than twins.

"I work here, so I can care for them at home." Caroline laid the little dress on her lap and began stitching one of the side seams. "It shouldn't be any more difficult for me than it would've been for Addie."

"That may be true." Maggie sipped her tea and wondered if Caroline was still seeing Mr. Bennett. "You haven't mentioned Gilbert. He did call to make sure you were all right during the flood, didn't he?"

"He sent Mr. Grey over to see about repairing the water damage." Caroline threaded the needle through the soft fabric and grinned. "You were right about him. He was so high-handed and insufferable the other evening that I told him just what I thought of him." She shrugged and added, "I don't think he'll be back." And that was a relief.

Caroline drew the thread through the material. She didn't want to hear Gilbert's opinion about her keeping the babies—or anything else she did. She really should have paid more attention to those niggling doubts she'd had about him, especially when she saw that her cat *and* her dear friend didn't like him.

Momentarily fascinated with Caroline's sewing, Maggie watched her ply the needle. "I don't recall ever seeing him smile, let alone hearing him laugh." She grinned. "He's not nearly good enough for you."

Caroline skimmed her hand over the little dress she was sewing. "With Livvie and Robert, I'll be very happy."

Maggie noticed Caroline stifle a yawn and smiled. "You can hardly keep your eyes open."

"I would like to get some rest before the twins wake up."

"And Sam said the reverend would be here at nine in the morning."

"I'm glad he agreed to come here. I didn't know his

church had been flooded or much else that's happened recently. The only time I've left the house in the last few days was to go to Dr. Lindley's."

Maggie reached over and clasped Caroline's free hand. "Reverend Vincent said he would also go to the cemetery with us after the christening."

Caroline looked at her. "I believe Addie would have wanted it that way." She poked the needle through a fold in the dress and set it on the small table. As she stood up, she said, "You can sleep in my room. I left a clean nightgown for you on the bed." Tucker rubbed her ankle and went to the door.

"Thanks." Maggie picked up the tea tray. "I forgot to ask Sam to bring some of my things over." She carried the tray with their cups and teapot into the kitchen.

Caroline let the cat outside. "Leave those. I'll wash them in the morning. Oh, if you don't close the bedroom door tight, Tucker might join you during the night."

"That won't bother me. You aren't going to sit up with Mrs. Williams all night, are you?"

As Caroline regarded the coffin, she struggled to prevent the yawn pulling at her jaw. She should sit up with her, but she was so sleepy and tired. "No, but I'll feed the twins in here."

"Good. You're going to need all the rest you can get. I'll see you in a while."

Caroline added water and another piece of cinnamon to the kettle, and more wood to the fire. "The babies don't make much of a fuss, yet. I hope they won't wake you."

Maggie grinned. "They better. I want an excuse to hold them again."

Sam and Jeremiah had brought out the gentler side of her, Caroline thought. When she was ready for bed, she let Tucker back inside and turned the lamp wicks down on the way to the sewing room. Before she lay down, she watched Livvie and Robert a moment. Their looks were nearly identical, but their personalities were not. "Sweet dreams, my little ones."

When the twins woke for their feeding, Caroline hadn't wanted to bother Maggie, but she was grateful for her company and help both times. In the morning Caroline roused to the aroma of coffee and bacon. She added wood to the small woodstove for the babies, quickly slipped into her dark green dress, combed her hair back in a plain bun, and set out her wide-brimmed serge bonnet.

She found Maggie and Sam cooking breakfast. "Good morning. What time is it?"

"Hi." Maggie pulled out Sam's pocket watch. "Just after seven-thirty, almost sunrise. The tea should be ready." She tucked the watch back into her husband's pocket and smiled at him. She had missed him during the night. Odd, she thought, a few months ago, if anyone had asked, she would've said she couldn't share her bed with anyone.

Caroline couldn't miss the intimate exchange. Maggie and Sam's deep affection for each other was wonderful, and Caroline wanted nothing less for herself. "You two didn't have to make breakfast."

Sam chuckled. "I'm being selfish. That shack we moved into after the stern-wheeler went aground doesn't have a kitchen. Jeremiah and I were hungry for a big breakfast, and I figured both of you might be, too." He picked up a plate and dished out eggs and his special pan-fried potatoes.

Caroline beamed at Maggie. "He's a gem. If you ever tire of him, let me know." Caroline helped serve, and they enjoyed a hearty meal. Afterward she checked on the twins. While she and Maggie were doing the dishes, Jeremiah ran into the kitchen.

"Mrs. Dobbs, there's a man here to see ya. Says ya know him."

"Please tell him I'll be right out." Caroline dried her hands, saying, "Must be Reverend Vincent," and went out to meet him.

Daniel was glad to see Mrs. Dobbs had friends staying with her. She came out of the kitchen brushing at her skirt and looking more rested than the day before. "Morning, Mrs. Dobbs."

"Mr. Grey, hello." She hadn't expected him so early, but she was glad to see him. She glanced at Maggie and Sam. "I would like you to meet Mr. Grey." Caroline made the introductions.

Daniel shook hands with Mr. Adams, then turned back to Mrs. Dobbs. "I hope you won't mind, but I stopped by the undertaker's and told Mr. Fogarty I'd take Mrs. Williams to the cemetery. When would you like me to return for her?"

"Thank you. I appreciate your help. Reverend Vincent will be here at nine. He'll christen the twins and go to the cemetery with us. I would've gotten word to you, but I didn't know where to find you."

"That's all right. I'll be back in a while."

She reached out and put her hand on his arm. "Please don't leave, Mr. Grey—unless you have another appointment." He had moved Addie so tenderly, and Caroline still appreciated his consoling words. He was a plain-spoken, realistic man, and she liked that. "We have coffee and tea, and you can sit outside if you'd rather." She glanced at Maggie and Sam. "The reverend should be here any time."

"We could use a witness, if you wouldn't mind." Sam slipped his hand over Maggie's arm. "We have the honor to be Robert and Livvie's godparents."

Daniel met Mrs. Dobbs's gaze. "It'll be my pleasure." He gave her a hint of a smile and added, "And that cup of coffee sounds good." She smiled, the kind of sweet smile a woman gives a man that makes him feel very proud to have pleased her.

"I'll get it for you." Caroline turned toward the kitchen and paused. "Maggie—Mrs. Adams—is the captain of the *Maggie*, a stern-wheeler on the Willamette." She went to pour his coffee.

"Was," Maggie amended. "She was washed aground during the flood."

Daniel smiled. "That's why you seem familiar." He shook his head. "Yes, I saw her. That's a shame. She was a good boat. Are you going to rebuild?"

Sam shook his head. "No. We're going down to California."

Daniel's attention momentarily strayed toward the kitchen, then back to Mrs. Adams. "That's too bad. I've heard good things about you. You'll be missed."

"Very kind of you to say so, Mr. Grey." Maggie excused herself to check on Jeremiah.

Caroline returned with a tray. She handed Mr. Grey the cup of coffee and set a plate of rolls on the dining room table. "These are still warm."

"Thank you." Daniel thought he had a firm hold on the saucer, until her fingers lightly brushed against his. Lord, it had been a long time since a woman's touch had felt so tender. Oh, there had been a couple ladies who hadn't concealed their interest in him, but Caroline, he thought, was different.

She smiled at him and lowered her hand. "I'd better see about the babies."

Maggie returned to the parlor while Caroline was speaking with Mr. Grey. "I'll lend you a hand." As Maggie crossed the room, she overheard Mr. Grey ask about the salvage rights to the *Maggie* and kept walking. Sam could handle that. Even though it'd been a week since her riverboat was shoved aground, she still didn't want to think about her beloved old stern-wheel as a pile of rubble.

When Maggie came into the sewing room, Caroline pointed to Robert. "He usually wakes first, but he doesn't cry right away. He acts as though he's looking around, but babes can't see much so soon."

"He's trying." Maggie peeked at Livvie. "I hate to wake her, but she must be wet."

"Oh, that reminds me." Caroline reached under the table and set out two large squares of material. "I cut a couple pieces of oilcloth for our laps—so they won't soak us, too."

"That's nicer than setting them in bowls. I'll remember for the next time I hold someone's baby." Maggie began changing Livvie. "I like Mr. Grey. I think Sam does, too."

Caroline smiled. "He's a nice man. Did I mention his son is working with him?"

Maggie shook her head. "Have you met Mrs. Grey?"

Caroline looked at her. "I hardly know him. He only started working on my roof a few days ago, but I told you that. His wife's a fortunate woman."

"Hmm." I wonder, Maggie thought. I wouldn't want Sam gazing at Caroline the way Mr. Grey had.

5

"*IN THE NAME* of the Father, the Son, and the Holy Ghost, I christen you Robert Farris Williams, Jr.," Reverend Vincent said, sprinkling water over the baby's head.

When the water dripped on his head, Robert jolted and let out a healthy wail. Caroline rocked him in her arm and whispered to him until he quieted.

Reverend Vincent stood in front of Maggie, who held Livvie. "In the name of the Father, the Son, and the Holy Ghost, I christen you Olivia Caroline Williams," he said, sprinkling water on her head. Livvie cried out, and Maggie shifted the baby to her shoulder to quiet her as Reverend Vincent closed his Bible and said a prayer for Robert and Olivia.

Caroline kissed Robert, and then she leaned over and pressed a kiss to Livvie's cheek. "Addie must be smiling now." Tears blurred Caroline's vision, but she quickly dried her eyes.

Reverend Vincent cleared his throat. "Mrs. Dobbs, do you want me to begin the requiem now?"

Caroline looked from Maggie to Sam to Mr. Grey. Each gave her the barest nod. "Yes, please."

Reverend Vincent stood by the coffin, Bible in hand, and recited, "I am the resurrection and the life . . ."

After the reverend read the Twenty-third Psalm, Caroline spoke about Addie's determination, strength, and love for her children. Reverend Vincent concluded the service with a prayer.

Caroline gently rocked Robert in her arms and looked at Mr. Grey. "After we bundle up the twins, we can leave for the cemetery." The twins were so small and shouldn't be taken out so soon, but when they were older she wanted to be able to tell them that they had attended their mother's burial.

Daniel nodded. "We can use my wagon."

Maggie held Livvie in one arm and took Jeremiah's hand. "Come with me, honey. Where's your jacket?"

"Back there, on a chair." Jeremiah stopped and tugged on Maggie's hand. "Where're they takin' her?"

Maggie dropped down to his level and combed her fingers through his hair. She still had to remind herself he was only six years old. "We'll take her to the cemetery and her coffin will be buried deep in the ground."

"In the dark?"

"She won't wake up, honey. She's in Heaven with your mama and papa." She kissed his cheek. "Help me wrap up Livvie so she won't get cold."

"Okay. And Robert, too. They're so little."

Caroline and Maggie cradled the babies under the sides of their capes as they rode to the Mountain View Cemetery with Reverend Vincent in his buggy. Sam and Jeremiah went with Mr. Grey. High clouds blocked the sunlight, but it was warmer than usual for December. They made their way up the gentle slope of the rolling hillside. The jostling didn't appear to bother either of the twins, but Caroline realized she couldn't take them out by herself, not until they were walking.

When they entered Mountain View Cemetery, Daniel saw

Mr. Fogarty standing by an open grave and pulled up alongside. "Mr. Fogarty." Daniel set the brake and stepped down to the ground.

"Hello, Mr. Grey." Mr. Fogarty nodded to the other gentleman and walked to the back of the wagon. "I hope this plot will be all right."

The open grave was on the far side of two other recently covered sites. Daniel watched the reverend's buggy come to a stop opposite the pit. "Here's Mrs. Dobbs. You should ask her."

Jeremiah jumped down from the wagon and ran to the buggy ahead of Sam. "Mama, can I ride back with you and baby Robert?"

"Yes, honey, I think we'll all go back together."

Sam handed Caroline and his wife down. "Caroline, Mr. Fogarty needs to speak with you."

"Thank you, Sam." Caroline walked over to Mr. Fogarty. Although they had never met, she had seen him and couldn't easily forget the tall solidly built gentleman. "Mr. Fogarty, thank you for taking care of the arrangements."

"Mrs. Dobbs," Mr. Fogarty said, tipping his tall-crowned black hat. "I hope this site meets with your approval."

There was a beautiful old fir tree nearby, woods beyond and to the west, a wonderful view of the Willamette River—and what had been Lynn City a week ago. From that height she could see the destruction the flood had caused, fallen trees, deep trenches where the land had been flat, and the debris . . . She stared beyond the waterfall. Was Addie's farm within sight? "It couldn't be better, Mr. Fogarty."

"Good. Dr. Lindley spoke to me the other day. He didn't hold out much hope for the poor woman. Will there be others attending?"

"I don't believe so. She was brought to me after being

rescued from the river. She must have friends, but I didn't know how to get in touch with them."

Mr. Fogarty nodded. "I'll see that a notice will be published in the *Argus*. Mr. Craig won't charge for it. With the office flooded he couldn't get a paper out last week, but he's working on publishing one this week covering the flood an' all." He motioned to the marker resting against a nearby pine tree. "I made a simple gravemarker."

Caroline read the neatly chiseled lettering: MRS. WILLIAMS, DIED DEC. 9, 1861. "That is very nice. Mrs. Williams was a good woman. When her children are older, they will appreciate your thoughtfulness."

"Oh, I didn't know she had children."

She smiled at Robert, sound asleep in the layers of blankets cradled in her arms. "Mrs. Williams passed away not long after giving birth to the twins." The poor man looked uncomfortable. "I'm sorry, Mr. Fogarty, I thought Dr. Lindley had mentioned the twins."

"No—he was in a hurry. I understood she'd been recently widowed, that Mr. Williams had drowned in the flood."

"That may be true. We didn't hear any more about him." She excused herself and joined Mr. Grey, Maggie, and Sam. "I think we should begin the service now."

"Yes, of course."

Daniel admired her strength and her sense of obligation. Her husband had been a very fortunate man. He walked over to Reverend Vincent and spoke to him for her.

Caroline and Maggie, with Jeremiah, waited in silence while Sam and Mr. Grey positioned the coffin at the side of the grave. As Caroline watched Mr. Grey, she recalled his first name, Daniel, a good strong name. Daniel Grey. She liked it. And she was very grateful for his help.

Reverend Vincent opened his Bible and read from the

Holy Scriptures. "The Lord gave and the Lord hath taken away. . . ."

Staring at Mrs. Dobbs, the curve of her cape that shielded the infant, the reverend's voice reading the all-too familiar Scripture carried Daniel back six years to another burial. Arletta, his daughter, had lived only long enough to draw a few weak breaths before she slipped away. His sister-in-law hadn't allowed him in to see his baby until after she had stopped breathing. He had managed to keep that memory out in the far corner of his mind, until now. Suddenly Daniel felt Mr. Adams touch his arm, and returned to the present.

As the men lowered the coffin into the ground, Caroline was comforted by the knowledge that Addie was in a better place, where she no longer felt pain or sorrow. Reverend Vincent recited the Committal, and as he intoned the Benediction, Caroline silently renewed her promise to raise the twins.

After they finished eating dinner, Caroline refilled Sam's and Maggie's cups with coffee. "I appreciate both of you helping me, and I wish you didn't have to leave so soon."

Maggie rested her hand on her husband's. "Sam was expected at the ranch last month. The flood's the only reason he's still here. Now that the roads are drying, we should be able to get through. We can't delay the trip any longer."

"I understand." Caroline sat down at the table across from Maggie. "Please do write. We can keep in touch."

"Agreed, and you'd better tell me all about those twins of yours." Maggie took a drink of her coffee and looked at Sam.

He nodded and stood up. "We really should leave, Maggie. We have a little more packing to finish." He looked from Caroline to Maggie and shook his head. "You two shouldn't part with such long faces. Five days apart by stagecoach isn't that far."

Maggie knew he was right. Besides, she was never one for long good-byes. "He's right. Who knows, he may need to come back up here to buy more sheep."

Caroline smiled. "I've wanted to see California. Now I'll have someone to visit."

She found Jeremiah's coat and promised to take good care of Tucker and the twins. Sam gave her a big hug and said he expected to see her soon. Then she looked at Maggie and couldn't prevent the sudden tears that blurred her vision. "Mr. Grey was right—you will be missed, but knowing you, you'll help Sam build the best sheep ranch in the West." She moistened her dry lips. "You'll have to learn how to spin and weave cloth from some of that wool."

Maggie chuckled, determined not to cry. "If I do, I'll send it to you."

Sam and Jeremiah stepped outside. Caroline smiled and gave Maggie a hug and walked out with her. "Have a safe trip. When you can, write and tell me about it."

Maggie nodded. "I will. And kiss Livvie and Robert for me." She hurried down the steps, paused to pet Tucker, then joined her husband and son.

Jeremiah looked back, and Caroline waved to him. "Come inside, Tucker. I don't want you following them." The cat darted under her skirt. As she was closing the door, she noticed her signpost. Tomorrow she would hang out her dressmaker's sign. After all, she had a family to feed. The thought came naturally, but at the same time she realized how different it was for her, and she smiled.

Robert and Livvie—my family.

Caroline finished cutting out another six dresses and a dozen nappies. She had laundered the soiled clothes and hung them on the clotheshorse set up by the fireplace in the parlor. Most women began putting together a layette during pregnancy. She gazed at the sleeping twins. When she had finished enough of the necessities, she would make special dresses for them for Christmas.

She carried the drawer out to the parlor and set it near the hearth without waking the babies. The afternoon seemed to pass in the blink of an eye. Before she knew it, Daniel Grey had returned with his son and was working on the roof. The footsteps and hammering were reassuring sounds. By the time she put the sewing aside, she had finished two dresses.

She reheated a piece of leftover chicken and a biscuit for supper. When the food was warm, and smelled inviting, Livvie and Robert woke up. Caroline gave each a kiss. "Does my supper smell good?" While she prepared their bottles, she wondered if the aroma of her food had roused them.

After she had changed and fed the twins, she ate her supper at the dining room table. So much had happened in the last two days, but now she was alone with Livvie and Robert. As Caroline stared into the parlor, she tried to imagine the twins walking around.

While she cleaned up after supper, she heard Daniel Grey's hearty laughter. It was a deep, rich sound, one that added warmth and homeyness to her formerly quiet house. She wanted to repay his kindness and decided to invite him and his family for supper the following evening. Martha would be there to help in the afternoon, so she could manage.

Caroline waited until Daniel Grey and his son stopped working. She hurried to her room, got her soft wool shawl, and wrapped it around her shoulders as she rushed outside to meet them. Ethan was climbing up to the wagon seat, and

Daniel Grey was putting the ladder in the back of the wagon.

"Hello, Mr. Grey."

Daniel smiled and tipped his old hat to her. "Evening, Mrs. Dobbs." It was nearly dark, and with the light from the house behind her, he couldn't see her face as well as he would've liked. "Is everything all right?"

"Yes, we're fine, thank you." She walked over to the side of the wagon. "I would like to have you and Mrs. Grey and, of course, Ethan, over for supper tomorrow evening. You've done so much for me." She didn't think her invitation was strange, but when he looked surprised—or taken aback—she quickly added, "I wanted to repay your kindness, but if you would rather not, please say so." She glanced at Ethan, and he appeared as uncomfortable as his father.

Daniel wasn't in the habit of explaining his family's business to others, but most everyone had heard that Emmaline had left him within a week after she disappeared. That was five years ago. He had been whispered about, had noticed pitying glances, and had received veiled sympathy. But there was no reason Mrs. Dobbs should've known. No one had mentioned Emmaline for a long time. He looked at his son and cleared his throat. "Mrs. Grey isn't with us any longer. If you wouldn't mind just the two of us, we'd be pleased to have supper with you, Mrs. Dobbs."

"I didn't know— Please accept my sympathy." When she glanced at Ethan, he turned away, the poor boy. "Would six o'clock be convenient, Mr. Grey?" Now she was even more determined to make a special supper for him.

"Yes, ma'am. We'll be here." Daniel climbed up beside his son and started home.

"Pa, she thinks Ma's dead. How come you didn't tell her different?"

"I will, son, but then wasn't the right time." Daniel spoke

the truth but not all of it. He didn't like talking about Emmaline, and he especially did not want to explain his wife's absence in front of his son. The boy had been hurt enough by her.

Daniel followed Abernathy Creek on his way home. If only he hadn't accepted her invitation to supper or if he had thought of some simple explanation why his wife had been *away* for five years, Mrs. Dobbs wouldn't've misunderstood his meaning. Hell, he didn't understand it himself.

Caroline settled the full skirt over her many petticoats and buttoned up the bodice. The cinnamon poplin dress had a plain fitted bodice with a lace collar, full sleeves, and a dropped shoulderline. It was comfortable and modest, which seemed appropriate.

She checked on Livvie and Robert. They had awakened when Caroline was about to change for supper. Each had taken part of a bottle, and she hoped they would sleep for a while. Caring for them wasn't difficult, it was a joy, but she wasn't yet used to allowing extra time in her plans for them waking when she thought they would sleep. But I will adjust, she thought, going into the kitchen.

Daniel and Ethan Grey had stopped working early, and she felt certain they would return on time. It was almost six o'clock. The creamy parsnip soup would be done soon, the beaten biscuits were ready for the oven, and the chicken and noodle casserole was bubbling when she put the gingerbread in to bake. She put the coffeepot on the stove and the dish of chicken scraps on the floor for Tucker. She set the bowl of butter on the dining room table, inspected the setting one last time, and had to admit she was a little anxious.

If I had known he was a widower, she mused, would I have invited him for supper? Why not? That had nothing to do with the kindness he had extended her. She added another log to the fire in the fireplace and stopped to gaze at her babies. The sound of a wagon quickened her pulse. Tucker jumped up to the front window and cried out. She licked her lips and smiled at the twins. "Maybe our company's arrived."

She resisted the impulse to peer out of the window and waited for the knock. When she opened the door, Daniel and Ethan had their hats in hand. "Good evening. Come on inside." They had spruced up, and she took that as a compliment.

"Mrs. Dobbs." Daniel handed her the flower he had carved for her. It was a small token he hoped she would like.

"Thank you, Mr. Grey. It is lovely." It was a delicate wood pansy on a short stem. "The wood is beautiful. Did you make this?" To a woman a pansy indicated *pleasant thoughts* or *think of me,* but she believed he meant it as a gesture of kindness, and for that reason it would always remind her of him.

"I like working with wood, and there aren't any flowers around right now. The alder polishes up real nice."

It was hard to believe his large hands could do such delicate work. She hung up their coats and hats and walked into the parlor with them, the pansy still in her hand. The petals were so fine she almost raised it to smell.

Before taking a seat, Daniel paused to look at the twins. "They sure are something."

Caroline smiled. "I think so, but I'm partial."

He glanced across the drawer at her. The way she beamed at the babies reminded him how he had felt after Ethan was born. Unfortunately, Emmaline hadn't been as taken with their son. "They'll outgrow that drawer soon."

"It should do them for another month or more," she said, meeting his gaze, "and give me time to see if I can borrow a cradle." His forest green flannel shirt brought out his brown eyes, and he had even tried to slick back the soft wave over his left ear. Uncomfortable with the direction of her straying thoughts, she quickly looked at Ethan. He was dressed in the same manner as his father and trying to be so grown-up. "How are you, Ethan?"

"Fine, ma'am." Ethan held his hand out to the cat. "Did you know he comes up on the roof with us sometimes?"

"No, but I'm not surprised. Tucker loves to see what everyone is doing." She sat in her rocker and put the pansy on the nearby table. "How are you doing with Mr. Peterson's store?"

Daniel sat in the sturdy armchair. "We've cleared away the damage and started on the foundation."

"Mr. Peterson must be anxious to reopen his store."

"He is. But with almost all of the mills washed out, most folks are worried about replenishing their supplies of flour."

"I imagine it will take a while for the stores to restock the shelves." Caroline noticed Tucker eyeing her, the way he did before he would jump up to her shoulder, and rubbed him behind the ear. "It's a shame about Governor Abernathy's store. Do you know if he's going to rebuild?"

"Some say no. There wasn't much left but rubble. I heard even his account records are gone. He rode by Peterson's the other day." Daniel shook his head. "I've never seen him so downhearted. The city wouldn't be the same without his brick store." He watched her rub the cat's ear with one curved, slender finger, and he understood why the animal purred so contentedly.

Caroline peered into the drawer and smiled. Neither of the twins had awakened, and she hoped they wouldn't until after they had finished eating. She looked at Daniel Grey. This moment was awkward no matter who her guests were. She needed to serve their meal, which meant leaving her company to their own devices, something no good hostess would do, but she did not know how to avoid it. "If you will excuse me, I'll see about supper." It wasn't long before she had filled the water glasses, set the tureen of soup on the table, put the casserole on the warming shelf, and placed the biscuits in the oven to bake.

She invited Daniel and Ethan into supper. Daniel sat on her right, his son across from him. She ladled the parsnip soup into the bowls and passed them out.

Ethan inhaled the steam rising from his bowl of soup. "This sure smells good, doesn't it, Pa?"

Daniel grinned at his son. "That it does." He looked at Mrs. Dobbs. "My cooking's filling and hot, but it doesn't look or smell this good."

"I'm glad you like it." Caroline swallowed a spoonful of soup. "Ethan, have you heard when school will reopen?"

"Next week, I think." Ethan looked across the table at his father. "But I'll be workin' after school."

Daniel gave him a nod. "As long as you keep up your schoolwork, you can work with me."

Caroline did not feel comfortable prying into people's lives, but she knew so little about Daniel Grey. "I hope you won't think me rude, Mr. Grey, but I am curious about your work. Have you built many of the buildings here in town?"

He swallowed the soup and shook his head. "I'm a cabinetmaker by trade. Making furniture is what I like best, but I've worked as a carpenter, and a cooper when there was a shortage of barrels here."

"Your furniture must be in demand. The long trail from the States was marked with family treasures."

"You were fortunate to keep so much of yours."

"We only brought a few pieces. Mr. Dobbs built the frame for the sofa, and I upholstered it to cover the rough wood." She removed the empty soup bowls and served dishes with generous helpings of the casserole. When she returned with her plate, she passed around the basket of biscuits with the butter and set the casserole dish on the table.

Daniel spooned butter onto his plate and handed the bowl to his son. "I noticed your sign out front today." He glanced at the drawer in the parlor. "In a few months you'll have your hands full. Surely they won't always be so quiet." He spread butter on a biscuit and took a bite.

"I wanted the ladies to know that I'm still in business." She shrugged and reached for a biscuit. "Most will be recovering from the flood for some time, but one or two women may need a new dress or want help with remaking one." The gingerbread smelled done, and she went into the kitchen to set the pan on a cooling rack.

Daniel regarded his son and smiled at Mrs. Dobbs as she sat back down. "You'd think he hasn't eaten in a week."

She managed not to laugh. "Then he must like my cooking."

"Yes, ma'am. I wish you'd tell Pa how you made this chicken and noodles so good."

Caroline looked at Daniel and smiled. "I'm sure you don't need any advice. He's almost as tall as you."

Daniel had thought his son had accepted his mother's desertion long ago, but listening to him, he realized he was wrong. Ethan sounded as if he still missed her. Daniel eyed his son with a slight smile. "You can cook anytime you want."

Ethan scooped the last bite on his fork and looked at Caroline. "I want to make this, if you'll tell me how."

"I'll be happy to give you the recipe and help you."

After they finished supper, she cleared the table and served the gingerbread. She had just taken a second bite when one of the babies whimpered. "I'll be right back."

She went into the parlor and stepped over to the drawer.

Livvie quieted at once. "Hi, sweetie." As Caroline picked her up, the baby stared at her. "You want to see what's going on?" She took one of the two squares of oilcloth from the end of the drawer and sat down at the table with the baby cradled in her arm, the oilcloth covering her lap.

Ethan gulped down his bite. "Which one is that?"

"This is Olivia. Livvie, meet Ethan and Mr. Grey."

Ethan stared at the baby. "Gee, she's so little."

Daniel chuckled. "Hard to believe we were that small once, isn't it?"

Robert woke up, and Caroline grinned. "These two will have to learn to take turns."

"I'll hold her for you." Daniel wasn't sure why he had offered, except he hadn't held his daughter. He had seen other women with infants and hadn't felt any need to hold them. It must be Mrs. Dobbs, he decided. Fifteen years ago when he married Emmaline, he had wanted a large family. However, she had told him she didn't want a passel of younguns. He had forgotten about that—until now.

"Thank you." Caroline placed the baby in his waiting arms, amazed by his tender expression. He was so different from Gilbert.

6

$\mathcal{D}$ANIEL HOISTED THE last bundle of shingles up to the roof. He had told Mrs. Dobbs he could do the repairs in four evenings, but after a week, he hadn't finished the roof. To his credit, he had replaced a large section of roof sheathing he hadn't included when he gauged the work.

Ethan hammered the nail down and reached for another shingle. "Pa, when we get these shingles on, can I go fishing? Tim and Leroy said they'd be on the Abernethy— where the old oak fell down."

"Sure." Daniel nodded and opened the bundle of shingles. "We should be done here soon. Maybe you'll catch enough for supper."

Ethan nailed the shingle and picked up another. "I saw the cradle in your shop. You cleanin' it up for Mrs. Dobbs?"

"Yeah. We don't need it, and she does." Daniel concentrated on laying the shingles, but his mind kept drifting back to the cradle he had made for Ethan. The boy had slept in it until the first time he climbed over the side. However, Mrs. Dobbs would need more than one cradle.

"She gonna keep it?"

"I don't know—" Daniel frowned at his son. "I haven't even given it to her, yet. Don't you want me to give it to her?"

Ethan pounded the last two nails in as if he were trying to send them through the roof. "Not *give*, Pa. Can't you just let her use it?"

"I could. But I thought you'd taken a liking to her." His son had a generous nature. It wasn't like him, Daniel thought, to ignore someone's need—or be so angry.

"Well . . . yeah, but didn't you make it for Ma and me?"

"I did." Daniel looked at his son and said, "But she doesn't need it and Mrs. Dobbs does." So, that was it. His mother. He couldn't blame the boy for wanting to keep things that would remind him of her, but Daniel knew where to place the blame—squarely on Emmaline's shoulders.

His memory of their last conversation hadn't faded after more than five years.

"You weren't happy making furniture back home. No, you had to drag me cross country—with only a few dear things of my own, while you bring all of your precious tools—to live in the woods. I can't take being stuck out here. You're happy with your precious trees and your workshop, but I'm not," Emmaline had said. *"I shouldn't've married you, but I'll remedy that. I'm leavin'."*

She packed her clothes, told Ethan good-bye, and rode off on one of their two horses. Daniel hadn't heard from her since, though he had learned that she had boarded a ship bound for San Francisco.

"Cleanin' up the cradle's better than making coffins, huh, Pa?"

"Sure is, son." Daniel smiled at him and picked up another stack of shingles. Tonight I'll start another cradle, he thought, for Mrs. Dobbs. He had made enough coffins for a while.

While Livvie and Robert slept, Caroline folded the dresses,

linens, and nappies as she took them off of the drying rack. Daniel and his son had arrived midday to complete the roof. He assured her the window repairs would be finished long before Christmas. As she carried the stack of clean laundry to her room, she wondered if he realized that Christmas was eleven days away.

She returned to the parlor with a needle, thread, and the cut pieces of white cambric for two infant dresses. By the time Robert woke up, she had stitched the shoulder and side seams and set the gathers around the neck of one dress. She picked him up before his sister woke and carried him to her bedroom.

The wet clothes were dropped in the bucket. She wiped him off with a wet towel and dried him. He waved his arms, and she caught his little hands and kissed them. "I do believe you've grown in the last few days. Your mama was so proud of you and Livvie." And one day I'll tell you how privileged I felt to be a part of your birth and to raise you. She finished dressing him, wrapped him in a blanket, and held him while she mixed the sweet milk and hot water for the bottles.

She fed Robert, holding him, the sucking bottle, and the leather finger in the small opening, which was meant to hold a rubber tube attached to a nipple. She couldn't help wondering how she would manage when the twins were larger. I'll need a kind of sling, she decided, to hold them, one at a time, against my chest so I would have both hands free. As she fed Livvie, Caroline thought about the different materials she had on hand and knew which fabric she would use to make the sling.

Tucker rubbed against her leg, then jumped on the table near her rocking chair and watched Livvie. "What do you think?" He meowed, walked over to the drawer and looked in at Robert. "Wait till they are walking around. Both of us will be busy then."

She was stitching the decorative pleats on one small sleeve, and noticed Daniel walk past the front windows. He had the confident easy stride of a man who had nothing to prove. She smiled as she put down the sewing. She wouldn't call him handsome but neither was he homely, and she had grown fond of him.

A moment later he knocked on the front door. She smoothed her hair back, patted her cheeks, then stood up and brushed her skirt. When he didn't enter, she opened the door and stepped back. "Hello. Won't you come inside?"

"If you don't mind."

"When my sign's out, everyone usually just walks in." As she closed the door, she noticed the bare signpost. "I forgot. It's Sunday, and I didn't hang up the sign." She led the way into the parlor. "You must be thirsty. Can I get you and Ethan something to drink?"

"Thank you. I'll take a glass of water." He could've had a dipper at the well, but he wanted to see her. He talked with his son and the men he worked with, but when he was with her, he felt better than he had in years. "Ethan finished a while ago and went fishing with a couple of his friends." He liked the feel of her home. It was comfortable, warm, and it smelled inviting.

"I'm glad. A boy needs to spend time with his pals."

"We don't usually work on Sundays, but your roof had to be finished." He smiled and shrugged. "This weather can't hold much longer."

"You're right, but after all of the rain, the sun is certainly welcome." She waved her arm toward the chair and sofa. "Have a seat. I'll be right back." She went to the kitchen, filled two glasses with water, and returned to the parlor. Daniel was standing by the hearth in front of the drawer smiling at the twins on the bench. She handed one of the glasses to him. "How is Mr. Peterson's store coming along?"

He walked around to the armchair and sat down. "We'll be closing up the walls tomorrow and put in the windows when the glass arrives." He drank half the glass of water and noticed the cat watching him from the far end of the sofa.

She sat in her caned rocking chair and set her glass on the small table between their chairs. "Are you able to get your supplies from Portland?" The armchair seemed well suited to Daniel, and she liked that.

"Some. Others are being shipped from Astoria, and two ships left last week for San Francisco to bring back more." The cat had moved closer to Mrs. Dobbs. Caroline sounded friendlier. He had already started thinking of her as a friend, but he couldn't allow himself to go beyond that. And with her, it would be easy. "The twins look like they've grown some."

"I thought so, too, but it's hard for me to tell. They're only a week old. I'm sure they will feel heavier before long."

"Have you had any luck with borrowing a cradle?"

"I'm afraid not. The women I've asked had already lent them out." As she spoke, she recalled that he had said he was a cabinetmaker. "Mr. Grey, when you finish Mr. Peterson's store, will you go back to making furniture?"

He nodded. "I enjoy working with wood too much to give that up." The cat was now watching him from underneath the small table between their chairs. He lowered his right arm and let his hand hang down for the animal to smell. "We have Ethan's cradle, and I've cleaned it up. Would you like to use it?"

She slowly smiled. "I appreciate your offer, Mr. Grey. Yes, I would like to borrow it—at least until I can make other arrangements." She sipped her water. "I was about to ask what you might charge to make one."

"It would depend on the wood. Mahogany, pine, or walnut? And on the design. Spindles take time to shape, unless you wanted a simple box style. . . ." He had already chosen the alder for the second cradle and had decided to make it in the sleigh-bed style, same as the other one. He would have to put her off until Christmas so he could surprise her.

"Spindles would be too fancy," she said, interrupting him, "but a simple pine box type would serve the purpose. It won't make any difference to them." And she couldn't afford to be prideful. What she hadn't the means to provide, she would make up with affection, love, and a good home.

"Cradles are more for the mother's convenience than the baby's. Ethan's is large enough for both twins for a while. I'll bring it over tomorrow." The cat rubbed against his hand. He smiled and stroked the animal.

"That would be wonderful. Thank you, Mr. Grey." She started rocking. Having a second bed for the twins in the bedroom would be convenient, she thought, but that could wait. She needed the drawer back in the chest so she could put away her clothes. "Would you have time—in the next few weeks, next month—to make a plain box-type cradle?" It shouldn't cost too much, at least she hoped not. However, weighing the price against the thought of carrying the cradle, with both infants, from room to room made the expense much more reasonable.

"I don't see why not." Good, he thought, she hadn't pressed him to make it soon.

"They are so small right now, but I always seem to plan ahead."

"With twins, that's a good idea. You'll have your hands full with them in a couple years."

She gazed at Livvie and Robert and grinned. "I'm looking forward to that." Tucker jumped in her lap and curled up. She glanced at Daniel. "That may sound odd, but I have wanted—" Good grief, whatever possessed her to almost share her most intimate thoughts with him? "I'm sorry. I was rambling."

He nodded. "They'll get into your sewing before you know it." His attention strayed to her hand as she petted the cat. Although the animal had a soothing effect on her, watching her slender fingers caress the cat had a decidedly unsettling effect on him. He drained his glass of water. "I want to take another look at your windows before I go." He stood up and set the glass on the table.

Tucker vaulted to the sofa, and Caroline walked Daniel to the door. "Thank you for finishing the roof."

"Would you like to see it?"

"Yes, I am curious." She glanced up at the edge of the roof. "Can I see it from the yard?"

He smiled at her. "I don't see why not," he said, holding his hand out to her.

It was an everyday gesture, one she should not have given a second thought to, and wouldn't have, if she hadn't seen the flash of humor in his dark eyes. I'm far too old to behave as if I were a schoolgirl, she thought, and put her hand in his. His broad fingers were surprisingly gentle. When she started to walk down the walkway, he released her hand.

He walked at her side to the wagon. He could have taken her arm, but there was no need, unless he admitted that he just wanted to feel the warmth of her again. He turned back to face the house. "The new shingles will weather and blend in with the others."

She stared at the roof. He had repaired more than she expected he would. "You replaced most of the shingles. It's almost a new roof."

"Once we removed the old wood, I found more water damage underneath."

"How much?"

"Four sheathing boards were damp, warping. I replaced seven in all."

She clasped her hands at her waist and could almost hear the clink of the coins stacking up. "Are those boards large?"

"They're eight feet long, 'bout six inches wide. Good and strong."

She walked over to where she could see the side of the house. "Was the damage worse on the back side?"

"No. You shouldn't have to worry about it for a long time. It's almost as good as new."

"From here, it does look like it." We'll be dry, she thought. And I will pay more attention to it in the future. "How much do I owe you?"

"Nothing, till I've finished all of the work."

She unclasped her hands and felt the blood rush back into her cold fingers. "Not even for material?" When one of her customers wanted a dress made from an expensive fabric, she arranged to have them pay for it before she cut out the dress.

He chuckled. "Hold on to your money a few more days." He took the measuring stick out of his tool chest, tapped the stick on his forehead in a friendly salute, and headed for the side of the house. He almost felt as if he were working at home. Almost.

Daniel applied another coat of his special polish to the cradle and rubbed it into the wood. This was the fourth coat he had put on, and would be the last. As he worked, he recalled the night he had presented the cradle to Emmaline, the pride he'd felt in having made the handsome bed for his child. She said it was nice, but she'd wanted one of those pretty cradles with spindles all around the sides. He pointed out that the one he had made would provide more warmth in the winter.

He rubbed harder. It was gratifying to see the beauty of the mahogany come to life. He buffed it until he was satisfied with the deep luster and covered it with a clean cloth. It was late and he was tired, but he looked over the measurements he had taken one last time. That one would be made with alder grown on his land. He closed the door to his shop and walked across the yard to the house. The fire in the fireplace had burned down to embers, and Ethan was sound asleep in his room.

Daniel banked the fire and went to his room. He shed his clothes and stretched out under the covers. When he closed his eyes, he saw Caroline smiling at him. She was a breath of springtime, and he drifted to sleep with the sound of her silvery voice clear in his mind.

After a fitful night's rest, he awoke looking around his room, searching for . . . What? He couldn't quite remember. He rinsed his face with cold water from the pitcher and felt more alert. He pulled on his trousers, woolen stockings, and his shoes before going to the kitchen. He had added it on to the cabin seven months before Emmaline left, but it hadn't been enough to keep her home.

The bacon sizzled in the iron skillet, and flapjacks bubbled on the griddle. He was putting the eggs into the pot of boiling water when Ethan came in yawning. "Good morning. Sleep well?"

Ethan poured himself a cup of coffee. "You always ask me that. What if I said no? It's too late to do anything about it." He grinned and picked up a piece of crispy bacon. "Did you start on the Henrys' table last night?"

"I'll get to it in a day or so." Daniel shrugged and turned

the flapjacks onto a plate. "Trestle tables aren't complicated."

"Don't forget, you told them you'd deliver it well before Christmas." Using the big fork, Ethan lifted the bacon from the skillet and dropped the strips on a plate.

Daniel glanced at his son. "They'll have it in plenty of time." Sometimes the boy sounded more like the father than the boy. "Did you finish that drawing you were working on after supper?"

"Nah. But I think I know what's wrong with it now."

"Good for you. That's half of the work." Daniel removed the eggs from the boiling water and broke two over each stack of flapjacks. "You'll have to walk over to school and see when it'll start up again."

"Okay." As he sat down at the table, Ethan darted a glance at his father. "Freddy signed up with the Clackamas Company the other day."

"He's barely two years older than you. Did his father know?"

"S'pose so. But the Union needs more men." Ethan cut a bite of flapjacks with his fork. "That's what the sergeant said."

"I heard that the Oregon troops won't be leaving the area."

"You're wrong, Pa. You gotta be 'cause Freddy says he's goin' to help President Lincoln fight those secessionists."

"They aren't fighting here. Hope he won't mind mucking out the horse stalls and shining boots. Guess he thought life in the Oregon Regiment would be more exciting than working on his pa's farm." Daniel ate a bite of egg and flapjacks. That boy'd be better off staying in school. He was glad Ethan seemed to be following in his own footsteps.

When they finished eating breakfast, Daniel washed the dishes and his son dried and put them away. His life hadn't turned out the way he had thought it would, but he had a fine son and his work. He had only one disappointment, and there was little he could do—short of a scandal—to change that. He hitched the horse to the wagon and called to his son.

As Ethan crossed the yard, he saw his father put the covered cradle under the seat. He hurried that last few yards and climbed to the seat. "You still gonna give that cradle to her?"

The boy sounded so much like his mother that Daniel fixed his son with a furious glare. "She's borrowing it. One day your child may use it. But I made it, and I'll not leave it in the rafters when Mrs. Dobbs has need of it." He snapped the reins on the horse's rump.

Ethan stared at his shoes and gnashed on his lips. A couple long, silent minutes later, he gulped and said, "Sorry, Pa," just louder than a whisper.

Daniel loosened his stranglehold grip on the reins. "Good. You should be." The sky above was clear, but there were clouds moving up from the south. Damn. They didn't need any more rain.

"Does she know?"

"What? That you didn't want her to use *your* cradle?" Daniel shook his head. "Why would I tell her—" At least the boy had the good grace to be ashamed. For that, he was grateful.

"Thanks, Pa." Ethan looked down the road that cut through their land. "She was nice. I don't want her to feel bad 'cause of me."

"She won't—unless you tell her." Daniel leaned back and surveyed his trees. Two Douglas firs, one of the tall white oaks, and a couple maple trees had fallen in the last storm. He planned to trim one of the firs, bring it into the house, and decorate it for Christmas. His prized alders were fine. When he cut them down, he chose with care so he didn't weaken the stand of trees. Their wood made beautiful furniture.

"Pa, can we stop by Mrs. Dobbs's house on the way to Mr. Peterson's store?"

Daniel glanced at his son. "That's fine with me." He'd just as soon not wait until later. It had been so long since he enjoyed looking forward to seeing a woman that he felt a little foolish. They were hardly friends, and that was the most he could hope for, he thought. It would have to be enough.

He pulled up in front of Caroline's house. The cat was sitting in the front yard as if it were on guard. He stepped down and lifted the cradle from the wagon.

Ethan looked at his father. "Can I go in with you?"

"I wasn't going to stay but come up to the door with me." Daniel followed his son to the door and waited for Caroline to answer his knock. Was she bright-eyed in the morning? Did her reddish-brown hair hang down her back in waves? What was— He'd lost his senses. Even though he didn't have a wife, he was married and must remember that.

Tucker walked over to Ethan, and Ethan bent down to pet him. "Pa, maybe she's not up yet."

"I can leave it here. I'll be back later to fix the windows." Daniel was setting the cradle on the doorstep when the door opened.

Caroline didn't know who to expect so early in the day, but seeing Daniel bent over on her doorstep struck her as funny. She grinned. "Good morning. Won't you both come in?"

Daniel stood up holding the cradle. "We're on our way to work, but we thought you would like to have this. I'll just set it in the parlor for you."

She stared at the cradle. He hadn't exaggerated about the size. He put it down in front of the fireplace. The cradle resembled a sleigh bed. "It's beautiful, Mr. Grey." She ran her hand over the satin smooth, curved end. "It looks new. Ethan must have been a very quiet baby."

"Hardly," he said, laughing. "Good wood wears well." She was crouched down, her dark gray skirt billowed out around her like a cloud, and a red ribbon held her hair back from her face. He glanced up and saw his son watching from the doorway. "It's been a long time since he used it."

"I will take very good care with it." Tucker ran in and jumped into the cradle. Caroline smiled at Daniel as she stood up. "He might as well look at it now. It'll be the last time he gets in there."

Ethan walked over to them. "He won't hurt it. He's just nosy."

She glanced at the cradle, then at Daniel and at his hands. The small bed was a work of art. He was a true craftsman. No wonder he enjoyed making furniture. "Would you like a cup of coffee? It won't take long."

Daniel looked from his son to Caroline. "Better not now. But I'll be by later to start on the windows."

"Thank you for bringing the cradle. I really appreciate it." She smiled at Ethan. "Did you try making the chicken and noodles recipe yet?"

"No, ma'am, but I will soon." Ethan went outside and waited on the stoop for his pa.

"I will see you later then, Mr. Grey." He smiled, a broad boyish toothy smile, and his eyes crinkled at the outer corners. She met his gaze for a moment and wondered why she hadn't noticed how attractive he was before then. Tucker ran under her skirt, and she remembered that Ethan was waiting outside of the open door. "There isn't a grander cradle west of the Mississippi. I'll make it up for the twins."

"I'm glad you like it, Caroline." He nodded and belatedly

realized what he had said. He'd feared thinking of her by her given name could lead to trouble. As he waited for her reproach, his heart pounded. She remained silent, except for the smile that said more than words.

7

CAROLINE KNEW BABIES were not usually as quiet as the twins had been, but that wasn't the case now. Robert's sharp cry had pierced the air only moments before Livvie began wailing. Tucker jumped to the back of the sofa, where he could guard them from a safe distance.

"Shh," Caroline said, settling Robert in the crook of her left arm. She scooped up his sister with her right arm and sat down in her chair. She gently rocked them and murmured until they quieted.

Caroline wondered if they were upset by the separation now that Livvie slept in the cradle. If that was the cause of their discomfort, she believed the change would be easier now than in a few months when they were older. As she rocked, she looked for differences between the twins. Livvie's fingers were just a little narrower than Robert's, and his feet were a tiny bit longer than hers, but their hair was the same dark brown as Addie's.

A wagon stopped in front of the house. She managed to rise with a baby cradled in each arm and walked over to the window. Daniel. He was early, and he was alone. That should not make any difference, she told herself. In another day or so the repairs would be complete. He wouldn't have a reason to call, and she didn't have the funds to pay him to fix anything else. She wouldn't see him again. When he started up the walk, she put Robert down in the drawer. She opened the front door and stepped back so Livvie wouldn't feel the draft.

Daniel stopped on the threshold. "Is it all right if I come in?" Caroline was standing in the doorway to the parlor— rosy cheeked, her skirt swaying as she gently rocked the baby in her arms. She had changed since their first meeting. Much had happened since that day, but she seemed more at peace, happier.

"Please." Livvie whimpered, and she rubbed her stomach to quiet her. "Did you finish early?" She had planned to have a small pot of coffee ready for him, later, but she was nonetheless happy to see him.

"A little. Looks like it might rain soon. I wanted to take care of one or two of the windows for you." He peered at the baby in her arms. "Which one is this?"

"Livvie. I just put Robert down. It isn't easy holding both of them at the same time."

"Mind if I hold him?"

She smiled at Daniel. "I think he would like that." She knew Gilbert would never have made such an offer. Daniel picked up the baby and held him in the crook of his arm. What a wonderful sight. She had only seen one other man show such tenderness to an infant.

Daniel ambled across the room with the tiny treasure in his arm. "He just wanted to see what's going on." He loosened the blanket so the baby could move his arms, and looked at Caroline. "You'll have a special Christmas with these two."

"A quiet one, but definitely merry." She pressed a kiss to Livvie's forehead. "What about you?"

"The same. My family's back in Michigan, Clair County. We usually manage to trade letters for Christmas." He moved the baby to his shoulder and patted his back. "Doesn't look like there'll be much snow in the mountains this Christmas."

"Not after the warm spell." Watching the tender way he held Robert gave Caroline the feeling that Daniel would like to have more children. He's not too old to marry again and have more, she thought, but maybe he's still mourning his wife. "Do you miss the snow?"

"Sometimes." He looked at her and smiled. "It was fun when Pa put runners on the wagon, or I'd walk into the woods. It was so quiet."

"We'll probably get some snow in the next month or so." Livvie had fallen asleep, and Caroline put her in the cradle. "Do you want me to take him now?"

"No, but you'd better." He lifted one of the baby's hands. So tiny. "Well, my boy, you rest, and I'll get some work done." He handed the baby to Caroline and watched him snuggle against her neck. That lucky little babe. "I'll start on the back window." He went to the hall and looked back at her. "The window has to come out. I'll leave the door closed."

After Robert dozed off, she put him down in his bed and finished stitching the sling she had cut out. It wasn't her best work, but it was serviceable. She put on a pot of coffee and started preparing her supper. Daniel made a couple of trips through the house. She thought about asking him to have supper with her, but decided against that idea. The last time there had been a reason—or an excuse—but she had none now. She set the pan of garden soup on to heat, put a slice of smoked ham in the small skillet, and prepared the bottles for the babies.

Daniel went back into the house. She wasn't in the parlor with the twins, and he sure wasn't about to walk down the hall to the back room without telling her. "Caroline—"

"Yes—" She met him at the door to the dining room. "Finished already?"

"With the back window. Can't do any more outside tonight, but I want to check the inside of the other windows."

"Do you need my help?" She glanced into the kitchen.

"Not if you don't mind my looking in the other rooms."

"That's all right. Would you like some coffee when you're done?"

"Sounds good." He went down the hall and checked the window in the bedroom. Must be hers, he thought. Although there were stacks of baby things on every flat surface, the room was very neat. He looked at her bedroom window and went into the parlor. That window seal was in the worst condition; water had run down the wall and stained it. He packed the space between the glass and the bottom rail with a piece of twine and went outside to repeat the process.

Caroline moved her supper to the side of the stovetop and made a pot of tea for herself. She set two cups on the worktable and put out the sugar bowl, a spoon, and a small pitcher of milk. The front door closed and a moment later a cry pierced the calm. She hurried into the parlor, but by the time she reached out to pick up Livvie, Robert started wailing, too.

We will work this out, Caroline thought, carrying Livvie to the bedroom to change her wet clothes. If they had to take turns, surely they wouldn't know any different and would adapt to it. Clean and momentarily dry, Livvie quieted a little. Caroline kissed the baby's soft cheek. "You will have supper very soon." When she returned to the parlor, Daniel was holding Robert, trying to calm him. "Thank you for helping, but I'm afraid they are going to have to learn to be patient with me."

"I know. But I'm easily taken in by babies." *And certain pretty smiles*, he thought, gazing at her.

She smiled. "I'll remember that." She put Livvie in the cradle and turned to Daniel. She stood toe to toe with him, close enough to hear the husky rush of air he exhaled as she slid her hand under the baby and brushed the soft fabric covering his muscular arm. A delicious wave of pure pleasure flittered through her stomach. It had been so long since she had experienced that wonderful sensation that she was surprised by it and nearly snatched the baby away from him.

He tried to move his arm out of the way but nearly ended up with it trapped between the baby and her nicely rounded bosom. He didn't need to know what she felt like. His imagination had been doing just fine, but now he would have the memory to haunt him.

"I'll be right back." She hurried down the hall to her bedroom, praying he hadn't heard the pounding of her heart. She kissed Robert's little clenched fists and began changing his wet linens. As she washed and dried him, she wondered what Daniel had been like when he was a baby. A young boy. Suddenly she remembered that he was a widower—for five years. Maybe her instincts weren't that wrong. She went back to the parlor and put the baby down in the drawer. "I'd better feed them. Would you like coffee now?"

"That would be fine." When she turned to go to the kitchen, he followed her. "I'll need to come back the next two or three evenings. Tomorrow I'll start to work on the parlor window. I may have to open up the wall."

She glanced over at him. "It's that bad?" She filled a cup with coffee and set it in front of him.

"Afraid so. I'll replace the sashes, but the marks on the wall look as if they've been there a while."

"Yes. I noticed them the first time last spring and wiped

up the water." She shook her head. "I forgot about the leak, until a couple weeks ago."

"I'll take care of it." He glanced down at his hands. "Do you mind if I wash up?"

"There's a pan in the dry sink. You can use that towel on the side." Nice, she thought, having him in the kitchen and around the house. She had grown used to living alone, but that didn't mean she preferred her solitary life.

After he had dried his hands, he picked up one of the little bottles on the table. "This is what you use to feed them?" It was shaped like the body of a blackbird and about the same size.

"Yes. We were fortunate that Martha was able to find them." She mixed the prepared milk with hot water and filled the other bottle.

He turned it around. "Can they drink out of this end?"

"Not yet," she said, grinning, but there was no reason he should know anything about sucking bottles. "I was using pieces of chamois for nipples but they got too stiff, so I made a few of cloth." The cloth-covered wads seemed to be working. At least the twins weren't getting too much milk at once and choking, and they seemed to be satisfied with about the same amount as a couple days ago.

"It sounds complicated." He handed the bottle to her and added a spoon of sugar to his coffee.

She filled the second bottle and set both on the tray, along with the small plate with the nipples. "I feed them in the parlor," she said, picking up the tray. "It's more comfortable than in here."

"Can I pour your coffee?"

"No, thank you. I'll have a cup of tea after I've fed Livvie and Robert." She walked back to the parlor, set the tray on the hearth, and one bottle and small plate on the table between the chairs. Livvie was sobbing, and Robert had his fist in his mouth.

Daniel sat in the armchair and watched her stuff the wad of cloth about the size and length of his thumb into the bottle. It was a clever idea. The only infant he had seen nurse was his son at his mother's breast, a memory he had treasured.

Choosing which baby to care for first was a frustrating decision for Caroline. Robert tended to be the more patient one, but he shouldn't have to always be second because his sister was more demanding. After she tied the ends of the sling around her neck, she kissed Livvie and placed Robert in the sling. He nestled against her. It was a perfect fit.

Daniel stared at the hammocklike contraption. It was clever and the baby looked content. "I never knew there was so much to know about bringing up babies."

"I admit I've tried to solve problems I have never thought about before. It might have been easier if they were my natural children, but we are doing very well." She put the cloth nipple in the small opening of the bottle, tipped it until the fabric was wet, and lightly pressed it to Robert's lips. "And I couldn't love them any more."

As Robert sucked on that nipple, Daniel saw the pleasure and satisfaction in Caroline's eyes. "He sure is hungry. Looks like his sister is, too, and she doesn't mind letting you know."

Caroline looked at the cradle. "Maybe if I could rock her it would help." That's the answer, she thought, for both of them. She slid her foot over to the rocker on the cradle and gave it a gentle tap.

Daniel grinned. If she'd had another pair of hands, they would also be busy with two babies to care for. "I don't mind holding her for you."

"Thank you, but I—" She paused when she noticed the

way he was gazing at the baby. He really wanted to hold her, she realized. "I would appreciate your help." She had to be careful, otherwise she could easily become spoiled.

He held Livvie on his shoulder and wandered around the room with her. "This's a nice house. Did your husband build it?"

She nodded. "Mr. Stiles and Mr. Tibbles crossed the country in the wagon train with us. The three men decided it would be easier for them to work together on three houses than for each of them to build his own." Caroline tipped the bottle back. Robert was getting stronger, sucking on the nipple with more energy. Thank goodness. She wanted to be a good mother, and in her mind that meant seeing him and his sister thrive, not simply survive.

"When was that?"

"A little over five years ago."

He stopped in front of the fireplace. The stones were well set, the mortar still strong, and it was straight. "They did good work."

"Thank you." She glanced over at the fireplace made of stones she had helped gather, then watched Daniel walking with the baby with such ease. "How long have you lived here?"

"We came across in fifty-four." Almost eight years ago, he thought. Ethan had turned five during their journey.

Daniel turned, and Caroline couldn't miss the hard set of his jaw. "I hope I'm not speaking out of place, but both of us have lost our partners. Or is it still difficult for you to talk about her?"

"Yes, it is. That's why—" He sat down on the sofa facing her. "I have to clear this up. Last week when you asked about my wife, I said she wasn't with us any longer. And she's not." He started patting the baby's back. "Everyone knows. I haven't had to explain this in years." I'm rambling, he thought, just spit it out. "She isn't dead, Caroline. She left me five years ago." Caroline looked puzzled, and he waited for her to speak.

She felt stunned, but she tried to piece together what he had said. "You're telling me you are married? And you let me believe you had been widowed?"

"I didn't mean to, but yes. I don't like talking about it, especially in front of Ethan. He was sure his ma left him even though I told him it was me she didn't want any part of."

When Robert pushed the nipple away, Caroline set the bottle down and put him on her shoulder. "It must have been difficult . . . for both you and your son." Daniel was married, she kept thinking. She had just begun to realize that her feelings for him could be much deeper than mere friendship. Even worse, she had believed he might return her regard. She stood up and walked over to the side window.

It was easy to see that she was upset, but he wished he knew *what* she was thinking. He glanced down at Livvie and brushed his lips over the baby's cheek before he came to his feet. "I'll leave now."

"Yes. Maybe you should." He had been nice, she thought, almost too good-natured and helpful.

He laid the baby down in the cradle. He walked to the door and turned to her. "I told you the truth. At the time I didn't think it'd make much difference. I didn't know—" *That I would come to care for you,* he had come close to saying. However, it was probably best, for her, if he didn't tell her how he felt. She deserved better than the esteem of a married man, and he couldn't offer her any more than that. "I'm sorry. I'll fix that window tomorrow."

She nodded and waited until he had closed the front door behind him before she put Robert down. Daniel's wagon rumbled up the street, and she let out a long shuddering sigh. Married. She cared for another woman's husband, and she had thought she had reason to believe he was interested in her, too. Fool, she thought.

Daniel fitted one dovetailed side to the head end of the cradle. It was late, but after he had finished cutting out the pieces needed for the cradle, he didn't want to stop until he had put it together. However, the more he tried to concentrate on the crib, the more Caroline's discomfited expression haunted him. He had believed he could mask his feelings—from her and from himself.

Since he hadn't succeeded, he would show her that he wanted only to be friends. After he had fitted the sides to the ends of the crib, he placed the bottom board inside on the lip and nailed it down. When the two rockers were attached, he applied the stain. The cradle wasn't an exact replica of the first one, but most people weren't likely to see the difference. Most important, it would be hers—to keep, lend, or give away.

The following morning Caroline slept until the babies woke her. Having fed them every two or three hours around the clock for nine days, she had learned to nap whenever she could. In fact the last time Martha had come over to help, Caroline had slept. She had finally worked out a routine— feed the babies when they were hungry, rest anytime she could, and sew for as long as she could keep her eyes open.

Once Livvie and Robert had been changed and fed, Caroline washed and dressed. She ate a bowl of mush in the parlor with the twins and talked to them. She knew they didn't have any idea what she was saying, but they quieted at the sound of her voice, and it helped keep her thoughts from straying to Daniel. Married.

About two that morning, when she had been up with the babies, she remembered what he had said about his wife. The woman had left him. She couldn't help but wonder why. He seemed to be a gentle man, hardworking, and he didn't look like a man who drank excessively. Of course, she hardly knew him. Maybe there was more . . . or maybe she just shouldn't think about him. She certainly had no intention of carrying on with . . . She laughed. Her imagination was running wild. He hadn't suggested anything of the sort.

After breakfast she hung out her dressmaker's sign and put the little brass bell back over the door. Back to normal. It even looked drizzly out—very normal for December. She set to work stitching the pieces together for the second infant dress.

About midmorning the bell rang out and Mrs. Kinney, her next-door neighbor, stepped inside. Although age had rounded her shoulders and grayed her hair, it hadn't slowed her pace any.

"Hello, Mrs. Kinney." Caroline put down her sewing and went over to the older woman. "I haven't been over to check in on you since the flood." Mrs. Kinney was a hardy soul. She had outlived four husbands and said that was enough.

"There's no need. I understand you have been busy." Mrs. Kinney looked around the room and walked over to the cradle, then saw Robert in the drawer. "Good gracious, two. Couldn't believe the poor woman'd had two of them. Both boys?"

"No. Robert is sleeping in the drawer, and Livvie is in the cradle." Caroline smiled at the twins.

"One of each. That's good but a lot of work. What're you gonna do with them?"

Caroline motioned for her to take a seat and sat in the rocking chair near the babies. "I am going to raise them.

Mrs. Williams, their mother, and I agreed before her passing. But why do you ask? Hardly anyone knows about them. I haven't put an announcement in the newspaper."

Mrs. Kinney sat down on the sofa. "No need to. Mr. Moss helped pull that poor woman from the river. Doc Lindley saw them and their ma, you sent Martha to buy those sucking bottles, and Reverend Vincent presided over the service at the cemetery." She chuckled. "That's half the town."

Caroline realized that she was staring at her and quickly glanced at the twins. "What are people saying?" It honestly hadn't occurred to her that anyone would give her a second thought. After the flood, wouldn't there be more to think about than her situation? Besides, she mused, what I do is my business alone.

"The folks've been talking 'bout who'll take the infants. Some say they'll have to be separated, some say not." Mrs. Kinney stared at the babies. "Not bad looking. Good size for two born at once. Reverend Vincent won't have any trouble t'all finding them homes."

"No. I daresay he wouldn't, if they needed one." Caroline looked Mrs. Kinney in the eye. "I will raise Robert and Livvie. No one could love them more than I do."

"I see." Mrs. Kinney shrugged. "Ain't none of my never-mind. Mr. Hoyle said you'd never give 'em up."

Caroline smiled. Mr. Hoyle was the neighbor on the other side, a quiet man who wrote poetry and accounts of pioneer travel. She didn't know him much better than Mrs. Kinney, but he evidently was more understanding. "Would you like a cup of tea?"

"Thanks, but I gotta git." Mrs. Kinney stood up and walked to the front door. "If you need a hand, don't think twice b'fore asking."

"I won't, Mrs. Kinney." Caroline opened the door and Tucker ran inside.

"You don't let that cat near those babies, do you?"

"He doesn't get too close, and he lets me know when they are waking up."

Mrs. Kinney shook her head. "That animal'll suck the breath right out of those babies if he gets the chance." She started down the walkway. "You mind what I say if you care about those two."

Caroline closed the door and the bell rang softly, but the twins didn't seem to mind the sound. She went over and kissed each of them. "We will be just fine, my little ones." She smiled at Tucker. "That includes you, too." She knew he would never harm the twins, but she couldn't say the same for some people.

Daniel hammered a nail into the wallboard. Mr. Peterson would soon be able to start moving stock into his store. Daniel picked up another board and finished the south wall. After he closed up the last wall, he carried a half dozen of the extra boards out to his wagon.

Ethan ran up to his father. "Pa, can I go back and help Mr. Stanton some more?"

"If he needs it. Did you get the walls cleaned off?"

"Yeah, and the desks, too. Well, just about, but the floor's still muddy. Is it okay? He said he'd make a fire, and we could cook supper when we're done. Can I?"

Daniel chuckled. "Sure. When will you be finished?"

Ethan shrugged.

"I told Mrs. Dobbs I'd be over to work on the parlor window. I'll stop by the school on the way back home." He felt as if he had just been putting in time all day until he would see Caroline. He wasn't sure how she'd feel about him today, but he had been looking forward to seeing her.

He remembered how his mother would chase his father out of the house when she was angry, then later, after she had had a chance to think it over, she would talk it out with him. He could only hope Caroline would be as fair.

"Thanks, Pa."

Daniel went back inside the store. The counters had been salvaged, but there were still cupboards and a lot of shelves to put up. He checked the plans, picked up the measuring stick and began marking where the cupboards and shelf brackets would be mounted on the wall.

After he had marked off the placement of the cupboards, he folded the measuring stick and closed up the store. It was close to sundown. He had waited long enough.

8

$\mathcal{I}$T WAS JUST after three o'clock when Caroline put Livvie down in the cradle and sat in her rocker to feed Robert. Dan— No. Mr. Grey should be there in a little while. Would he bring his son? The boy was nice, but his father had deceived her. She was willing, now, to allow that he hadn't started out to, but he didn't correct her misunderstanding when she believed that his wife had died—not until much later. That was unforgivable. Well, almost, but she couldn't think of how he could possibly talk his way back into her good graces.

There was a tap on the door just before it opened. She watched the entry. It wasn't Mr. Grey. It was one of her ladies, and she smiled. "Mrs. Tillson, how nice to see you." Robert turned his head away from the bottle, and Caroline set it on the table. Mrs. Tillson hadn't been in to have a dress made for at least a year.

"And you, Mrs. Dobbs." Mrs. Tillson went into the parlor and stared at Robert. "Those are the babies—the twins I've heard about, aren't they?"

"Yes, Mrs. Williams's infants." Caroline put Robert on her shoulder and gently rubbed his back. "How may I help you, Mrs. Tillson?" Livvie whimpered. Caroline slid her foot over to one rocker of the cradle and carefully rocked it.

Mrs. Tillson stepped over to the cradle. "Pretty little dears, aren't they?"

"I think so, too." Caroline watched Mrs. Tillson, wondering if she had come to learn gossip or if she did want to have some clothing made. Or maybe she just wanted to visit. "Did you have much damage from the storm?"

"Nothing to speak of. Did you?"

"Some, but it's being repaired."

Mrs. Tillson nodded. "I know this's short notice, but do you think you could make a dress for me before New Year's?"

"I'm not sure. What did you have in mind?"

"Oh, nothing too fancy. A soft wool would be warm. What do you think of that claret color? Would it look good on me?"

"Claret?" Caroline eyed Mrs. Tillson. "Indigo blue, or wine red or dark green would be nice. In fact, I have a dress you may like. I'll be right back." After putting Robert down in his bed, Caroline went back to the sewing room and searched through the cupboard where she stored folded yard goods and unfinished garments. She found the one she wanted and returned to the parlor.

Holding up the basted-together wine red dress, she said, "Do you like this? It would be easy to take in for you." She held out one sleeve to her. "This wool is very soft." It had a plain fitted bodice with bishop's sleeves and a generous skirt. If she didn't sell it, she just might make it over for herself.

Mrs. Tillson rubbed her fingers and thumb on the fabric. "I do like it. How come you haven't finished it?"

"Mrs. Evans ordered it and didn't return for her fitting."

"Elvira Evans?"

"Yes, Mrs. Tillson."

"But my dear, she ran off and left poor Mr. Evans just a

month ago. He even put a notice in the *Argus*. Said she ran out and he won't pay her debts."

Caroline nodded. "I saw that, too, but I wasn't sure then if she had left town."

"Some women never take to life here, but she did have a good eye for nice clothes." Mrs. Tillson stared at the dress. "A bertha collar would be perfect, wouldn't it?" She smiled. "I'll take it, Mrs. Dobbs. Can you have it ready by the thirtieth?"

"Yes, Mrs. Tillson. If you have the time, I can do the fitting now and you can pick it up in thirteen days," she said with a smile.

"I knew if anyone could make me a dress in time, you would."

It was always reassuring when a customer confided her confidence, Caroline thought. "Come back to the sewing room with me, Mrs. Tillson." She grinned at the twins. One dress at a time, she thought.

The fitting went well, and half an hour later Caroline walked her customer to the front door. "Have a happy Christmas, Mrs. Tillson."

"And you, Mrs. Dobbs."

As Caroline stepped back and started to close the door, Mr. Grey drove up in his wagon. His son wasn't with him. She clenched one hand in the folds of her skirt and fervently wished she wasn't glad to see him. She shouldn't be. Then he smiled and waved at her. Surely he didn't believe she had forgotten their conversation last night.

Daniel picked up his toolbox from the back of the wagon and headed up the walkway. The sign was out, and Caroline looked the same as the first time he met her. Distant, reserved. She stepped away from the door, but she did leave it open for him. He went inside and closed it. A bell jingled overhead, and he glanced up. I'm just the carpenter, he reminded himself, and entered the parlor.

He set the toolbox near the hearth and looked at her. "Hello. Is it all right if I start on that window now?"

"Yes, of course. I'll take the twins into another room." She picked up the drawer and carried it down the hall to the sewing room. She put the drawer across the bed and glanced up as Daniel came in carrying the cradle.

"Where do you want me to set this down?"

"There, at the end of the bed," she said, motioning to the end closest to the woodstove. She was glad for his help, and yet, she wished he hadn't moved it for her. It seemed childish, but she didn't want to be any more beholden to him than she was already.

As he made his way along the length of the bed, she stepped back beside the woodstove. He set the cradle where she wanted it. When he straightened up, he was less than an arm's reach from her, close enough to notice the rise and fall of her chest and hear her ragged breath, close enough to slip his arm around her waist. "It's sturdy—and heavy. I'll put it back in the parlor for you after I finish."

His voice seemed to vibrate in the small room. She clutched the piece of firewood and concentrated at the wave of his hair at his temple, instead of looking him in the eye. "Thank you." She opened the door on the woodstove and put the wood inside and started the fire.

He stepped into the hall and closed the door. He had hoped she would at least be willing to talk to him, give him a chance to tell her about his wife. Maybe he had been wrong, and she really didn't care. He went into the parlor and started removing the lower sash from the casing.

He had replaced the bottom rail of the window frame and was resealing the glass when he heard Caroline in the kitchen. Something, maybe a spoon, clattered on the floor, a cupboard door shut, and he thought he heard her say something. He finished repairing the window and put it back into the casing. By the time he had taken off the stained wallboard, he had decided he needed to talk with her.

He grabbed a rag, wiped off his hands, and walked into the kitchen. She looked over at him brushing a wisp of hair out of her eyes as if surprised to see him. "Having trouble?"

She glared at him, snatched the towel off of the back of the chair, and sopped up the milk she had just spilled. "Is there something you need?" The only problem she had was with him.

"As a matter of fact, there is. I'd like to take up our conversation where we left off last night."

"What else is there to say?" She studied him for a moment. He looked as innocent as a little boy—with cake crumbs on his shirt. "You are still married, aren't you?"

He nodded. "I won't deny that. When she left, she said she was going back home. That was five years ago." He shrugged.

There was unmistakable sadness in his voice, but Caroline could only imagine his agony. Nonetheless, she wouldn't allow that to override her common sense. "Did she get there?"

"I don't know."

"You haven't heard from her?"

He shook his head. "A seaman from the *Willoughby* said she'd asked about passage around the horn to New York."

"Did you write? Go after her? Try to find her?"

He caught and held her gaze. "I had no money to chase after her. She took what little we had set aside, and took one of our two horses and sold it for passage to San Francisco. I don't know how she came by the rest needed to make such a journey." He held his hand out to her, then lowered it.

Caroline forced herself to look away from him and ask

what she had to know. "Why did you want to tell me about her?" She couldn't change his circumstances and honestly had no idea what he wanted from her, although she didn't think he was seeking her sympathy.

He paced the width of the kitchen and stopped across the worktable from her. "Your understanding. Ever since I told you I was still married, you've acted as if I had cholera or yellow fever."

She stirred the simmering beef soup, while her thoughts swirled in a dizzying fashion. She cared for him more than she had a right to—he was a thoughtful man, seemed to be gentle, a talented cabinetmaker—and none of that changed the fact that he was married. "I do understand, Mr. Grey, and I am sorry. It must be very difficult for you and Ethan. However, I think it would be best if we didn't—"

He stared at her, and came close to betraying his pleasure in what he believed she was about to say, then he interrupted her. "Would friendship be so unseemly?"

"I don't feel unfriendly toward you, Mr. Grey." No, definitely not, she thought, and if I'm not careful, I may wish I had never met you.

"That's a good start." He returned to the parlor.

"And the end," she said, more for her benefit than his.

She heard Daniel go outside, and a moment later Tucker ran into the kitchen looking rather scruffy. "About time you came back. And just in time for supper. Where have you been since yesterday?" He meowed, raised his chin, and sniffed, then wove a figure-eight in and around her ankles. She rubbed behind his ear and set the plate of scraps down for him. Daniel came back inside, and she was curious to see exactly what he was doing, but she didn't want to encourage conversation.

Never in her life had she behaved in such a rude manner, but if she weren't careful, she would surely regret it. Tucker finished eating, and she returned to the sewing room. Livvie and Robert woke up, and Caroline fed them. She was walking with Robert, when there was a soft tap on the door. She opened it, expecting Daniel to announce that he had finished his work.

She was holding one of the babies, and she positively glowed. Daniel didn't think he could ever tire of watching her. "Reverend Vincent is here to see you. I asked him to wait in the dining room."

"The reverend? All right, thank you." On her way through the kitchen she moved the pot of soup to the side of the fire before she continued into the dining room. Reverend Vincent and a woman she had seen but had not met were waiting for her. "Good evening."

"Hello, Mrs. Dobbs." Reverend Vincent gave her a nod and held his hand out toward the woman at his side. "I'd like you to meet Mrs. Fairfield. Mrs. Fairfield, Mrs. Dobbs."

Caroline smiled at her. "I'm glad to meet you, Mrs. Fairfield. Won't you both have a seat? I'm sorry the parlor is in such disarray. Would you care for tea?"

"Oh, no, Mrs. Dobbs, we can't stay very long. Please, sit down with us." Mrs. Fairfield stepped to Caroline's side and looked at Robert. "Healthy-looking baby. Which one is this?"

"Robert Williams, Junior." Caroline waited for her guests to be seated and sat at the end of the table. "How can I help you?"

Mrs. Fairfield glanced at the reverend before she spoke. "We've been concerned about you. Taking care of twins must be difficult for a woman alone with no help."

Caroline smiled at Robert and rubbed his back. "It is, at times, but if I had a husband, there would be much more to keep me busy, wouldn't there?"

"I . . . daresay you're right," Mrs. Fairfield admitted.

"Would you excuse me? I won't be long." Caroline didn't believe theirs was a social call and did not care for the direction of Mrs. Fairfield's questions. Caroline kissed Robert, put him in his bed, and returned to the dining room. "Now," she said, taking her seat, "is there something I can help you with, Mrs. Fairfield? Reverend Vincent?"

"Yes—" Reverend Vincent cleared his throat and folded his hands on the table. "Mrs. Dobbs, you've given these infants a good Christian beginning, and the town is grateful. I'll see they are placed with devout families."

Caroline stared at him a moment. "That won't be necessary. I promised their mother I would raise them as my own, but thank you for offering to help." She heard Mr. Grey cross the parlor, and she looked at the doorway as he came into the room. What now? she wondered.

Daniel gave her a slight smile and nodded. He had overheard the self-righteous preacher. If the man were really interested in helping her, he'd ask what he could do. Besides, there were families who had lost everything in the flood. Weren't they enough to keep him occupied?

"Oh, well—" The reverend looked at Daniel and, in turn, to Mrs. Fairfield, then added, "If you should change your mind, Mrs. Dobbs, please let me know. You're not alone in this."

Yes, I know, Caroline thought. She glanced at Daniel and had the feeling that he understood and hadn't been surprised.

Daniel stepped over to the table. "Has anyone come to you about the babies? Complained about their care?" He didn't put much store in the reverend. The man had a habit of sticking his nose in other people's business and gave little practical advice, from what he had heard.

"No . . . Some of us simply thought that Mrs. Dobbs had more than done her duty by the infants. It's my understanding that she . . ." He faced Caroline. "You didn't know Mrs. Williams before she was rescued from the river and brought to you."

"That is true. However, we became close during the time she spent with me." She glanced at Daniel and back at Mrs. Fairfield. "She said she had no relatives. Of course, if Mr. Williams has survived, he would take his children."

"Yes, yes, but I don't see there's any chance of that. Not after almost two weeks now, bless his soul." Reverend Vincent pushed back from the table and stood up.

It seemed to Daniel that the reverend didn't have much to keep him busy if he had nothing better to do than interfere in Caroline's life. Daniel leveled his attention on him, then on Mrs. Fairfield.

Mrs. Fairfield looked away from Daniel as she came to her feet. She pushed her chair under the table and looked at Caroline. "Thank you, Mrs. Dobbs. If you change your mind, please let us know. We want only what's best for those children."

Daniel stepped into the entry and opened the front door.

"So do I, Mrs. Fairfield, above all else." Caroline walked them to the door. It was standing wide open. She met Daniel's gaze. It had been a long time since she'd had a man's support.

After Reverend Vincent and Mrs. Fairfield left, Daniel closed the door. "Has anyone else wanted to take the babies away from you?"

"I've hardly seen anyone, but news about the birth of twins has surely spread. Even my neighbor, Mrs. Kinney, was curious, and she hasn't called on me until now." She wandered into the parlor. "Twins aren't commonplace. Half the city probably has heard about them."

"True. But I don't see why anyone would want to give you trouble, unless they are childless and want what you have." Someone would have to be pretty mean-spirited to do that, and he couldn't imagine anyone thinking Caroline wouldn't be a good mother.

"They likely just wanted assurance that I would care for Livvie and Robert." She stepped over to the window he had fixed and ran her hand over the new wood. "The seams between the pieces of wood are perfect." When he came up beside her, so close that her skirt spilled over his pant leg, she lowered her arm and felt the heat of his body on her shoulder. She took a deep breath. Having lived alone for the past two and a half years had made her much more aware of his nearness.

He shrugged, but he was glad she appreciated his workmanship. "I'll paint that tomorrow and get to your bedroom window, too."

She stared at the new section of wall and tried not to brush against him. "I didn't realize the water had spread so far."

"Over time it soaks in, but the studs were okay. The windows shouldn't leak for a long time."

"I guess that would be good news if I knew what 'studs' were."

He chuckled. "They're the boards that make up the inside of the wall."

She looked at him and quickly averted her gaze to where the cradle had been.

When she suddenly sobered, he followed her line of sight and guessed what still bothered her. "Don't worry." He would've liked to put his arms around her, give her a reassuring hug. Instead he smiled. "With a little luck, they'll have someone else to save tomorrow."

He sounded so confident. She hoped he was right, but she had to ask, "Do you believe they can take the twins away from me?"

"I don't see how. I'd say you have more right to raise them than strangers." He started collecting his tools and put them back in the box. "Besides, the reverend and Mrs. Fairfield are only two people. They might not have talked to anyone else about their idea."

"You're right." She rubbed her hands together and shivered. "It just hadn't occurred to me he would question my keeping Livvie and Robert. I hardly know him." She added two logs to the fire and watched the flames take hold.

"I thought you did. You asked him to baptize the babies and give the service for Mrs. Williams."

"She didn't know many people here, and I had heard of him." Although at the moment, she couldn't recall exactly what she had heard. "Thank you for speaking up for me."

He grinned and picked up the box of tools. "Just being a friend, Caroline."

She held her hands out to the fire. He had been a friend. "I appreciate it." She turned her back to the fire. Daniel was a good man. He had kind eyes and a generous nature. Could she think of him as a friend? She had to try. "I made beef soup. Would you like to have supper with me?"

"Smells good, but I have to pick up Ethan and get back home. Thank you for asking, though." He set the box of tools by the front door and walked over to the hallway. "I'll bring the cradle out for you."

She went into the sewing room with him and brought Robert and the drawer out to the parlor. She straightened the blankets over Livvie and Robert. "I'm surprised they're still asleep."

He watched her tend the babies. Years ago that's how he envisioned his wife, but she wasn't Caroline or like her in any way. "Better eat before they wake up." He opened the front door and grabbed the box of tools. "Good night,

Caroline. I'll finish tomorrow." They were back on friendly terms, and he wanted to keep it that way.

Daniel completed the work on Caroline's house the next afternoon and returned to Peterson's store. She'd been surprised when he had arrived so early in the day and, he believed, was disappointed when he left not long after midday. Understanding her discomfort with him being a married man, he thought it best not to give in to his desire to be near her. When school was out, his son joined him, and they worked until past nightfall. It was a cold, moonless night, and the ride home felt longer than usual.

Ethan pulled up his collar and shoved his hands into his jacket pockets. "Are we still going to have a tree for Christmas?"

"We'll stop work early tomorrow and choose one." Daniel glanced at his son and smiled. He had made the boy's gift before the flood and hid it. With Christmas only a week away, he was as anxious to give it to him as he imagined his son was curious. "Do we have enough popcorn to string?"

Ethan smiled. "We better get more." He moved closer to his pa. "Michigan's so far away; you think Grandma's letter'll get here by then?"

"Yep. We'll hear from her and your grandpa. They haven't disappointed me yet."

"When I'm done with school, I wanna go back and stay with them a while. I hardly remember what they look like."

"Start saving your wages. Who knows, maybe we can go together. I'd like to see them, too."

Daniel pulled up to the barn. He tended to the horses, while his son went inside to start supper. They took turns feeding the cows and chickens, and with the milking and egg collecting. He stored the pail of fresh milk in the springhouse and helped Ethan get supper on the table—warmed baked beans and bacon sandwiches.

After they had eaten and cleaned up the kitchen, Daniel went out to the workshop. On each piece of furniture he made, he inscribed his name on the back. On the cradle, he signed it on the inside of one rocker. Caroline may never see it, but that didn't matter. He put another coat of finish on the cradle and on the Henrys' trestle table. Part of his mind was on the furniture, but his thoughts kept drifting back to her. Did she sew all day and evening? She had stood up to the reverend, but what made her laugh? So many questions he had no right to ask.

The next day Daniel stopped working before sundown and took Ethan out to choose which of the fallen fir trees they would cut to size for the house. Daniel had finally narrowed the choice down between three trees. "Well, which will it be?"

Ethan walked around each tree, then walked over to another. "I like this one."

"It's crooked, but I can build up a base."

"No—that makes it interesting. Reminds me of an old man, only he needs a cane."

Sometimes that boy has a strange way of seeing things, Daniel thought, taking the ax to the trunk. He cut off the top about six feet from the crown and the two of them loaded it into the wagon. One tree that his son had dismissed had a full top that would be just the right size for Caroline's parlor.

Ethan climbed over the wagon seat and looked back at his pa. "What're you cutting another tree for? We don't need two."

"I thought Mrs. Dobbs might like this one." When he had cut off the top five feet, Daniel put it in the wagon with the other one. Caroline was so busy with the babies, he didn't think she had time to look for a tree.

9

CAROLINE FINISHED ATTACHING the left sleeve to the bodice and held it up. Except for the bertha collar, which she would put on last, it was complete. She stood up, arched her stiff back, and walked around the house. It had turned cold and started snowing, perfect for a brisk walk.

The twins were too little to take outside, and Martha could only manage one afternoon a week now that she was back in school. While the twins slept peacefully, Caroline wrapped her cloak over her shoulders and went outside. After three turns around the house, she went back inside, but she still didn't feel as if she could settle down.

Glancing at the clock, she realized why she felt so restless. It was almost five. The repairs on the house had been completed two days earlier. Daniel hadn't come by the night before, and she would not see him that evening or the next. She looked at the new part of the wall in the parlor. She hadn't known how much she had anticipated seeing him each day.

When Livvie whimpered, Caroline was glad the baby had awakened. Every day the twins grew more alert. Their hair was dark brown, like their mother's, and she believed their eyes would be, too, after they outgrew the newborn blue shade. She tried to imagine how they would look on their first birthday, running around in the yard, walking hand-in-hand with her through a field of spring blossoms. As she changed Livvie's clothes, the baby waved her arms and watched Caroline. She tied the tapes on the nappie and kissed each of the baby's feet. Robert was still asleep when she went back into the parlor.

Cradling Livvie in one arm, Caroline decided to put her into the sling so she could hold her while she mixed the milk. It worked beautifully, and she soon returned to her rocking chair to feed Livvie. Robert woke up before Livvie had finished with her sucking bottle, and Caroline spoke softly to quiet him.

She had just finished feeding Robert and was patting his back as he lay across her lap, when she heard the wagon stop in front of her house. It sounded like Daniel's, but she decided that was wishful thinking. Robert burped, and she sat him up on her lap. Tucker ran to the front window and settled on the ledge purring. When the knock sounded on the door, she gave a start, and Robert cried out. "Shh, there's no need for you to worry."

She moved him to her shoulder and went to answer the door. Daniel and Ethan were standing on her doorstep holding a fir tree. "Hello. What brings you here at this time of night?"

Daniel motioned to the tree. "I didn't think you'd have time to get one."

"No, I don't—" As she stared at the tree, he set it on the doorstep. It wasn't any taller than she was, and the bottom boughs were wide. "You brought this for me?"

"If you want it, it's yours." He brushed one hand down the tips of the branches. "It's nice and full. And it's still fresh. Ethan and I cut the trees last evening."

"Thank you, it's beautiful. Please, come in." She pushed the door wide open and stepped back. "I'm not sure if I have anything to put it in. . . . How about a pail? With rocks to weigh it down?"

"You won't need that. I nailed a couple boards on the bottom to stand it up."

"What a good idea." He really is a special man, she thought, and his wife must be a fool, or a featherbrain, to have left him.

Daniel carried the tree into the parlor and paused to take a glimpse at the babies. He glanced at Ethan, standing just inside the parlor door. "Come over here and look at Robert an' Livvie. She is in the cradle, isn't she, Caroline?"

"Yes, though they probably should take turns until you can make a second one, but there's no hurry." Ethan seemed uncomfortable, so she smiled at him. "Babies grow slowly, at least the first few weeks."

Ethan nodded, but he didn't look at either of the twins. "Where do you want us to put the tree, Mrs. Dobbs?" The cat walked over and rubbed against his leg. He bent down and petted him.

"I don't know, Ethan, let me see." She glanced around the parlor. With the twins' beds, there wasn't much extra space. "What do you think about that front corner on the other side of the fireplace? I can move the candle stand." She watched Daniel as he studied the twins, then he looked over at her, and she was startled to see the longing in his eyes.

"Pa?" Ethan moved over and tapped his father's shoulder. "Pa, want me to put the tree in the corner?"

Caroline stepped around them and moved the little stand to the far corner of the room. The fir tree was fragrant and added a bit of seasonal spirit.

"That's all right, I'll do it." Daniel raised the tree up above the furniture, stepped around the furniture and set it down where Caroline wanted it. He stepped back up to the window and glanced at her. "What do you think? Want me to turn it around?"

"Perfect. It's too bad the twins are too young to appreciate it."

"They'll enjoy one next year."

"Please, sit down. I'll get something to drink." She went to the kitchen, started a pot of tea, and set the tray on the worktable. There hadn't been time to make any sweets, but she had a few leftover biscuits. She split them open, spread berry preserves over the top, and set them on a plate. When she carried the tray into the parlor, Tucker stood up on his hind legs batting at Daniel's fingers. He had made another conquest.

She set the tray on the table and moved the plate of biscuits in front of Ethan. "The berry preserves turned out pretty good, but I'm partial to them."

"Thank you, ma'am."

She poured their tea and set the cups out within their reach. "There's the sugar and I'll get milk if you want."

"This's fine." Daniel took a sip of tea and peered at the babies. "They don't seem to mind having their own beds."

"They were fussy the first day, but they're fine now." She couldn't resist smiling. "They share the drawer at night. It is easier to move from room to room."

He stared at the cradle. Wheels would make it movable, but then she couldn't rock them. "It would be." She was alone, no man to lift heavy things for her. He had seen her bedroom and knew there wasn't enough space for two cradles.

Ethan held a bite of biscuit down for the cat and petted him. He glanced from his pa to Mrs. Dobbs and turned his attention back to Tucker. "Want another bite?" Tucker stood up and curled his front toes over one of Ethan's fingers.

As Caroline sipped her tea, she noticed the exchange.

Daniel appeared very much at home in the armchair, watching his son. Then he turned and smiled at her, and it felt as if he had reached out and put his arm around her waist. The cup rattled on the saucer she held. She quickly put it down on the table. "Have you decorated your tree?"

"We started but ran out of popcorn." Daniel looked away from her heated gaze and ran his finger around the neck of his shirt. "Ethan put two strings of polished acorns on the tree."

"I imagine they're pretty." Caroline leaned forward and picked up a biscuit half. Ethan was petting Tucker. "Does he have a cat?"

Daniel shook his head. "One wouldn't last very long out in the woods." And after his dog died, his wife found one excuse after another why they shouldn't get a new one. Ethan had finally given up asking. Next spring, Daniel thought, I'll see about getting one for him.

"Pa, shouldn't we go home? It's gettin' late."

Maybe the boy was right. "Yes," Daniel said, glancing from his son to Caroline. "It is later than I thought."

Ethan picked up his schoolwork and stood up. "Thank you, Mrs. Dobbs."

"You're welcome, Ethan." The words were no sooner out of her mouth than he bolted outside.

She walked Daniel to the door. As he stepped over the threshold, she reached out and put her hand on his arm. "Would you like company while you string the popcorn? Tomorrow night? I'll have plenty for both trees." She couldn't recall the last time she had been so bold, but she wanted to see him again and not just in passing on the street. It was Christmastime, and she wanted to spend part of it with a friend. Daniel.

He felt her slender fingers tighten, ever so slightly, and he smiled. "I'd like that, Caroline."

"Good. Come anytime after work." She grinned. "We're not going anywhere." Her heart pounded in her ears, and it felt wonderful.

The next day Caroline made popcorn to string for the tree. The bell over the door rang. She came out of the kitchen to see who had entered about the same moment Tucker jumped on one of the chairs at the dining room table. Mrs. Kinney, Mrs. Croy, who still had thick black hair and was the size of a young girl, even though she was well into her sixth decade, and Mrs. Hubbard, the taller of the three older ladies, led the way into the parlor. "Hello. Please, go on in." Since each of the ladies had a bundle or package, Caroline assumed they had been shopping, overheard talk of the twins, and called to satisfy their curiosity. She didn't mind. The more people who saw them, the sooner the rumors would fade away.

"I'll just dry my hands and join you."

"Take your time, dear," Mrs. Croy said. "We're in no hurry."

Caroline went to the kitchen. After she had dried her hands, she smoothed her hair back and went into the parlor. All three ladies were whispering over the twins. She stopped by the end of the cradle. "They are so good."

Mrs. Hubbard handed her a small package. "Those are for the babies." She perched on the sofa at one end, her gloved hands folded on her lap.

Caroline smiled and glanced at the present resting on her open hand. She knew Mrs. Croy and Mrs. Hubbard to greet in a store or on the street but not well enough to consider them friends. "Thank you, Mrs. Hubbard." Sitting in her rocking chair, Caroline unwrapped the cambric and found two pairs of infant slippers, one a dark green, the other a soft yellow. "They are lovely. They'll need these before long." She put them on top of the cambric on the table.

"Here, dear—" Mrs. Croy handed her gift to Caroline. "Newborns need so much. I hope you can use those."

Caroline unfolded the calico and held up one of the two bib aprons. "These are beautiful." She smiled at the older woman. "The embroidery stitches are very fine." Each had sprigs trailing along the hem. The woman's kindness was a wonderful surprise.

"Thank you, dear. My eyes aren't what they used to be a few years ago."

"No one could tell by this, Mrs. Croy." Caroline took a deep breath and laid the bibs by the slippers. "Would you like tea? I was about to pour myself a cup."

Mrs. Kinney eyed the other two women before speaking. "No, thank you, Mrs. Dobbs." She handed Caroline her package.

Caroline was tempted to say that all this wasn't necessary, but she didn't want to offend the women. The last gift was bulky. She pulled the loosely tied string and opened the calico wrap. Toys. She smiled at Mrs. Kinney as she held up the cloth ball. "For Robert?"

"Don't imagine he'll use that for a while."

"It's his first toy." Next to the ball was a cloth doll. "I'll save this for Livvie until she's old enough to be careful with her." The doll had a linen mob cap with crocheted trim over yarn hair; a doily had been fashioned into the bodice, and the skirt was strips of cloth topped with an apron. "She's wonderful. Thank you very much . . . all of you." She held the doll on her lap and rocked the chair slowly.

"Mrs. Kinney mentioned," Mrs. Hubbard said, with a glance at her friends, "that you plan to keep the infants."

"Oh, yes, I do. I helped Mrs. Williams with the birthing, and I couldn't give them up, even if she hadn't asked me to raise them." Caroline clutched the doll, wondering how many people she would have to tell before others would quit asking.

Mrs. Croy moved closer. "By now, dear, you must realize how difficult it will be to care for those infants. Why, you'll need two of every item for one child. And once they're past the age of eating bread and milk, how will you feed them?"

Caroline stared at her. "I will see that they have all the nourishment any child could need or want."

"Mrs. Dobbs, we understand how you must feel." Mrs. Hubbard looked directly at Caroline. "However, we hope you'll understand and want what is best for the infants. We can place the babies with good families before Christmas. God-fearing families. Would you deny them that?"

Caroline didn't look away and hoped that Mrs. Hubbard realized how very angry she was becoming. "Livvie and Robert do not need another family. They have one. Just as this is their home and will be until they wish to leave."

"Dear, we had hoped—"

"As all of you can see, the twins are happy and healthy. If you overhear any gossip about us, please put their minds at ease." Caroline stood up, effectively cutting off Mrs. Croy, and put the toys on the calico under the tree. "Thank you for calling and for your generous gifts. I understand how busy you must be."

"You're making a mistake, Mrs. Dobbs, and those orphaned infants will pay the price for your ill-placed pride." Mrs. Hubbard walked around Caroline's little rocking chair and straight to the door.

Mrs. Croy stood up and stared at the tree. "Toys belong under Christmas trees. They make it so much more festive, don't they, Mrs. Dobbs?"

"I think so, too, Mrs. Croy."

Mrs. Kinney followed the others to the door and paused. "If you need anything, just holler out the window."

"Have a nice Christmas, Mrs. Kinney." Caroline hoped she wouldn't need her help. She closed the door, determined to disregard their comments.

She stepped into the parlor and gazed at the tree. It did look nice with the toys beneath the full lower boughs and the twins nearby. She put the other two gifts on their wrappings by the toys. Her Christmas spirit had definitely returned.

Daniel set the jug of cider under the wagon seat. "Ethan, come on, boy—" The clouds parted and the new moon gave a sliver of light on the snow-covered ground.

Ethan closed the front door and ran across the yard. "Why do I have to go with you? You're the one who wants to see her. I still have schoolwork to do."

"Get in the wagon. You can do it at Mrs. Dobbs's house as easily as here." Daniel climbed up to the bench seat and picked up the reins.

Ethan went back to the house for his schoolbooks, paper, and pencil.

Daniel turned the wagon around and stopped long enough for his son to climb aboard before he started down the road. "Who stuck a burr under your skin?"

"I just don't understand why you want to spend so much time with her."

"She's a nice lady."

"You're still married to Ma. *Does she know that?*"

"Yes, son, I told her about your ma and me. Besides, Mrs. Dobbs and I are only friends. Don't you want me to have any friends?"

"Oh, Pa—you got fellows to drink with. That's not why you're seeing her, is it?"

Daniel shook his head. "Son, you've got a lot to learn."

"You might be surprised what I know," Ethan mumbled.

Daniel looked at him. They talked about everything, but maybe it was time he asked a few questions. Not tonight, later when the boy wasn't so riled. He turned onto Caroline's street and stopped in front of her house.

Ethan got down and grabbed his bundle. "Can't I walk over to Jay Yancy's house?"

"No." Daniel stepped down to the road and looked at his son. "And Ethan, don't ask me later, in front of Mrs. Dobbs."

"Yeah, Pa."

Daniel got the jug from under the seat and walked to the door a pace ahead of his son. When he saw Caroline standing in the doorway, he almost regretted insisting his son accompany him. Her forest green dress made her eyes a shade darker and her hair lighter. "Good evening."

"Hello." She motioned for him to enter and smiled at Ethan. "Is that schoolwork?"

"Yes, ma'am."

She closed the door after him. "You're welcome to do it in the parlor with us or you can sit at the dining room table."

"The dining room, I guess."

"All right. When you finish, you can help us, but I'll bring you a bowl of popcorn to nibble on." She showed him into the dining room and lighted the lamp. "Do you need anything else?"

"No, ma'am." Ethan put his bundle on the table and unfastened the strap.

"Okay." She went to fill a soup bowl with popcorn and set it on the table for him. She left the door open, which was her habit unless it was very cold and she didn't want to waste heat on that room, and Tucker darted under the table.

She almost called him back, then thought Ethan might like company.

Daniel was holding Livvie and telling her about the Christmas tree when Caroline came into the parlor. He didn't know much about women's fashions, but he liked the way the top of her dress showed off her nice curves. "You look very pretty. I like that dress." Her cheeks turned pink, and he grinned.

"Thank you." She had hoped he would but wasn't bold enough to tell him. She walked over to him and peeked at Livvie. "Did she wake up?"

"No. I just wanted to hold her. Do you mind?"

"If she doesn't, I don't see any reason I should."

"I see Livvie and Robert have new toys." He nodded toward the tree.

"Mrs. Croy, Mrs. Hubbard, and Mrs. Kinney came by to see them and brought gifts." The rest she didn't think he needed to know.

He glanced at the three large bowls and basket of popcorn. "Is all that for us to string?"

"Mmm-hmm. I wanted enough for both of our trees."

He chuckled, and Livvie rubbed her face on his shirt, then settled again. He kissed the little cap covering her head and laid her back in the cradle. "We'd better start stringing if you want us to empty those bowls."

"The needles, scissors, and thread are on the table." Caroline glanced at the sofa but chose to sit in her rocking chair with the table between her and Daniel.

He took his usual seat and moved one of the bowls closer. "Do you have any special method of doing this?"

"Just leave enough string at each end in case you want to tie it onto a branch." She threaded a needle and tied the first piece on with the thread.

It took him a little longer to thread the needle. When he

tried to tie on the first piece, he pulled too hard and it crumbled apart. "Now I see why you made so much." He ate a handful and succeeded on the second attempt.

Grinning, she scooped up a handful of kernels. This wouldn't have been half as much fun without him. "What we don't need, I'll feed to the birds." She poked the needle through three pieces. "How is the Peterson store coming along?"

"I'll put up the last shelves tomorrow. Mr. Peterson's already started stocking the store. Wants to be open a few days before Christmas."

"So many businesses have suffered." She glanced up at the same moment Daniel's lips parted, and he popped some of the puffs of corn into his mouth. She wished she hadn't seen that.

"Many have reopened already. Moss's livery is back in business. Almost every day another store opens its doors." He sat back and put the bowl between his legs. Her rocking chair gave out a soft creak. She likely had grown used to it. He hadn't, and he wondered if he would have the chance to become accustomed to the sound.

"I don't know what I'd do if I lost everything."

He looked at her. "You'd do whatever had to be done. That's how survivors overcome hardship." The faint grating of the rocking chair seemed to beckon his attention—or it could have been wishful thinking.

"I still can't believe all but a couple of buildings in Linn City washed away." She scooped up another handful of popcorn and started feeding the needle through each one.

"Have you read last Saturday's *Argus*?"

When she wasn't tending the twins, she had been sewing, which left no time to read. She grinned. "Not yet. Why?"

"There was a note about a 'Wonderful Dame,' a woman who's knitting stockings for the soldiers in the Union army.

Seems eighty-five years ago she did the same for the men fighting the Revolution."

"Good gracious, she must have been a small girl then. Was her age given?"

"Mmm-hmm." He gently pushed popcorn down the thread. "Said she's ninety-five."

"Such a long life—" Livvie cried out and seemed to wake herself up. Caroline set the popcorn string aside, slipped the oilcloth under Livvie, and picked her up. "This won't take long."

One day that little baby would be a grown woman. He wondered if she would take after Caroline—her smile, her way of looking straight into a person's eyes, her gift for making people feel welcome. "I'll be here."

After she had changed Livvie's clothes, Caroline made sure there was enough hot water to mix with the milk and stopped in the dining room. "How is your schoolwork coming along?"

"Okay. I'm almost done."

"Good. Come into the parlor when you finish. There's plenty of popcorn." She moved Livvie to her shoulder. "Can I get you something to drink?"

"No, thank you," he said, without looking up from the paper in front of him.

"There's water in the kitchen if you change your mind." Caroline returned to the parlor.

Daniel smiled at her. "Robert's still sleeping. I almost woke him, but thought you might not appreciate that."

"It is easier when they don't want to be fed at the same time." She picked up the sling and sat on the rocker.

"I'll hold her while you fix her bottle."

"You are a rare man, Mr. Grey." She put the baby in his arms. It was impossible to avoid brushing his chest with her hand, but the most uncomfortable moment was when she felt his breath on her cheek. A shiver reeled down her back, and she hurried to the kitchen. Friends shouldn't notice such things, she told herself.

He sat back and smiled at the baby. "Your mama felt that, too," he whispered, and kissed the baby's forehead.

Ethan went into the parlor and dropped his schoolwork on the sofa. "Why're you holding that baby? She's their mama, and she's got you doin' woman stuff."

"Sit down, boy." Daniel pointed to the sofa. "And watch what you say. I can still warm your backside."

Ethan sat at the far end of the sofa glaring at his shoes. "Don't see what's so special 'bout those babies anyway. They can't even talk."

"You sound like you're four years old." Daniel shook his head. "I held you, fed you, and have been proud of you—until right now."

Ethan worked his jaw as he stared down. "I don't see why you're making a fool of yourself for her."

"Son, you've got a lot to learn about life and women. One thing to remember: Always do what *you* think is best. It doesn't matter what anyone else says. You've a rare gift for drawing buildings and houses. Don't let anyone take that away from you."

"Are you trying to tell me *you like* holding that baby?"

"Yes, I do." Daniel looked at his son. "What does a foal do?"

Ethan frowned at his pa as if he'd lost his mind. "Follow his ma around."

Daniel glanced down at Livvie. "She can't do that, so her parents have to hold her."

"But *you're* not her pa."

"No. The poor little babe doesn't have one, and it's easier for Mrs. Dobbs if she doesn't have to hold her while she fixes their feeding bottles." When Daniel stroked Livvie's downy cheek with the back of his first finger, she latched on to his fingertip and started sucking. "She's stronger than she looks."

Caroline returned to the parlor carrying the tray. She set it on the hearth and turned in time to see the baby sucking on Daniel's finger. She couldn't help staring. She had never seen a man show such tenderness to an infant.

"Your mama's here, Livvie." He glanced at Caroline. "You came just in time to save the end of my finger." She was watching him with the oddest expression. He loosened his finger from the baby's grasp and scooted forward on the chair. "Caroline—"

She blinked and regained her composure. "Good. We wouldn't want anything to happen to your hands." *Oh, please,* she silently pleaded, *let the floor open up and swallow me.*

10

$\mathcal{A}$FTER ROBERT FINISHED his bottle, Caroline put him on her shoulder and rocked her chair as she patted his back. Ethan had been quiet all evening. Christmas wasn't a time for brooding, and she thought that maybe he felt left out.

"Ethan, would you help us string popcorn? You can take it home for your tree." She looked at Daniel, and he tipped his head ever so slightly.

Ethan stared at her as if he were surprised she had seen him sitting there on the sofa. "Yeah—" He started to turn his head toward his pa but seemed to change his mind. "Yes, ma'am."

She slid one of the bowls of popcorn in front of him, then handed him a needle and the spool of thread. "Don't forget to eat some." Robert burped, and she kissed his temple. After she put him down to sleep, she faced Daniel and Ethan. "Can I get you something to drink? Maybe I've eaten too much popcorn, but I'm thirsty."

Daniel pushed the puffs onto the needle and down the thread before he set the string aside. "I brought cider." He reached down and picked up the jug. "Ethan, do you want water or tea or weak cider?" That sparked his son's interest.

"I can have cider?"

"It's Christmastime and you're a young man now. Don't see why you can't have a small glass with us." Daniel stood up and looked at Caroline. "How about you? Cider or tea? I'll pour."

"Warm cider sounds good." She stepped around her chair. "I'd better set the pan out for you."

As Daniel followed her, he paused at the door. "Ethan, do you want yours cool or warm?"

Ethan shrugged. "Warm I s'pose."

"Okay." Daniel went into the kitchen and set the jug on the worktable."

Caroline set a pan on the table. "Is that big enough?"

"It'll be fine." He uncorked the jug and filled the pan more than half full.

Rationing the precious spice, she took one stick of cinnamon from the spice box and held it over the pan of cider. "Do you mind?"

She was used to living alone, he thought, and it showed. He chuckled. "I like cinnamon, too."

The sound of his deep laughter made her smile. That was one of the things she had missed living alone. There'd been advantages—less laundry to do, smaller meals to cook when she was hungry, she could come and go as she pleased—but she had missed sharing special moments, until Daniel came into her life. They seemed to appreciate many of the same things, and she did like his smile. She stirred the cider. "Mmm, this smells good. Did you make it?"

"No. I get it from Mr. Boggs up on the Clackamas." He stepped over to her side. "He's got a nice orchard. Apple, pear, and peach trees so far. He said he wanted to plant some cherry trees next fall."

"His orchard must smell wonderful in the spring. I was going to plant an apple tree, but I haven't gotten around to it." He was so near to her, but she couldn't allow herself to think about that. Trees. They were talking about trees. Where there are fruit trees, there must also be bees. "Does he also collect honey?"

"I don't know. If you'd like to, we can ride up there next spring and ask."

"Yes. I would like that." By then the twins would be old enough to take with them. Oh, yes, she thought, glancing at him, I will look forward to that, but it was so far away. "Daniel, would you like to have Sunday dinner with me? You and Ethan, of course."

The table was ready, and Caroline had just set the casserole dish with blackberry pudding on the cooling rack. She mixed the sugar and butter for the sauce and set it aside to be finished before serving. The carrots and potatoes were almost tender, and chickens would be ready to take out of the oven soon.

Tucker came in and rubbed around her ankles. "You've already eaten and you can take a nice walk while we dine." She went into her bedroom and checked the mirror to make sure there weren't any smudges on her face or on her dress. The magenta stripe may not have been the best choice when she would be cooking, but she liked it and that was reason enough.

She walked into the parlor and added more logs to the fire. She was restless waiting for Daniel to arrive. However, Robert and Livvie were happy, awake and looking around. Caroline spoke softly, nonsense really, but they seemed to like the sound of her voice. Sometimes, she thought her heart might burst from the joy they had brought into her life.

A wagon stopped in front of the house, and she smiled at the twins. "I believe Daniel and Ethan are here."

When the knock sounded, Tucker ran ahead of her. She

opened the door and smiled at Daniel. "Hello." He surely was a welcome sight.

"I hope we aren't late."

"Not at all." She gently shooed Tucker outside before she closed the door. He could be a real pest when she served chicken. She followed Ethan into the parlor. "It's so cold. I've had the fire going all day."

"It's comfy." Daniel took off his jacket and held it out to his son. "Ethan—" He smiled at Caroline and noticed the Christmas tree. "You've added more decorations to the tree. It looks real pretty."

She glanced at the tree. "I remembered I had stored them in the back room and not the attic." There weren't many, only a few small tin horns, a tiny drum, balls made of yarn, and the little cloth dolls.

"I smell something good. Chicken?"

"Yes. I hope you like it roasted." She ran her hand down the side of her skirt. "Please make yourself comfortable while I set the table."

Daniel glanced at his son. The boy was trying to ignore the babies but had looked at them at least twice. Left with Livvie and Robert for a short while, Ethan might change his opinion about them. Besides, Daniel wanted to steal a few minutes alone with Caroline. "Mind if I help you, Caroline?"

She met his gaze and smiled. "Not at all." She led the way into the kitchen and put on her apron. "How are you at browning potatoes?" He gave her a teasing, wide toothy grin, and she felt her heart leap to her throat. *He's married, he's married,* she silently repeated, *he's married,* and I'm too old for romantic fancies. She set the iron skillet on the stove and added butter. After she spooned the potatoes into the pan, she held the spoon out to him.

"I'll take the challenge." He slipped his hand over hers,

holding it a moment before taking the spoon. "Do you have an old towel I can put over the handle?"

"Yes—" She handed him the one she used and grabbed another for herself. When she checked the carrots, he stood behind her, so close she felt the heat of his body on her back.

He leaned forward to turn the potatoes so he could inhale another whiff of the delicious scent she wore. "Mmm, you smell nice."

"Everything does in the kitchen." She slid the pan to the side of the stove and quickly stepped over to the oven before he heard her ragged breath.

He grinned and kept turning the potatoes. "How brown do you want these? Light? Dark? Or somewhere in between?"

She couldn't look at him, but she wondered why he was baiting her. "However you like them will be fine." She took the roaster out of the oven and set it on the worktable by the platter, then put the pan of biscuits in to bake.

He spooned a little salt from the cellar and sprinkled it over the potatoes. "Have you seen any more of your customers?"

"A couple have come by, but no one seems to have much Christmas spirit this year."

"Most of the people I've talked to are having a quiet family supper." He looked over at the table. "Is that blackberry pudding?"

"Do you like it?"

"Oh, I do. I tried making some once." He shrugged. "It was so sweet I put it out for the bears."

She chuckled. "Do you and Ethan take turns cooking?" As she separated the legs and wings from the birds, she put the pieces on the platter.

"Usually. Depends on what we have for supper. For the most part our meals are fairly plain." He glanced at her. "We're easily pleased." He stirred the potatoes and moved the skillet to the side of the fire. "These are ready unless you want them charred."

"I'll get a bowl for them."

She took two serving bowls out of the cupboard and set them on the table. It was almost eerie how well they worked together, she thought, side by side as if they were used to each other's ways. Soon their meal was on the table. The biscuits were fresh from the oven when Daniel sat down at the table with Ethan.

"Help yourself to the chicken." Caroline passed the dish of carrots to Ethan. "I just want to see if Livvie and Robert are sleeping." She went into the parlor and peered at the twins. They were sleeping. Now she could sit down and eat without feeling guilty.

Daniel enjoyed watching her tend the babies, seeing the glow on her face. If only Emmaline had been more like Caroline.

She returned to the table. "Thank you for watching the twins, Ethan. Did they fuss?" She set one potato on her plate and passed that bowl to Daniel.

Ethan dished a helping of vegetables onto his plate. "They didn't cry, just looked around."

"Robert and Livvie just started doing that." She put a piece of chicken on her plate. "I didn't think they would notice much of anything at their age."

"My son did." Daniel grinned at Ethan. "Almost from the day he was born." Daniel helped himself to the potatoes and set the bowl down near the platter. "One night I was holding him against my chest. I think he was all of three or four days old. He nearly scared the bejeebers outta me." He chuckled.

"Pa—" Ethan frowned and shoved the bowl of vegetables at him. "She don't want'a hear about that."

"How do you know?" Daniel dumped a helping of carrots

on his plate without looking. "You haven't even heard this story."

Ethan groaned and stuffed a large bite of chicken into his mouth.

"Like I was saying, I'd leaned back on the chair, and he was lying on my shoulder. All of a sudden, he pushes his little hands on my chest, straightens out his arms, and holds himself up. Then he looks at me as if to say, 'Look at me.'" Daniel shook his head. "I couldn't believe how strong he was. I was sure I'd drop him."

Caroline smiled at Ethan.

"He used to look around the room at everything, and I'd tell him the name of whatever had caught his interest."

"That's a good idea. The twins seem to like hearing voices." Caroline ate a bite of the crispy potato and glanced at Daniel. "These are tasty."

He grinned. "Glad you like them on the dark side."

Ethan glanced up. "He cooked these?"

"He browned them."

"Shoulda known. He always cooks 'em too long."

Caroline smirked but said nothing to interfere with their good-natured teasing. When she had finished eating, she went into the kitchen, put on the coffee, and began separating the eggs for the sauce she had started for the pudding.

Daniel waited for his son to get done eating and stood up. "Come on, let's clear the table for her."

"We gonna wash dishes, too?"

"That would be nice. She fixed dinner."

Ethan picked up his plate and the bowl of carrots. "You helped and left me with those babies."

"You didn't have to do anything." Daniel stacked his plate on his son's and picked up the platter.

Ethan shrugged. "Can I go to Jay's house?"

"Mrs. Dobbs is fixing a special dessert. Come on." Daniel

motioned for his son to follow suit as he carried the platter and other bowl into the kitchen.

Caroline added the beaten egg whites to the sauce and gently blended all of the ingredients. When Daniel and Ethan came into the kitchen a second time bringing more dishes from the table, she was embarrassed. "Daniel, please don't clear the table. I'll do that in just a moment."

"You're cooking. We don't mind lending a hand." When Caroline wasn't looking, Daniel eyed his son.

"We'd do as much at home."

"Thank you." She took three small dishes from the cupboard and spooned blackberry pudding onto each one.

Ethan licked his lips and glanced at his father.

Daniel gave his son an *I told you so* look.

Caroline spooned sauce over the pudding and glanced at Ethan. "You do want pudding, don't you?"

"Yes, ma'am."

She grinned at him. "I do, too. Let's eat." She handed one of the dishes to him and one to Daniel. He was smiling at her, but she had no idea why. "I hope it tastes as good as you think it will." The first time she had made an apple pie for Mr. Dobbs, he said it didn't taste like his mother's. She'd told him if he wanted his mother's cooking, he shouldn't have married and could move right back to his parents' home. He never compared her cooking to his mother's again.

Daniel poked his finger in the sauce and licked it off.

As Caroline watched his tongue slide upward, then his lips close around his finger, she felt much like a moth circling a flame. Even though his wife had left him, Caroline knew she could not indulge her fantasies. Loving him would cause her grief and pain, and it wasn't in her nature to carry on with a married man.

He smiled at her. "Delicious."

"Oh—I'm glad you like it." She picked up her dish, certain her cheeks must be crimson, and went into the dining room.

Ethan scooped another bite with his spoon and grinned at Caroline. "This is real good."

"Thank you, Ethan." She took a small bite of the pudding with a dab of sauce but hardly tasted it. Glancing at Daniel through her lashes, she was relieved he seemed more interested in his dessert than in her.

Daniel ran the edge of his spoon around the bowl. "My pudding didn't taste anything like yours."

Ethan scraped the bottom of his bowl and gulped down his last bite. "Pa, can I go see Jay now? I'll be back by sundown."

"It's all right with me, but you should ask Mrs. Dobbs's permission."

"Ma'am?"

She smiled at him. "Yes, go see your chum."

Ethan sprang to his feet and nearly overturned his chair. "Sorry."

When Ethan dashed out, Tucker ran inside and directly into the dining room. He jumped up on the chair Ethan had used and glared at Caroline. "You had supper earlier," she said. Hooking the toe of her shoe around the leg of the chair, she pulled it all the way under the table. Tucker yowled at her and darted into the kitchen.

Daniel laughed. "Your cat does let you know how he feels, doesn't he?"

She laughed. "He can be loud. Sometimes he reminds me of a willful child." She ate another bite of pudding. "You don't mind cats?"

He shook his head. "No. They're interesting animals. My aunt Effie had a black and white cat. At times I was sure it was grinning at me."

A man who admitted he liked cats was unusual, but she had already decided that Daniel was not an ordinary man. "Did Ethan put the popcorn strings on your tree?"

"Yes, and he made another with the extra you sent home with us."

She glanced at his empty dish. "Would you care for another helping of pudding?"

Daniel leaned back on the chair and smiled. "I would if I had room for it. You're a very good cook, Caroline. If I ate this way all the time, I'd be big as a barn."

She grinned. "I would, too, but I don't make desserts like this every day." She scooted her chair back and stood up. "The coffee should be ready. Go on into the parlor, and I'll bring it in to you."

He stood up, too, and pushed his chair under the table. "I wish you wouldn't treat me like company. It seems kinda funny since there's only the two of us."

But it's so much easier to keep my distance that way, she thought. "All right, Daniel." She stacked the dirty dishes and carried them into the kitchen.

"Where do you keep the cups?"

She had started across the room when he gently touched her arm, startling her. She glanced over her shoulder and was nearly nose to nose with him. If she relaxed, her mouth could easily brush across his. But she couldn't, and held her back ramrod straight. "Daniel?"

He had only meant to stop her from waiting on him, but God help him, he wanted to kiss her. Only one chaste kiss, he thought. Then her breath fanned his lips, and his taut muscles felt like iron bands. One wouldn't be enough—"I'll get the cups. Just tell me where you keep them."

"That cupboard," she said, almost whispering, and pointed to it.

He skimmed his hand down her arm to her hand and gave

her a gentle squeeze. "You'd rather have tea, wouldn't you?"

The baby's wail almost startled the wits out of her. "Yes—I think that's Livvie. I'd better—"

"You go on. I'll find the tea and bring our drinks into the parlor." She nearly bolted from the room, or from him, and he shook his head. He didn't want their friendship to be uncomfortable for her, but it was clear that she was aware of his desire for her.

He found the tea and brewed a small pot for her. While she prepared the feeding bottles for the babies, he held Robert and rocked Livvie in her cradle. While Caroline fed each one, he enjoyed watching her. She was caring, loving, and passionate. His idea of the perfect woman had been a faceless vague image with certain characteristics he wanted in his spouse, until he met her. Now he couldn't turn away from her. He wanted her to be part of his life, and he wanted to share in hers. Furthermore, he wanted his son to see, firsthand, that a man and woman could be happy together.

Caroline stopped rocking Livvie long enough to take a drink of tea. Daniel hadn't said much to her. He appeared content with a shared smile. "Your cradle is so lovely. Do you get many requests to make them?"

"No, it's been stored away. You're the first to see it in years. I'm glad you like it." Glad didn't come close to describing how he felt. Her praise did wonders for his self-esteem.

"I'll be happy to tell my ladies that you made the cradle." Addie would have loved it, Caroline thought. She couldn't have been any more grateful to Daniel for the loan of it.

"I did take an order to make an open cupboard, and I have another store to rebuild."

Livvie had gone to sleep. Caroline kissed her and put her

down in the cradle. "Daniel, you don't have to hold Robert until he falls asleep."

He glanced down at the baby. "I'm not coddling you, am I?" He pressed his cheek to the baby's head and put him down in the drawer. "Ethan should be back any time," he said, wandering over to the window where the cat was sitting.

"Does he ride into town to visit his friends?"

"No. He sees them at school and sometimes afterward."

She added two more logs to the fire and closed the drapes over the windows. It was nearly dark out and icy cold. "Would you like another cup of coffee?"

He nodded. "Thank you." He rubbed the cat behind its ear and followed her into the kitchen. "I'll cut the pieces for the other cradle after Christmas. Are there any changes you'd like me to make?"

She refilled his cup and looked at him. "Oh, no, but I thought you understood that the bed was to be a plain design and made from pine. In a few months it will stay in my room—" She swallowed, wishing she could take back that last word. "I mean, no one will see it, so you needn't spend too much time on it." She quickly turned around and faced the stove.

"I understand, Caroline," he said with a smile. "I think I know what you want."

The coffeepot clattered on the stove before she let go of it. My nerves are a jumble, she thought, all because I want him to kiss me. Admitting it, if only to herself, didn't ease her anxiety at all. She picked up the teapot and filled her cup on the worktable. "Are you ready for Christmas?"

"Yes. Ethan and I always exchange letters with my family at Christmas. I picked up the packet of letters yesterday, and we'll read them Christmas morning." He sipped his coffee. "How about you? Any special plans?"

"I finished the new dresses for Livvie and Robert. I think we'll spend a quiet day together." Last year Maggie and Lucy Graffe had come over for Christmas dinner. However, both had moved away, but in their place would be Livvie and Robert. Caroline knew she wouldn't feel lonely, not with them, and she could ask Daniel if he wanted to have dinner with her. There was one knock at the front door, and Ethan called out.

"We're in the kitchen." She glanced at Daniel. "I think he just made it before dark."

"I wonder if you'll be so lenient in thirteen years."

Ethan was walking into the room, when she grinned at Daniel. "I'll look forward to your visit then and you can see for yourself."

Ethan held out a bunch of mistletoe dusted with snow to Caroline. "This's for you."

"Thank you." She looked at Daniel. There was only one man she wanted to kiss underneath that bit of greenery. She dropped the mistletoe on the worktable. Ethan would expect, and rightly so, to see the mistletoe hanging over a doorway, but she would feel terribly self-conscious with Daniel there. Better to avoid the problem altogether. She wouldn't invite Daniel and Ethan for Christmas dinner.

"Pa, I put a whole crate of it in the wagon. Jay said we could sell it. It's okay, isn't it?" Ethan glanced from Caroline to his pa.

Daniel had seen the glimmer of longing in Caroline's eyes before she had dropped the mistletoe. "Yes, son, that's fine with me." He picked up the thick sprig of mistletoe and glanced at her. "If you have some string, I'll hang this up for you."

11

THE NEXT MORNING, even though Caroline hadn't invited guests for Christmas, she baked as if she had. It was part of the holiday spirit. She had a small store of dates and used half to make two loaves of bread. She tied one with a red ribbon and put it in a basket for Daniel and his son.

The mistletoe still hung where Daniel had tacked it up—in the parlor and in the kitchen. She had avoided it when she bid him good night. She thought about taking them down, but there was no danger of her being caught under either with a man. She had been surprised when he put one piece over the kitchen door to the hallway. An odd place but a safe one, she decided.

She made several pans of gingerbread, one for each of her neighbors, and added another to Daniel's basket.

While Livvie and Robert slept after their midday feeding, Caroline paid her yearly, and brief, call on Mrs. Kinney to wish her a Happy Christmas and give her a gingerbread cake. Mr. Noyle took his constitutional each afternoon, rain, shine, or when the wind blew with enough force to snap twigs off of the trees.

Caroline waited until she saw the familiar brown tweed overcoat and dark woolen trousers, and went out to meet him. "Hello, Mr. Noyle."

He smiled and met Caroline in the front yard. "How nice to see you out, Mrs. Dobbs," he said, tipping his bowler. "I understand you have had some excitement in recent weeks."

"Yes, you could say that." She handed the wrapped bread to him. "I hope you still like gingerbread."

"Oh, my, yes, Mrs. Dobbs, especially yours." He held it up and took a whiff. "I am afraid you are spoiling me, but I thank you."

"You are welcome, Mr. Noyle. Are you still working on the history of the valley?"

"Indeed I am." He shook his head. "The flood was a horrendous disaster, but I have found so many stories of courage and heroism and, unfortunately, sorrow." He looked toward her house and smiled. "I see Tucker is on sentry duty."

She laughed. "He doesn't miss very much. I hope he hasn't bothered you."

"No, no. He only visits on the mornings I have ham or sausage for breakfast and when I have fresh cream."

"I'm sorry." She looked over her shoulder at Tucker and could have sworn he was smiling. "Please, don't let him bother you. He eats enough at home without begging from you."

"It is an even trade, when you consider how entertaining he is and clever." He chuckled. "Actually, I look forward to his visits."

Caroline shook her head. "Well, don't feel you have to feed him or let him into your home."

"Oh, he earns his tidbits by catching mice and moles." He eyed the gingerbread. "If you will excuse me, I am going inside and have a slice of your delicious bread."

"Have a Happy Christmas, Mr. Noyle."

"And you, Mrs. Dobbs."

She hurried back into the house, but Tucker stayed at his

post on the front stoop. "Behave yourself and don't be a pest," she said, as if he listened to her, and closed the door.

The next day was Christmas Eve. Caroline made sugar cookies and added a spiral row of lace to each of the baby's new caps. She hummed "It Came Upon a Midnight Clear" and "Oh Tannenbaum," and she envisioned what the holiday might be like in the coming years, when Livvie and Robert were old enough to enjoy it.

Caroline had just passed under the mistletoe above the parlor door on her way to the kitchen to see about supper when she heard a wagon stop nearby. Although she told herself to ignore it, her heart pounded, and she waited for Daniel to come to the door. He wasn't expected, and she hadn't even invited him over for a Christmas toast, but that had no bearing on her desire to see him.

There was a noise outside the door, then it opened, and she turned just as Martha came in carrying a large milk can. "Martha, let me help you." Caroline rushed to the girl's side and took hold of one of the handles. "I wasn't expecting you this week since Christmas falls on Wednesday, but I am glad you came by."

"Mama said you'd need this. She also said she'd be real pleased if you'd come to supper tomorrow." They had reached the kitchen, and Martha set down the can by the worktable. "We'd all like it if you'd come, Mrs. Dobbs."

"Thank you, Martha, but it's too soon to take the twins out, especially in this weather." Caroline picked up the empty milk can she had washed out. "I'll put this by the front door. Come with me." She set the can in the entry and went into the parlor.

Martha followed her and stopped when she saw the tree. "You got a Christmas tree after all. It sure is a pretty one . . . and with toys under it." She stepped over to the twins and smiled. "Isn't that doll nice. Did you make it, Mrs. Dobbs?"

"It was a gift from Mrs. Kinney." Each time Caroline thought about Mrs. Kinney's gifts, she was surprised anew. "Your petticoat is finished. I wanted you to have it before Christmas, but I had no way to take it out to you." While Martha looked at the twins, Caroline went to the sewing room. She returned with the petticoat and handed it to her. "I appreciate your help."

Martha held up the petticoat and grinned. "It's the prettiest one I ever had, Mrs. Dobbs." She hugged the slip to her. "I'll come by next Tuesday, if it's okay with you."

"That will be fine, Martha."

"Well, I better go. Papa's waiting for me."

"Please, just a moment—" Caroline went to the kitchen for coins to pay for the milk and quickly returned. "This is for your mother, for the milk, and thank her for me."

"I will," Martha said, and dashed outside.

Caroline waved to Mr. Penny and closed the front door. Before the twins woke up, she went into the kitchen. The milk had to be stored, a fresh mixture of sweet milk prepared, and she needed to fix something for supper. The supply of wood in the house wouldn't last the night, and she brought more inside. Later that evening Caroline wrote a letter to her cousin Marylou and told her about the twins.

When Livvie and Robert awakened for their middle-of-the-night feeding, Caroline kissed them and wished each their first Happy Christmas. In the morning she let Tucker out, lighted the fires, and started heating water for tea and their baths.

Christmas and New Year's mornings Caroline's gift to herself was to don her best dressing gown, brush her hair back, and curl up on the sofa with a cup of hot chocolate. This Christmas while she sipped her drink, she talked to the twins about their mother. She wanted them to grow up knowing about her and understanding how much they were loved.

After their second feeding Caroline dressed them in their new slips, shirts, flannel petticoats, white cambric dresses, and lace-trimmed bonnets. The twins were so beautiful. She wanted to take them on an outing, show them off the way any mother would, but they were too young, and she wasn't yet sure how she would handle both of them at one time.

Daniel finished brushing his shoes and slipped on his jacket. "You about ready, Ethan? I want to finish calling on people before suppertime."

"Yeah, Pa. You hungry already? We just ate dinner."

Daniel shook his head. "Folks don't want company when they sit down to eat."

"Oh." Ethan grabbed his jacket. "Do you think Gramma and Grampa will really come here for a visit?"

"That's what they said. But it's an awfully long journey to stay for only a few weeks. They wouldn't be able to return home before the snow'd make traveling impossible." Daniel was as concerned as his son. His parents' letters had sounded cheerful and newsy as always, but he wished he knew why they would travel across the country just to pay a call.

"How come you didn't take the table to the Urwins yesterday?"

"Mr. Urwin wants to surprise Mrs. Urwin." Daniel slicked back his hair, again, and looked at his son. "Afterward, we'll stop by Mrs. Dobbs's and come back home."

"Can we stop by Jay's house? I want to show him the desk box you made me. No one's got a nicer one in the whole state."

Daniel smiled at him. "I'm glad you like it. The drawing

you made of our house is very good. I'll make a frame for it tonight and hang it right over the fireplace." The drawing was good, professional. His son had a rare gift, and he would see that the boy got the best schooling and training possible in Oregon.

"Well, can we?"

"I don't mind, but his family may have made plans."

"Oh, they didn't. Jay said they weren't doing much today."

"All right, but you can't stay very long." Daniel wrapped the little table in a clean piece of canvas and put it in the back of the wagon. After he did the same with the cradle, they left to make their Christmas calls.

When Daniel pulled up to the Urwin house, Mr. Urwin came out and motioned him to the side of his house. Daniel unwrapped the table and carried it over to him. "Merry Christmas, Mr. Urwin. Hope I'm not late, but you—"

"No—" Mr. Urwin hissed. "I don't want the missus to see this just yet," he whispered, and peered around the corner. "Thank you for bringing it over today, Mr. Grey. You have a nice Christmas, too." Mr. Urwin took the table from Daniel and hurried around the back corner of the house.

"Thank you—" Daniel said, wishing him luck with the surprise.

When he returned to the wagon, Ethan was running his hand over the surface of the wooden desk box. It will be interesting to see the drawings he makes on that desk, Daniel thought. His son had the ability to see buildings in a different way but had no interest in cabinetmaking. They were so unlike each other in that. He guided the horse toward town.

"I hope Grandma and Grandpa got our letters to read today."

"We sent them in plenty of time." Daniel glanced at his

son. "I'm sure they were poring over our letters this morning, too." The boy was growing up so fast, but there was still a little of the boy left. He hoped his son would enjoy a few more years before he had to be a man, but helping out during the flood and with the aftermath had changed him. Hell, it had changed just about everyone.

As soon as his pa pulled up in front of Jay's house, Ethan jumped down to the ground. "Don't come back for me. I'll walk over to Mrs. Dobbs's in a while."

"Ten or fifteen minutes, that's all. I don't want to impose on her hospitality." Or overstay his welcome, he thought.

Ethan shook his head, turned, and mumbled, "You won't," as he walked to the house.

Daniel held the horse to a walk for the two blocks to Caroline's house. He had tried to believe he wasn't anxious to see her face when he presented the cradle to her, but he hadn't been too successful. Exchanging gifts with his son had eased the eagerness, until he marched up her walkway and knocked on her door. Suddenly it opened. Caroline looked surprised, then a beautiful smile lit up her lovely face.

"Happy Christmas, Daniel. Please, come in." Wishes sometimes do come true, she thought.

"Merry Christmas, Caroline." She had left her hair down in a glorious cloud of auburn waves, and her eyes were as shiny as the chip of malachite in his mother's treasured broach.

Belatedly she noticed the odd canvas bundle he was holding, but wished she hadn't. After he stepped inside, she glanced at the wagon. "Isn't Ethan with you?"

"He's visiting with one of his friends, but he should be here before long." He went into the parlor and set the cradle under the tree.

She walked in as Daniel kissed Robert. Tears threatened

to blur her vision, but she refused to become weepy. "Have you read the letters from home, yet?"

"Oh, yes. Ethan and I read them aloud first thing, after I'd made coffee."

She pictured them sitting at a table, reading and laughing, and she smiled. "Would you like coffee?"

"Don't make a pot for me. When Ethan gets here, we'll go home." He was amazed by her lack of curiosity. His wife had almost pounced on her presents, but Caroline *wasn't* his wife.

"Won't you sit while you wait for him?" As she checked on the twins, she glanced at the canvas bundle by the tree. Maybe he had finished the second cradle for her.

"It sure smells good in here. Been baking all week?"

She looked at him and then she smiled. "It wouldn't feel like Christmas if I didn't. Are you sure you aren't thirsty? The tea is already brewed. Water? Or I do have blackberry cordial."

"Cordial sounds good, if you'll join me."

She nodded. "Be right back." She returned with their drinks and handed him one glass.

He held out his glass to her. "Merry Christmas, Caroline."

She raised her glass to his. "And to you, Daniel," she said, clinking hers to his.

He watched as she put the rim of the glass to her mouth, parted her lips, and sipped the cordial. It was easy to imagine her mouth on his instead of on the glass. He took a drink, not the gulp he needed, and sat down in the armchair. "Very good. Did you make this?"

"Thank you. It's my grandmother's dewberry recipe."

He looked at Livvie. "Now you have a daughter to pass it on to." A dreamy kind of smile came over Caroline's face, a very appealing look. He took another sip of wine.

"My grandmother would have liked that." She tipped the

chair back and rocked slowly. She glanced at the twins and couldn't help noticing the canvas. Why hadn't he said anything about it? It could be for someone else, she supposed, but why did he put it under her tree? A movement in the lower branches of the tree caught her attention. "Tucker, get out of there."

She was out of the chair and kneeling in front of the tree in a blink. Daniel chuckled. "He's just having fun."

"Mmm, yes, he is—with your basket." She swatted at the cat and picked up the basket. "It's only been under there for a couple of hours." She stood up and carried it over to him. As she said, "Happy Christmas," she set it on his lap.

"Thank you." There were several bundles, each with a ribbon. "Smells good. No wonder Tucker wanted a taste." The one on top had a bite taken out of one corner. He picked it up and laughed. "How was it, Tucker?"

"Oh, Daniel, I am sorry." She eyed Tucker, as if that would frighten him. He had taken a bite out of the gingerbread. He'd never done that before. "I'll get you another one—without teeth marks."

"This one's fine. It comes highly recommended." He broke off a piece for himself and held one down for the cat.

She stared as Tucker marched over and ate the bite. "I'll have a talk with him later."

"Don't on my account." He set the basket by the chair and went over to the tree. "This is for you." He watched her as he pulled off the canvas. Her lips parted, and she gazed at him, clearly stunned and pleased. He reached out to take her hand.

"Daniel—" She dropped down beside the cradle. "It's beautiful . . . and it matches the other one. But how did you finish it so quickly?" It was grand, far nicer than what she had asked him to make for her.

"I started this one a couple weeks ago." Her fingers

grazed the alder as if it were a living thing. He had never envied a piece of wood before, but he did at that moment.

"Thank you, Daniel. It really is lovely." She looked at him. "How much—"

"This's a gift. You liked the other one so much, I wanted you to have your own."

"But you can't. I asked you to make one, but this is a lovely piece of furniture, not simply an infant's bed."

"It's yours. I'll make the plain one. You can keep it in your room so you won't have to move cradles each night. Why don't we see if Robert likes it?"

Daniel held the baby, while she put the bedding into the new cradle. After she moved Livvie's cradle beside Robert's, she set the drawer out of the way. Caroline still felt dazed by Daniel's generosity, and grateful. He had given her a part of himself, and she would always cherish it.

He laid Robert down in his new bed and stepped over to Caroline's side. "They're happy babies." And I like being here, he thought. "You're a good mother, Caroline," he said softly. When she glanced up at him with her sparkling eyes, his need to touch her, feel her body next to his was nearly overwhelming. He put his arm around her shoulders and held her close. She felt soft and warm, exciting and tender.

He curved his fingers over her shoulder, and she leaned into his side. She was almost light-headed with joy. In her dreams she had imagined what his embrace might feel like. Now she knew. Heavenly. Her heart pounded and her breath seemed to catch in her throat.

She didn't resist and seemed to welcome his advances. It felt as if he had been waiting a lifetime to feel her warmth and affection, but strangely enough, he wanted more. There was no mistletoe overhead. It hadn't occurred to him to put any above the tree. He looked down at her. Surely she heard the thumping in his chest. "Caroline—"

She glanced up at him, and a heartbeat later his lips brushed over hers. It happened so quickly that she didn't have a chance to react the way she desperately wanted to or even put her arms around him. Then suddenly he walked to the doorway, and she looked over his head. She had been so sure she wouldn't be caught under the mistletoe, but that small bit of greenery wasn't what she should have been concerned about.

He grinned. "Just in case we need another excuse." As she came toward him, the rustling of her skirts sounded like a whisper. He trailed his fingertips down her cheek, along the curve of her jaw, and pressed his mouth to hers, gently at first, until he felt her hands move over his back. He forced himself to go slowly, to savor the scent of her skin, the sound of her unsteady breath, and his body awakening to the desire she aroused.

She parted her lips and welcomed his exploration. She had thought she would never again experience this rush of longing, hear her racing pulse, feel desirable and wanted. She was no innocent. She knew what this could lead to, where she wanted it to take them, where neither of them dare trespass, so she lost herself in their embrace. This was more than she had a right to and more than she had expected.

He drew her lower lip between his and traced it with his tongue, then moved to kiss her cheek, her temple. It wasn't fair to her to go so near that brink of desire where they would be tempted to do what was against their principles. He ran his hand down through her hair and cradled her head against his shoulder.

Once she caught her breath, she rubbed her cheek on his soft shirt. She could never look at him in the same way as before. For all of his strength, he was gentle, considerate, and oh, so seductive. "The only reason I let you put up the mistletoe was for Ethan."

He chuckled. "When he handed it to you, you dropped it like hot coals."

She leaned back and looked at him. "I didn't want you to think I expected you to kiss me under it."

"Really? I thought you looked like you were afraid I would."

"I was," she said with a grin that faded as she continued. "I was also worried about how I would react."

"You shouldn't've been concerned. You were perfect."

He mistook my meaning, she thought, but it didn't matter now. "We can't make a habit of this, Daniel, and it would be so easy."

"Do you want me to take down the mistletoe?"

She gazed at him. "Would it make a difference?"

"Not at all." He framed her face with his hands and brushed a kiss across her lips. "I wish we had met years ago—I wish I were—"

She placed her fingers over his mouth. "Please, don't say it." He pressed his lips to her fingers, and she lowered her hand.

He nodded. "I think I'd better find my son."

"All right." She picked up his basket and walked him to the front door. "I'll always treasure the cradle."

He skimmed the back of his hand down her cheek. "Would you mind if I came by in a couple days?"

"I'll make a pot of coffee."

He opened the door and stepped outside. "I don't like leaving you alone on Christmas."

"You're not, and I'm glad you came by today."

"Night, Caroline." He walked down the path before he decided to turn around.

She closed the door and watched him leave from the

parlor window. When she could no longer see him, she sat down in the armchair and gazed at the cradles in front of the little tree. One day she would give back Ethan's cradle, but the other one she would always have.

Daniel spent the day after Christmas in his workshop. He could still taste Caroline on his lips, hear the rustle of her skirts, and feel the curves of her body in his arms. Ethan had already given him odd looks and asked why he was humming. Daniel hadn't lied, but neither had he been completely truthful. That night his dreams of Caroline left him tired the next day and more frustrated than the day before.

After tending to the daily chores, Daniel and his son rode into town. He went by George Murphy's to see about reinforcing the foundation on his house, stopped at Thomas Lainge's to let him know he could start the work on the south wall of his home, and the last call he made was with Jens Ogden, who wanted an estimate on a warehouse on the south edge of town near the river. Daniel was given a set of plans, then he made notes and agreed to meet with him after New Year's with his bid.

They rode up through town and made a stop at Peterson's new store for supplies. When the goods had been loaded in the back of the wagon, Daniel settled back on the bench seat. As he started down the street, he looked at Ethan. "I told Mrs. Dobbs we'd stop by today."

Ethan stared at him. "Why do you keep seeing her? Don't you feel like you're cheating on Ma?"

Daniel eased back on the reins, slowing the horse's pace. "She walked out on me, son. She hasn't written one letter or bothered to let me know where she is in more than five years." He looked straight at his son. "Did you feel like you were betraying your ma when you liked Mrs. Dobbs?"

Ethan gulped, then nodded. "She's been nice to me, but I wanted her to be Ma."

Daniel nodded. "What do you remember about your ma?"

"She like to brush her hair and put on that fancy purple dress . . . and sing." Ethan smiled. "She had a pretty voice, didn't she, Pa?"

"Mmm-hmm. I liked to listen to her sing, too." It was easier on his ears than her screaming, Daniel recalled.

Ethan frowned. "You're tired of waiting for her to come home, huh?"

"Yes, and I don't think she will, son. But don't you go blaming Mrs. Dobbs. We're friends, and I hope we will remain friends. She's a very nice lady."

"You saying Ma isn't?"

"I didn't say she wasn't." Daniel knocked the dust off of his hat and put it back on. "Not everyone's cut out for this life." But I don't see why I have to pay for her change of heart, too, he thought.

Ethan turned on the bench. "You gonna go after her?"

"No, son. She's where she wants to be." Now it's time I figure out what I am going to do about it.

12

CAROLINE FASTENED THE last button on the cuff of Mrs. Tillson's dress and ran her hand across the back of her shoulders. "How does that feel?"

Mrs. Tillson moved her arms and slid her hand down the bodice to her waist. "It feels good, Mrs. Dobbs. How does it look?"

Caroline motioned to the full-length mirror. "See for yourself." She turned up the lamp wick and pulled the drape clear of the window.

Facing the mirror, Mrs. Tillson turned to her right, her left, raised her arms, and watched the skirt as she twirled around. "I do like it, Mrs. Dobbs. Thank you for having it ready in time for my New Year's party tomorrow evening."

"I'm glad you're happy with it." Caroline helped her change dresses and wrapped the new one for her. The twins were crying by the time Mrs. Tillson left. Caroline changed their clothing before she mixed the sweet milk with simmering water. While she fed one, she rocked the other in the cradle by tapping her foot on the rocker.

Having two cradles made it easier for her, and it also served as a constant reminder of Daniel, as if she needed one. He had come by with his son on Friday. It had been a short visit, and Ethan had gone outside with Tucker, while she and Daniel talked. He appeared worried and looked out of the window every couple of minutes.

The next day she had waited, hoped to see him, but he had not called. Sunday, the following day, had passed without a sign of him. Each day she became more anxious to see him, find out what was bothering him, hear his voice. When the twins had fallen asleep, she put another log on the fire and began pacing. She hadn't been out of the house for more than a few minutes in over a week. A walk. That's what she needed. She used to go out every day. She tossed her heavy cape around her shoulders and went outside.

A brisk walk in the cool air should put color in her cheeks and help clear her mind. Although she wouldn't go beyond either end of the block, she could cover the distance at a lively pace. She went down her side of the street, crossed to the other side, and walked to the corner, returned to her side, and completed the circuit. On her second trip around she greeted Mr. Noyle and continued on. She felt as if she were racing with herself, which made little sense.

She peeked in on the twins, to make sure they were sleeping peacefully, and resumed her walk. As she hurried up the other side of the street, she very nearly bumped into Ethan. He was with two other boys and looked as startled as she felt.

"Hello, Ethan. What a surprise running into you."

"Yes, ma'am." Ethan introduced his friends to her. "Is everything all right, Mrs. Dobbs?"

"Fine. And your father, how is he?"

Ethan glanced down before he looked at her. "He's been real busy . . . workin' on a house. Putting up a new wall."

"Please give him my regards. And have a Happy New Year, all of you."

She smiled at them and walked on. Ethan had been polite, but he clearly didn't approve of her inquiry about Daniel.

The boys' laughter rang out, but she didn't pause or look back. She made three more circles and returned to the house. Tucker was curled up on her rocking chair watching the twins. She petted him and kissed Livvie and Robert.

After pouring herself a cup of tea, Caroline set the flatirons on the stove to heat. As she took the laundry off the clotheshorse, she put the nappies in one pile and the clothing in another. While the twins slept, she sprinkled each piece of clothing with lavender water and rolled them up. Once she had set the wooden ironing board on the kitchen worktable, she started with the nappies. She had worked her way halfway through the stack when the bell rang out.

"Caroline—" Daniel didn't see her in the parlor and called out again.

Daniel. She could hardly believe it was him, but she would know his voice anytime. "In the kitchen—" She set the iron on the stove and looked at the door to the dining room as he came through. "Hello. Did you finish early?"

He chuckled. "It's dark out. Must be close to suppertime." Her hair was mussed, her cheeks were flushed, and her sleeves were rolled up. She looked beautiful.

She glanced at the window and grimaced. Where had the afternoon gone? "Did Ethan tell you he saw me earlier?"

He shook his head. "I took a roundabout route to pick him up."

"Oh." She turned to the stove to move the irons and smiled to herself. "How have you been?"

"Okay. You?"

"The same." Coffee. Hadn't she said she would have coffee for him? Or was that for last Friday? Never mind, she thought, and quickly put a pot on the stove. "Ethan said you were working on a house. A new job?"

"Yes. The Lainge place. One wall of his house was

damaged during the flood, and I told him I'd get to it when I finished Peterson's store."

Tucker ran into the kitchen, stopped in front of Caroline, and gave her one loud cry. "I'd better check on the twins. They probably woke up."

Daniel eyed the cat. "Does he always do that?"

"Usually." She went into the parlor, and sure enough Robert was awake. "Hi, sweetheart." He looked at her, and she grinned as she picked him up. "Aren't you the smart one."

Daniel followed her into the parlor. Sure enough, one of the babies was awake, though he couldn't be sure which one. Then he noticed the blue ribbon around one of the cradles. "What's the ribbon for?"

"So I can tell the cradles apart. That's the one you made for me." She kissed Robert's soft cheek. "Each day they notice more and more. They are growing so fast."

Daniel stepped over to her and held his little finger out for the baby to grab, and he did. "He's stronger, too." He rested a hand on her shoulder and brushed his cheek over her hair.

She froze, afraid of breaking the spell. His chest was against her back. A delicious ripple spread down through her belly. Thank goodness she was holding the baby. "I was hoping you would stop by tomorrow evening so we could toast the new year. But I didn't know if you had other plans."

None more important than yours, he thought. "What time?"

"Six-thirty? Livvie and Robert will have been fed by then."

He nodded. "I'll be here." He could only think of one better way to bring in the new year, but that would compromise her, and he would never do that.

She looked away but didn't move. "Ethan is welcome, too."

"He's having supper with some of his friends tomorrow. One of the boys joined the army, and the others wanted to get together before he leaves."

"Is he upset with me?"

"Did he say something to you?"

"No." She shook her head and sat down in her chair with Robert. "But I have the feeling he's angry. Maybe with me, or about me. He hasn't said anything to you?"

Daniel sat in the armchair. "We've talked. I think being around you reminded him of his mother, and when he realized he liked you, he felt guilty."

"I'm sorry. Losing his mother must have been very difficult for him."

"He was almost seven when she left. Of course his favorite memories are the good ones, when she was happy." He shrugged. "Guess that was better than making him as miserable as she felt. I just wish he could understand that she wasn't—isn't—perfect."

"Do you really want to take that away from him?"

"If it would open his eyes to her, yes. He wasn't a baby. When she was mad, she screamed something awful." He shook his head. "If only he didn't expect her to return."

What he said was as important to Caroline as what he had not. They had shared one kiss, that was all, and she must remember that—not what she might hope could be. "A mother would have to be terribly cruel for a child to want never to see her again. Maybe not even then."

"Well, he'll have to face the truth. She's gone, and she isn't likely to return. The sooner he understands, the happier we'll be." Damn, he had thought his wife was out of their lives, part of their past. Now he wondered if they would ever be free of her.

He had done a good job raising the boy so far, she thought, and she had no experience rearing children. However, she wished she knew how to ease the frustration and pain so apparent in Daniel's eyes.

He came out of his reverie, and Caroline was staring at him. "I'm sorry. I'd better leave. Ethan'll think I forgot about him." He stood and smiled at her. "You don't have to walk me to the door. I'll see you tomorrow." As he passed by her chair, he paused and brushed his lips over her forehead. It would be wonderful to take her to a party, dance and sing with her without any fear of gossip or damage to her reputation. You hold my heart in your hands, he thought, and it's never been safer.

The next day Caroline had just finished feeding Livvie and Robert when Martha arrived with another can of fresh milk. Caroline helped her carry it into the kitchen. "You look very pretty with your hair brushed back."

Martha grinned. "Mama said I was old enough to brush it back for the party tonight."

Caroline smiled at her. "You look at least eighteen." But try to remember you are fifteen, she thought.

"I hope Rupert notices me."

"Is he in your class?"

"Oh, no. This's his last year. Next fall he's going to the new Willamette University down in Salem."

She's smitten, Caroline thought, and hoped the boy didn't disappoint her. "You don't have to help me today. Go get ready for the party."

"It won't take me long to dress, and Mama said you need to get out, that a woman needs someone else to talk to besides her babies." Martha giggled.

"Your mother's a wise woman, Martha. I think I'll take her advice." Caroline stored the fresh milk and set the other milk can by the front door. "The twins have been fed and should sleep another two hours or so, but I'll be back before they wake up."

"Take your time, Mrs. Dobbs. I brought needlework to do, and I can change their nappies and keep them happy. Don't worry so."

Caroline heard the confidence in her voice and knew the twins would be in safe hands. "All right, I won't." She put on her cape, tucked her money in her skirt pocket, and picked up the flour sack to carry her groceries. "I'll see you later, Martha." Tucker watched her a moment before he jumped up to sit in the front parlor window. Sometimes she felt as if he expected her to tell him what time she would return.

Martha walked to the door with her. "Don't hurry back."

"I'll try not to." The sun was bright and the breeze barely ruffled her hair. What a beautiful day, Caroline thought, walking down the block. An item in the *Argus* mentioned that the steamer *Onward* had delivered tons of apples the other day.

She had made it her business to know what fabrics and shoes were available in the stores in case her ladies asked. However, she hadn't been able to browse through any of the shops since the freshet—that was how the newspapers referred to the recent flood. So many had had to close for a while to recover from it. Main Street had changed. Most of the storefronts were new, some of the buildings were, also, and some businesses were no longer there.

Her first stop was the Eagle Boot and Shoe store. Mr. Miner was waiting on a gentleman. She smiled at him and wandered along the aisle. There were French and pegged calf boots, ladies' kid slippers, enamel gaiters, children's shoes, and a good variety of hose in many sizes. She picked up a tiny pair of soft, kid shoes and smiled. Shopping with the twins would be fun.

The next store she visited was Mr. Peterson's Dry Goods store. It smelled of new wood and paint. Since Daniel had built the store, she took special interest in the building as well as the merchandise. Many of the shelves were empty but that was to be expected. It would take time to replenish all of the stock. She had looked through the bolts of yard goods and was running her hand along one smooth shelf when Mr. Peterson came up to her. "Hello, Mr. Peterson. I was just admiring the workmanship. Your new store is very nice."

"It is, if I do say so myself." Mr. Peterson chuckled. "Of course, I didn't build it, just paid Mr. Grey to do the work."

As she looked around, she smiled. "Mr. Grey is a gifted cabinetmaker. He loaned me the use of a lovely cradle he made. It really is beautiful."

"It would be if he made it," Mr. Peterson said. "What can I help you with today, Mrs. Dobbs? I understand you've taken in that poor woman's children."

"Mrs. Williams's twins, yes. I would like to see your embroidery thread."

"Right this way, Mrs. Dobbs. What colors were you looking for?"

"One cherry red, a buttercup yellow, and a cornflower blue."

He grinned at her. "Isn't often my customers know exactly what they want." He stepped behind the counter, took the appropriate packets of thread off the shelf, and set them on the counter for her. "Are those the right colors?"

She held up the red. "This is a bit darker than what I had in mind. Do you have it in a shade lighter?"

He looked again and handed her two more packets of red thread. "Will one of these do?"

"Yes," she said, setting one with the others she wanted. "I'll take these." She paid for her purchases and tucked the thread in her pocket.

"Don't be a stranger around here, Mrs. Dobbs."

"I'll try, Mr. Peterson." The heels of her shoes clicked on the hardwood floor and made her think of the many hours Daniel had worked there. The care he put into the furniture he made also showed in Mr. Peterson's store.

She walked up the street. A wagon rumbled by and momentarily drowned out the sound of the river surging over the waterfall. She saw Mrs. Obert across the street and smiled. Caroline looked in shop windows, spoke to people she hadn't seen in weeks, and was amazed by the amount of work that still needed to be done.

Her last stop was at Dannenbaum and Ackerman's. Their supply of vinegar was still good, though she didn't smell the cheese, and there weren't any buckets or smoked hams hanging from the nails on the rafters. The aisles were wider than usual with fewer barrels and sacks leaning against table legs. While she looked through the dress goods, the clerk came over to her. "Hello, Mrs. Payne."

"Mrs. Dobbs, how nice to see you. We've missed you." Mrs. Payne moved a pile of folded fabric aside for Caroline. "I hope you had a nice Christmas."

"Yes, thank you, and you?"

Mrs. Payne nodded. "Everyone I've talked to stayed home this year. I didn't even hear any carolers."

"Neither did I." Caroline admired a piece of soft wool and stepped over to a display of plain and Paisley shawls. "Maybe New Year's Eve will be merrier."

Mrs. Payne nodded. "Can I help you with anything today?"

Caroline took her list out of her pocket and handed it to her along with the flour sack. "Do you have fresh eggs?"

"Yes, ma'am. Mrs. George brought two dozen in just a while ago." Mrs. Payne glanced at the list. "I'll set aside half of those for you."

"Thank you, Mrs. Payne." Caroline wandered around the store until she came to a child's chamber pot with a small vine of sweet peas painted around the bowl. It was so pretty, she decided to buy it. The twins wouldn't need it for two years, but it would keep.

Mrs. Payne went over to Caroline. "Isn't that sweet? Almost makes me want another baby."

"I know what you mean." Caroline handed the small chamber pot to her. "I'll take that, too." She stepped over to the counter and paid for the items.

"Good. My husband would be grateful. Last thing we need is another child." Mrs. Payne wrapped the little chamber pot. "But I guess that's up to the Lord." She added it to the flour sack and slid the sack over to Caroline. "Do you want this delivered, Mrs. Dobbs? It's awfully heavy for you to carry home."

"No, thank you, Mrs. Payne. I'll manage." Caroline left the store holding the flour sack in her arms. If she weren't being such a pinch-penny, or hadn't spent more than she had planned, she would have had her purchases delivered. However, if all she had to do was tighten her purse strings to provide for her children, it was a small price to pay.

Daniel stopped the wagon in front of Jay's house and faced his son. "Have fun but mind your manners. Freddy's leaving to join his company is no cause to get rambunctious."

"Yes, Pa." Ethan jumped to the ground. "Have you changed your mind about coming to his parents' party? They said they'd sure like you to come."

"I already told you I was going to stop by Mrs. Dobbs's. I'll come back for you in a couple of hours."

"Well, you should at least come in and pay your respects to Jay's parents."

Daniel eyed his son. "I will, Ethan, when I return."

"Yeah, Pa." Ethan turned and ran up to the house.

The boy had been after him all day about staying for the grown-ups' party, but Daniel had said no and held his ground. He shook his head and set off for Caroline's house. That boy didn't give up easily. Must be a family trait. He could be just as relentless where Caroline was concerned.

When he arrived, Tucker was watching from the window, and Caroline answered the door with Livvie on one shoulder and Robert on the other. Just seeing her made him feel good. Coming home to her at the end of the day would be more than he could hope for. "Hello. How's our little girl?"

Our little girl? Oh, she wished . . . but that was only a saying. "Not very happy at the moment, I'm afraid, and she has upset her brother. Come on in." He walked past her, and the scent of wild mint lingered, one of her favorite fragrances. Then she realized he knew which twin was which. "How did you recognize Livvie? I have trouble telling them apart half the time."

He grinned. "Her voice." After he had hung up his coat and scarf, he spoke to Robert. "How're you doing?"

She patted the baby's back. "I don't think he knows why he's fussing. He's usually the happiest baby I've ever seen. I can't wait to see what they'll be like when they learn to talk."

He grinned at Livvie. "You and Robert'll probably talk until your mama wishes you hadn't learned so quickly." He looked at Caroline and wondered if he would be there to enjoy them with her. "Just like all other children. Want me to hold her for a while?"

"If you wouldn't mind—thank you." She handed the baby over to him, along with the piece of oilcloth. The baby quieted for a minute. "She likes you, but then you're a likable man."

"I'm glad you think so," he said, smiling at her before he turned his attention to the baby. He patted and rubbed the baby's back as he walked over to the armchair and sat down with the baby on his lap. Ethan had suffered a few bouts of colic, and Daniel had been the only one who could quiet him down. "How's that? Things look different this way, don't they?" The baby stopped crying for a minute and burped. "That feels better, doesn't it?" He met Caroline's gaze. "Just a touch of colic."

"I should have known." As she soothed Robert, she remembered her neighbor back home giving her baby pennyroyal. Her grandmother chewed on spearmint leaves or added the leaves to her tea. She didn't have pennyroyal, but there was a large mint bush outside the back door. She kissed Robert and settled him in his cradle. "I'll brew a cup of mint tea for her and get your coffee."

She returned a few minutes later and set the tray on the table between their chairs. "She's much better. You seem to have disarmed her." *He has the same effect on me,* she thought. "She may not need the mint tea."

He chuckled. "A little won't hurt, might help her sleep easier."

"That would be a blessing. She has about worn herself out." Caroline realized she had let the crying upset her, too. She added a little sugar to the mint tea. Livvie was content in Daniel's care, and Caroline didn't want to upset her again. "Do you mind holding her while I feed her a little tea?"

He turned Livvie around to face Caroline. "We're ready."

"I'll try not to spill any on you," she said, tucking the napkin under the baby's chin. Bending over his lap felt awkward. She kneeled in front of him and dipped the spoon in the tea. When the tip of it touched Livvie's lips, she opened her mouth, and Caroline dribbled a few drops in her mouth. "She swallowed it." Caroline grinned at Daniel. "This may take a while."

He cleared his throat, feeling almost mesmerized by her. "I'm not complaining."

She rested her left hand on his leg for balance. The muscle in his thigh tightened, and she glanced at her hand. And stared. The familiar way her fingers molded over his knee sent a shiver down her spine.

Her cheeks paled, then turned pink. He covered her hand with his. "It's all right." If it were possible, he would sit there all night as long as she left her hand on his leg, and the baby stayed on his lap. All too soon, she finished feeding the baby and stood up. A short time later Livvie fell asleep, and he put her down in the cradle. Caroline looked a little weary and oh, so appealing. He put another log on the fire. "You must be tired. How about that glass of wine? I'll wait on you for a change."

"Mmm, sounds good." She arched her back and looked at him. "I'm sorry about this evening. It's New Year's Eve. I've been looking forward to seeing you, and you end up holding a crying baby."

"I didn't mind, and the evening's not over yet." He gave her shoulder a gentle squeeze. Her back was probably stiff, and it would have been so easy to give her a massage to loosen up those stiff muscles—arouse others, and cross the boundary he had set for himself. "Rest. I won't be long."

She leaned back, set the rocking chair in motion, and closed her eyes. She was far from being tired. Her insides felt like jelly, and she was torn between wanting Daniel to stay and wanting him to leave so they might kiss good night. She rubbed the palms of her hands back and forth along the edge of the chair. Sitting there imagining his embrace, in more detail than was considered ladylike, was not the way to calm down.

Daniel returned with two glasses of blackberry cordial. "These glasses are larger than the ones you used, but I thought tonight you could use more than a sip." He handed one to Caroline. "Here's to 1862 bringing you the happiness you deserve."

I already have that, she thought, raising her glass. "I hope people discover your talent for making lovely furniture and order so many pieces you will be a full-time cabinetmaker and not a carpenter." Smiling at him, she tapped her glass to his and drank to their toasts.

As he watched her lips touch the rim of the glass, he took a healthy swig and sat down. "You've hardly been out of the house in weeks. Have you seen Mr. Bennett lately?" He knew he might regret asking, but it was the only way to find out.

"Not in two or three weeks. Why?"

"I thought he was keeping company with you." There, he'd said it. Now breathe easier, he thought.

She shrugged and took another sip of cordial. "He was, for a while, though I'm not sure why." Gilbert enjoyed his own companionship more than hers. "We decided not to see each other. That was before the twins were born." Is this Daniel's way of trying to find out if I have other gentlemen callers? No, it was just her mind grasping for a dream. "When have I had time to see anyone?"

He laughed, saluted her with his glass, and sipped his drink. He swirled the last swallow of wine in the glass. "It's not really my place to ask."

"We are friends, Daniel. You may ask me anything." She watched the smile that spread across his face, and grinned. "I can't promise that I'll answer, but you can ask."

I'm glad Bennett's a bigger fool than I had taken him for,

Daniel thought. They talked for a while longer, then he noticed the time. "I wish I didn't have to leave, but I'd better get Ethan before he and his friends think I've forgotten about him." He drank the last swallow of cordial, set the glass down, and stood up.

"I understand." She rose at the same time. "I'll probably be asleep when the new year arrives."

Gazing into her eyes, he stepped up to her and said, "Then for us, it's midnight." He wrapped his arms around her slowly, giving her time to check his advance, if that was what she wanted to do.

His arms wound around her almost hesitantly, until she closed the space and returned his embrace. She met his gaze and said, "Happy New Year."

"And to you." He covered her mouth with his. In his experience, New Year's kisses were a simple brush of the lips, but not this time. She held him with surprising strength and gave him access to deepen the kiss. She was sweet and bold and passionate—everything he wanted in a woman.

For the first time since her husband's passing, Caroline felt truly cherished. She tried to stand still, but he aroused her so she wanted to be closer and swayed against his body. Instead of appeasing her desire, it fueled her need for him. That need would never be satisfied, but his embrace came close to it.

He ended the kiss and held her against his racing heart.

He wasn't in the habit of making resolutions, but this year was an exception. Somehow, he would end his farce of a marriage. He wanted to honor Caroline, not disgrace her.

13

DIVORCE. THE WORD haunted Daniel's thoughts day and night during the following six days. He had never known a man who had been divorced. He'd read those short items in the newspaper, the ones that gave you a smile or a chuckle—"Mr. Brown claims his wife refused to cook his meals, wash his clothes, or act in a wifely manner." But he'd bet Mr. Brown hadn't laughed, and neither had Daniel.

He walked deeper into his stand of alders and let the wind bending the treetops soothe his frustration. Divorce was the only way he could be free of Emmaline. After she'd left, he had followed some advice passed along to him and put a notice in the *Argus*:

> "Whereas, my wife, Emmaline Louise, has left my bed and board without any just cause or provocation, this is therefore to give notice to all persons 'not' to harbor or trust her on my account, as I will pay no debts of hers contracting from and after this date."

When it was published, he cut it out and put it in the box with their marriage certificate. He could never be sure if the notice had really stopped her from charging any purchases to him, but he felt he had done something.

He needed to talk to a lawyer. He must have been thinking about it for a while, he realized, when he remembered reading one particular notice in the newspapers, W. C. Johnson, Attorney and Counselor At Law. It appeared in every issue, and Daniel almost felt as if he knew him. That's who he needed to see. After waiting more than five years for his wife to return, he was anxious to have it over with. Explaining it to Ethan was another problem.

And Caroline. He didn't need to close his eyes to relive New Year's Eve—feel her warm body in his embrace or taste the cordial on her tongue. Would she want to be seen with a divorced man?

Daniel turned back toward the house. Even if she never wanted to see him again, he needed to break with the past, for his sake as well as his son's.

Daniel drove the wagon to town and pulled up in front of Milwain's tin store. The Main Street House, opposite, still had the sign in the window: FOR SALE OR RENT. The building needed work, but Daniel wasn't interested in that job.

He climbed the stairs on the outside of Milwain's and entered Mr. Johnson's office. Bookcases lined one wall. The attorney was seated at his desk. "Mr. Johnson?"

As he looked at Daniel, Mr. Johnson slid his spectacles down his nose. "Yes, sir, attorney and counselor at law. How can I help you?"

"Daniel Grey," he said, holding out his hand. Mr. Johnson gave his hand a firm shake, and Daniel nodded. He had seen him around town, but they hadn't met. "Do you handle divorces, Mr. Johnson?"

"Please, have a seat." Mr. Johnson motioned to a nearby chair. "Yes, I can draw up a dissolution of marriage contract and file it with the county seat." He rubbed his left sideburn. "Is the divorce for you, Mr. Grey?"

"Yes," Daniel said, taking the seat.

"All right. Tell me the circumstances, why you want a divorce from your wife."

"It's pretty simple. Mrs. Grey left me more than five years ago."

"Were you both in residence here at that time?"

"Yes. We came over the trail in fifty-three. Arrived in the nick of time to file a donation land claim."

Mr. Johnson peered over the top of his spectacles at Daniel. "Did she tell you she was leaving? Why? Or did she just sneak off when you weren't around?"

"She took our son to school and left while I was working." Daniel chuckled, a sound harsh, even to his own ears. "She didn't like it here and especially didn't care for the land I claimed."

"I see. Did you have some sort of agreement when she left?"

"She said she'd never be back. Is that what you mean?"

"It'll do."

"Is that reason enough for a divorce?"

"Willful desertion for the period of three years is one of six causes." Mr. Johnson removed his spectacles and massaged the bridge of his nose before he continued. "Impotency, adultery, conviction of a felony, gross drunkenness, and cruel and inhuman treatment are the other five. Would you add any of those to your petition?"

The last one was tempting, but Daniel decided now wasn't a good time to test the attorney's sense of humor. "Desertion is enough, isn't it?"

Mr. Johnson nodded. "Do you know where Mrs. Grey is living now?"

Daniel shook his head. "I heard that she'd paid for passage to San Francisco."

"Did you try to find her?"

"No." Daniel shifted his weight on the wood chair. "Do I have to?"

Mr. Johnson shook his head. "I'll have the notice of intent published after we set a court date. I can also submit the same notice to the *Daily Herald* in San Francisco if you'd like. It's your choice on that one."

"Yes. At least I can say we tried to notify her." Daniel was tempted to tell him not to bother, but he needed to have everything done right. Slowly the "also" registered. "Excuse me, but did you mean that the same notice would be published here, too?"

"Yes, of course. Is anything wrong, Mr. Grey?"

"I had hoped it wouldn't be made public, at least for a while." Daniel stared at the door without seeing it. He hadn't planned on talking to Ethan or telling Caroline until near the court date.

"Don't worry, Mr. Grey. People won't think the worst of you. Isn't as easy for a woman. She might leave a husband who beats her and the children, and people gossip about her, as if it's her fault." Mr. Johnson pushed some papers aside. "No, after the first flurry of curious questions, everyone will forget."

Whatever he had let himself in for, Daniel hoped Mr. Johnson was right. "If it is necessary—"

"I assure you it is, Mr. Grey." Mr. Johnson went to his file cabinet and took out a sheet of paper. "I need you to fill out this short page. I'll need the names to complete the contract. You can use my desk."

Daniel read the questions before he picked up the pen and dipped into the inkwell. The only information he hadn't already told Mr. Johnson was his wife's full name and the date and place of their marriage. Daniel finished, set the pen back in the tray, and blotted his signature. He stood up and stepped aside.

Mr. Johnson quickly read the information. "Very good. I'll draw up the contract and write the notices. Can you return tomorrow, say in the afternoon?"

"Four o'clock okay?"

"Fine, Mr. Grey."

"I'll be here." Daniel glanced around the office. Mr. Johnson appeared to be a practical man. That was reassuring. "What is your fee?"

"We can settle fee and the expenses tomorrow."

"Expenses? What kind?"

Mr. Johnson gave a harsh laugh. "Don't worry, Mr. Grey. That will be the cost of posting the notice to San Francisco, about twenty cents. Shouldn't be more than fifty cents to have them published."

That would be the least of it, Daniel realized. "When can we go to court and get this over with?"

Mr. Johnson leaned back in his chair. "Since she might be several days to a week's travel time away from here, how about the last week of February?"

Daniel would have liked it to be over with sooner than that, but at least he knew when his marriage would end. "Yes, that should give her time to see the notice, if she's in San Francisco, and return, if she wants to fight it."

"I'll let you know what day you'll have to appear in court. If you haven't heard from her by now, you aren't likely to, Mr. Grey."

"That's what I thought," Daniel said with a shrug, "but she never did what I expected her to." He shook hands with Mr. Johnson. "See you tomorrow."

When Daniel drove the wagon up the street, he started in the direction of Caroline's house. He wanted to see her, talk to her, but he wasn't prepared to tell her about the divorce, just yet. He had a few days to go over it in his mind. At the next corner he turned the horse and rode away from her house. If he saw her now, he'd just blurt out what he had begun and that wasn't how he wanted to tell her.

Caroline smiled at Mrs. Wright. "Is that the dress?"

"Yes." Mrs. Wright handed it to Caroline. "I'm real partial to it. The muck washed out of the other two, but I couldn't get the stain out of the hem of that."

"This is dark, but have you tried a lye wash?"

"Yes, see," Mrs. Wright said, reaching over to expose a spot. "It started to take the color out, but it didn't hurt that mucky stain."

"How about fuller's earth? It might lighten it enough so it wouldn't be noticeable."

"No. I don't have any of that. Could you put some braiding or maybe some lace or fringe on to hide it?"

"If I can't bleach the stain out, Mrs. Wright, I'll see what I can do."

"Thank you, Mrs. Dobbs. It's not a fancy dress . . ."

"I understand. I have a couple skirts I wouldn't want to part with or toss in the dustbin, either."

Mrs. Wright stepped closer to the cradles and peered at the twins. "They are sweet, Mrs. Dobbs, and big for two at once." She smiled at Caroline. "When I was seventeen, a neighbor lady had a pair of babies at once, but they were scrawny little things, not like these two."

Caroline beamed at Livvie and Robert and didn't mind if her pride was showing. "They do have good appetites."

"They'll be twice the care and work. I heard you were keeping them." Mrs. Wright bent over the cradles, taking a closer look. "Which one's which?"

Caroline took a deep breath and let it out slowly. The woman was a customer, she reminded herself, and curiosity was natural. "Robert is on your left, and you did hear right.

I'll raise the twins as if they were my own—their mother wanted it that way."

Mrs. Wright nodded. "They're lucky babies." She walked around Caroline's chair. "I'd better get to my other errands. When should I come back for the dress?"

"I don't want you to make an unnecessary trip. If you have a few minutes, you could pick out the trim now."

"Yes, that would be easier."

Caroline led her to the sewing room and set out the trimmings she had. After Mrs. Wright had chosen one, Caroline walked her back to the door. "I'll get started on it now. I believe I can have your dress ready by day after tomorrow, after two o'clock."

"Oh, that's wonderful. Just in time for my Friday night meeting. Thank you, Mrs. Dobbs. I knew I could count on you."

When the front door closed behind Mrs. Wright, Caroline grabbed the woman's dress and marched to the kitchen. She knew she should be more tolerant with questions about the twins, her twins, but good gracious, she wished people would quit asking if she were going to keep them. Surely most everyone had heard she was by now. The twins were four weeks old last Sunday.

She scrubbed the skirt with her special soap, but the stain still showed. Next she treated it with soda, prepared a lye wash, and poured it over the stain but stopped when it started bleaching the fabric instead of the discoloration. She washed the skirt again, wrung it out, and hung it on the drying rack in front of the fireplace to dry.

For a moment she watched the sleeping twins and wondered when she would see Daniel. He had stopped by on Friday to show her the washstand he had made. It was beautiful, with turned legs and a scrolled backsplash. When she had told him how much she liked it, he had seemed distracted or worried about something. He had come inside only long enough to see the twins and notice that she had taken the tree down. He left to deliver the washstand and said he would see her in a few days, but he hadn't been by since then.

To her, a few days were two or three, not five. As she brushed the back of her hand over her lips, a tremor of desire slid down from her belly. She had thought she was beyond the age when passionate yearnings could shake her body and fill her dreams. She had been wrong. Very wrong, indeed. Nevertheless, she wasn't a beast and would have to control these wonderful feelings—or not see Daniel again.

Of course, if his wife returned to him, that would end her friendship with him. Then she began to wonder if his wife had any bearing on his disposition the other day. If she were back home, Caroline felt sure he would tell her. He was an honest man, and had admitted he was married, though not immediately.

Daniel dished out baked beans and pork onto their plates while Ethan put the sour-milk biscuits on the table. "Did you pour the milk?"

"Yes, Pa." Ethan picked up his plate and carried it to the table. "Can I stay over with Jay Saturday night?"

Daniel carried his plate to the table and sat down to eat. On Saturday the latest edition of the *Argus* would come out with his notice in it, and he wasn't sure what he would say until after they talked about the divorce. "We'll see."

"I told him I'd let him know at school tomorrow." Ethan gulped down a bite. "We have to write a paper on some news that's in Saturday's paper, and Jay's pa gets one every week."

"I do, too." Daniel took a bite. "I'll let you know in the morning." He would pick up his copy at the *Argus* office, as he did every week, cut out the notice and put it with the earlier one in the box. He wasn't sure why, it just seemed the right thing to do. "How are you doing in school?"

"I get good marks. Why do you always ask me?"

Daniel chuckled. "Is there anything wrong with wanting to know how you're doing?"

"Guess not." Ethan looked at him a moment. "Did you finish Mr. Lainge's wall?"

"Sure did, and I'm almost done at Mr. Murphy's." He looked at his son and grinned.

Ethan poked a chunk of biscuit in his mouth. "You see much of Mrs. Dobbs anymore?"

"Don't talk with your mouth full." Daniel drank some milk. "Haven't had time in the last week. But I plan on seeing her tomorrow evening." He picked up another biscuit and broke it in half.

"People are going to talk about you two if you don't stop going over there."

Daniel stared at his son until he caught his attention. "Ethan, what do you know about divorce?"

"Divorce? I heard divorced ladies were no better'n a fancy woman. That true?"

"Where did you hear that?"

Ethan shrugged. "I dunno. Around."

Daniel fixed him with a harsh stare. "It *is not* true."

"What're you getting all riled about?"

"The only reasons people divorce are because they have very serious problems."

"What's all this—" Ethan narrowed his eyes. "You're going to divorce Ma, huh?"

Daniel's gaze held, and he nodded.

"*Why?* Why'd you want to do that? So you can see Mrs. Dobbs?" Ethan jumped to his feet. "That's it, isn't it, Pa?"

"Sit down, boy." Daniel waited until Ethan had taken his

seat again. "Your ma's been gone over five years. That's a long time, son. She's living the way she wants to; don't you think I should have the same choice?"

"Well, yes—no—Ma could come home any day. Maybe she's scared to come back, afraid you'll wallop her or doesn't have money for stage fare . . . or—"

Daniel shook his head. "I have *never* struck a woman, and your ma was always good at finagling whatever she wanted, once she set her mind to it."

"But—"

"Son, she made her decision, and I have made mine. Probably should've done it years ago. We have to accept that she doesn't want to return and isn't going to." Daniel held his son's attention and added, "I want you to understand, Ethan, I *need* to do this."

Ethan stared at his pa. He opened his mouth, and then closed it.

"She wasn't happy here, and I wouldn't drag her back if I could. We can't have everything the way we want it."

"I love her, Pa. Don't you? You married her."

"When we married I did." Daniel wrapped his hand around his empty glass. "But things weren't the same by the time we settled here. As much as I liked it, she didn't."

"LeRoy's ma and pa fight all the time and they're happy."

"And they live together."

Ethan scraped his shoes on the floor. "When're you gonna do it?"

"I signed the papers Tuesday. Mr. Johnson will take them to court and get a date set for the judge to hear my petition."

"How soon'll that be?"

"Mr. Johnson said he would try for the last week in February. A notice announcing my petition for divorce will be in this week's newspaper. I wanted you to know in case anyone says something about it to you."

"You mean *everyone'll know?*"

Daniel nodded. "That's the way it's done. There was no way around it." He watched his son struggle with the news. "We can talk about it anytime. If you have trouble in school, tell me. We'll face it together."

"Are you going to tell your friends?"

"Not unless they ask, except for Mrs. Dobbs. I think I should tell her so she doesn't hear it from one of the ladies."

"You going to marry her?"

"I don't know, son. I'm not free to ask anyone to be my wife now."

After she had taken her sign down from the post in the front yard and had fed Livvie and Robert, Caroline changed from her dress to a wrapper and washed her hair. Brushing it dry in front of the fireplace was soothing. For the first time in the last three days, she wasn't listening for the sound of Daniel's wagon or hoping he would come through the door and surprise her.

Something was wrong, and she wished he would confide in her. If she had drunk more cordial on New Year's Eve, she could probably convince herself that she had dreamed their second kiss. She stood up and bent over and continued brushing her hair. Men. She didn't know much more about them now than she did when she was eighteen. She sat back down on the hearth and brushed her hair down over her shoulder.

Tucker came over to her and curled up on the hem of her wrapper. She petted him and was rewarded with his rumbly purring. A little while later, when her hair was almost dry, there was a knock at the door. Tucker leaped over to the window. Surely it couldn't be Daniel. She opened the door and there he was standing in front of her. "Hello. I wasn't expecting you."

Seeing her in that pretty yellow wrapper with her hair falling over one shoulder made him wish he had gotten the divorce a year ago. "I'm sorry I haven't been by, Caroline. I'd like to talk. Can I come in?"

She glanced down at her comfortable old wrapper and wished she hadn't taken off the belt. "I suppose it will be all right." Why couldn't he have come by earlier, before she had changed clothes and washed her hair, when she didn't look as if she were ready for bed? She walked back into the parlor.

He followed her inside and closed the door behind him. Unbuttoning his jacket, he decided not to take it off. She wasn't too happy with him, and he wouldn't be surprised if she told him to leave. "Mind if I sit down?"

"Of course not." She stepped back so he could pass. When he sat down in the armchair, she reclaimed her place on the hearth. "How have you been?"

"Busy . . . okay. You?"

"Fine." She tucked her feet under her skirt. "So are the twins." Daniel wasn't his usual smiling self, but she did not want him to think he could drop by and expect to be welcomed as if she didn't mind being forgotten about.

He turned on the chair to face her. Some men knew how to sweet-talk a woman, say anything and make it sound good. He'd never learned how to do that, and he ended up blurting out the first thing that came to mind. "Are we still friends, Caroline?"

She had wondered about that herself, and he was asking her? "I thought we were."

He stared at the fire a moment, then he met her gaze. "Tuesday, I signed a petition for divorce. The notice will appear in tomorrow's paper. Caroline," he said, lowering his voice, "I wanted to tell you before someone else did."

She stared at him, completely nonplussed. "I . . . didn't

know you had been thinking about— It's so final. Are you sure that's what you want?"

He nodded. "I've been thinking about it since New Year's Eve." He pulled off his jacket and tossed it over the back of the chair. "I should've seen a lawyer a long time ago."

She felt their embrace had been much more than a passionate kiss, but it never occurred to her that he would ever consider divorce. No wonder she hadn't seen him. She watched him through her lashes as she picked up her brush and pulled it through her hair. He sounded relieved, and yet she knew his decision had not been made easily. "I shouldn't ask you, Daniel, but I'm curious. What made you do it now?"

"You're not beating about the bush," he said with a grin, then he sobered. "I'm tired of being married and not having a wife. I can't even walk out with a woman without fear of tarnishing her reputation. Some men might wink or slap my back, while their wives would shut the woman out." He started to rise and changed his mind. He wanted to hold her and tell her how very much he loved her, but he wouldn't do it now, this way. "As much as I love my son, I want more. Is that unreasonable?"

"No. Oh, no, it isn't." She didn't have a child to ease the loneliness after her husband's death, but she knew what Daniel meant. No child could fill the space a departed mate leaves. There were more questions she could ask but not without sounding brazen. Tears started gathering in her eyes, and she resumed brushing her hair with brisk strokes. She didn't want to be the cause for his divorce or his unhappiness.

Daniel reached out and gently rocked each cradle. Caroline's reaction wasn't what he had expected, or even hoped for when he arrived. Could he have mistaken her feelings for him? If he hadn't, he wondered why she wasn't happy for him?

"Does Ethan know?"

"Mmm-hmm. We talked about it last night."

"From the way you sound, he didn't take the news very well."

He shook his head and leaned back on the chair. "He hasn't mentioned his mother in over a year. Now, suddenly he's almost talked himself into believing she'll come back." He watched the brush glide down through the silky strands of her hair. Here was another memory to keep him company at night.

"Does he understand that she will still be his mother, no matter what happens between you and her?"

"He must know. Whoever heard of a youngun divorcing his ma?"

"It may help if you remind him." She coiled her hair around her hand and let it fall in a spiral. "Does he blame me?"

"He's upset." The coil of hair spilled over one breast. He wanted to comb his fingers through those strands, feel the fullness of her breast on his palm . . . But he didn't need to torture himself further until he was free to touch her. "He asked about you—" No, he thought, this wasn't the time to bring up the other reason. "But he knows it was my decision."

"He will understand. It took you time to decide what you wanted to do. Give him the same chance."

"You're right." He grabbed his jacket and stood up. "I'd better go. Probably shouldn't have come over here tonight."

She put down her brush and followed him to the door.

He paused in the entry and turned to her. "I can let myself out." He stared at her dark hair resting over her breast.

As he reached out to her, she stood frozen, waiting to feel

his caress. He caught the hank of hair in his fingers, and she felt the warmth of his hand, but not his touch. A tremor slid down her spine, her heart leaped to her throat, and still she waited for him . . . to brush the back of his hand over her breast or put his other arm around her, she didn't know.

"Caroline . . ." Dear God, he needed to hold her, just hold her. But what if an embrace wasn't enough? He let the strands of hair slip through his fingers. "G'night—" He walked out of the house before he tempted his restraint any further.

"Night, Daniel." She glanced down at her hair and smiled.

14

ALTHOUGH DANIEL HAD not been far from her thoughts since he had left the night before, Caroline woke up Saturday morning still uncertain how she felt about his divorce. It was such a drastic action to take. She could imagine his frustration at being married and yet having no wife to keep him company or to share his dreams, hopes, and ideas with. He would be single, and before long half the women in the Willamette Valley would know it.

She couldn't help wondering if his wife would see the announcement or if it would make any difference to her if she did. One thing Caroline knew she must remember— they were friends, and he was not obliged in any way to keep company with her. Thinking that and believing it, however, were not the same.

She put her sign out, though not many women came by on Saturdays. She spent the morning cleaning the floors and polishing the furniture. She was in her room dusting the bedstead and Tucker was grabbing for the dusting rag when the bell rang out. She was brushing her hair back from her face when she stepped into the parlor. "Daniel—" She smiled and then noticed the newspaper. "Is it in there?"

He returned her smile and held out the *Argus*. "I brought this one over so you can see the announcement for yourself." The cat rubbed against his leg, and he stroked its back.

"Thank you." She opened the newspaper to the next-to-the-last page, where the notices were posted.

"Left column, halfway down. Under the drugstore advertisement." She had the prettiest hands, he thought, with long slender fingers. A gold band would look real nice on her left hand. So would emeralds, garnets, and pearls.

She read the item and closed the paper. "I've seen similar notices, but I usually don't read them. Are you worried about people seeing it?"

"Not for myself. But Ethan might overhear something he doesn't need to. There hasn't been any talk about his mother in years. I just hope it doesn't start up now."

She looked at the twins. She would feel just as protective for them. "Boys must have other things to talk about, and he seems to be close to you."

"You're probably right." He glanced at the babies. "Robert's awake. Mind if I hold him before I go?"

"Better let me change him first." She picked up Robert with the oilcloth under him and walked to the hall door. "This won't take long." She returned a few minutes later. Robert was wide awake and looking around, until he saw Daniel. "He's almost smiling at you."

Daniel held the baby up in front of him a moment. "Hi there, young man. How are you and Tucker getting along?" He dropped down to one knee and held the baby so he could see the cat. Tucker backed away, and Daniel stood up.

"If I didn't know better, I might think he understands you."

He grinned at Caroline, then he kissed the baby's cheek.

She shook her head but couldn't resist smiling at his silliness. "Would you like a cup of coffee?"

"I would, but I have to get back to work." He handed the baby to her. "I hired a couple men to help build Jens

Ogden's warehouse. We'll start next week and need to get as much done as we can while the weather's clear." He skimmed one knuckle over the baby's chin. "So I won't be able to come by very often."

"That's a big project. I'm happy for you."

He lowered his hand and gently caressed hers. "Kiss them good night for me."

He stood close enough to put his arm around her, and she could almost feel his touch. "I will." As she stared at him, he turned and left before she had the sense to walk him out. Oh, Daniel, she thought, I can't help loving you, but I hope you aren't making a mistake you will regret.

Saturday night Daniel put the last coat of polish on the plain infant beds for Caroline. He doubted that what he had made was what she'd had in mind. However, knowing she would keep these in her bedroom, he had made sturdy beds without rockers that would last the babies four or five years.

He worked later than usual and returned to the shop the next morning until midday, when he rode into town to give his son a ride home. There was a light rain and it was cold. He hoped he and the men would get the footing for the warehouse dug before the ground froze. They'd had a dusting of snow and could be in for a few more inches and freezing nights.

When he reached town, he went straight to Jay's house. His father was out front. Daniel got down and went over to pay his respects. "Hello, Mr. Yancy."

"Mr. Grey, hello. Sorry you couldn't make it to the party last night."

"So am I. Hope my boy behaved himself."

"He's a good lad." Mr. Yancy chuckled. "Of course, you put two boys together, and they have to get into something.

Mostly eavesdropping on the party. A harmless prank. Better that than all their talk of the rebellion."

"Oh, yes, the paper they were assigned to write."

"Think they spent more time talking about Freddy and joining up with the army." Mr. Yancy shook his head. "Be glad when they forget about that."

"I agree. At their age, it all sounds so exciting." Daniel glanced at the house. "Well, I'd better collect my boy."

"One more thing, Grey. Saw your notice in the paper and wanted to say it to your face. Thought your missus'd died a few years back. What you're doing is damned decent, if you ask me."

Daniel stared a moment before he understood the gist of Mr. Yancy's comment. "Thanks. I appreciate your saying so." When Daniel started up the walkway, Ethan came outside with Jay.

"Hi, Pa." Ethan glanced at Jay. "We were just going down by the river."

Daniel eyed his son. "I told you I'd come for you this morning."

"Yeah, but it's noon. I thought you might be at . . . visiting a friend."

"No such luck." Daniel eyed him, wondering if the boy was swaggering or if he had realized that Caroline was as nice as she appeared, then shook his head. "Thank Mr. and Mrs. Yancy, and we'll be on our way."

Ethan said his good-byes, grabbed his schoolwork, and joined his pa in the wagon. "Don't see why I had to leave."

"Don't overstay your welcome," Daniel said, glancing at his son, "if you want to be invited back."

"I didn't."

"Did you get your schoolwork done?"

"Yes, Pa. Mrs. Yancy said we couldn't leave the kitchen table until we did."

Daniel chuckled. "What did you write about?"

"I read that Colonel Sam Colt died at Hartford, Connecticut. He made the Colt pistols, but they didn't say anything else about him. Did you read about the slave trade?"

"This morning."

"That's what I chose. Captain Schufeldt did the right thing down in Havana, stopping the slavers from bringing those poor Africans to the States. Did you know they sell them for *three hundred* dollars each?!" Ethan worked his jaw a moment and added, "The war with the South should stop that."

Daniel watched his son out of the corner of his eye. He agreed with the boy, but he was concerned about anger in his voice. Sometimes he sounded more like a grown man than a boy. "What did Jay write about?"

"His paper's on the Utah convention in Salt Lake City to draw up a constitution. They want to take it to Congress so they can become a state this session."

"Did Jay see the notice about my divorce?"

Ethan shook his head. "He didn't read any more than he had to."

"Did you?"

"I'll see it later."

"Have you given any thought to what you'll say if someone asks about it?"

Ethan stared off to the side of the road. "Guess I'll say it won't make any difference. Doesn't look like she's coming home."

Tuesday morning after he had taken Ethan to Jay's house, Daniel drove to Caroline's. It was early to pay a call, but with two babies to feed, he was sure she would be up. At least he hoped so. He knocked on the door and stepped back to watch the front window. Sure enough, Tucker jumped up to the ledge. Caroline opened the door looking beautiful and not quite awake. "G'morning."

"Daniel—" She started to yawn and quickly covered her mouth. He was bright-eyed, smiling as if he had a great secret, and his breath formed little clouds in the cold air. "Come inside."

"I brought the babies' beds. It's too cold to leave the door open. Wait inside. I'll bring them in."

She nodded and watched him from the window with Tucker. She thought she had misunderstood him, but sure enough, Daniel lifted *two* cradles out of the wagon. Didn't he understand that she couldn't afford two? When he came back to the door, she opened it for him.

He carried the beds into the parlor and set them down. "You said you wanted plain cradles to keep in your bedroom." He glanced at them. They were as close to resembling boxes as they could be. "These are large enough to last Robert and Livvie for four or five years. I didn't put rockers on because in a year or so, they could tip them over, but I will if you want rockers."

"This's what you call plain?" She ran her hand along one edge. Instead of a flat cut on the side boards, they had a lazy *S* design near the head, and the edge was rounded and smooth as satin. There were wide openings on each side making handles to pick up each one.

"They're almost boxes." He smiled, but she was busy checking the beds. "I can fit rockers on the bun feet if you want them, maybe paint scrolling around the side?"

"No, they don't need that." She took a closer look. On the inside of each headboard he had carved the date of the twins' birth. She was so touched, she reached out and put her hand on his arm. "The beds are wonderful, and thank you for adding their birth date. That makes them even more special."

He let out a soft sigh. "I'm glad you like them."

"Daniel—" She realized she was holding on to him and lowered her hand. "I don't want to sound ungrateful— please understand—you made two. I believe I asked for one, but I know you won't have any trouble at all selling the other. They are lovely."

"Caroline," he said, resting a hand on each of her shoulders. "They are yours. I made them for you." He pressed a quick kiss to her forehead and leaned back from the temptation she posed. "With twins, you need two of everything."

"I realize that, but I cannot afford to buy everything in pairs." She didn't want him to let go of her. His hands were large and warm, and had the most fanciful effect on her.

"They are yours." He gave her shoulders a gentle squeeze. "Unless Robert and Livvie don't like them."

She shook her head, then rubbed her cheek on the back of his left hand. "You're impossible."

"Really?"

"Oh—you are making this difficult. I ordered one, and I *will* pay for it." Staring into his eyes, she felt as if she were caught in his snare. "All right, the other, we will accept with gratitude." She kissed his other hand, sure he heard the thumping of her heart.

He lifted his fingers from the back of her shoulders, but he couldn't release her. As his palms moved downward, he ignored his conscience and framed her sweet face with his hands. *I love you, Caroline,* he thought, and kissed her waiting lips.

She gave into the passion he inspired so easily. His lips and tongue teased her senses, while his fingers lightly played with her hair. She wrapped her arms around his waist and felt the corded muscles tighten beneath her fingertips. She pressed her body to his, from her breasts to her knees, and imagined how she would feel lying beneath him in bed.

He ended the kiss while he still possessed the willpower and held her close. "I'd better take the beds to your room while I still have the strength."

In spite of herself, she laughed softly and splayed her hands over his back. "You haven't lost it."

Caroline finished feeding the twins and sat on the edge of her rocker to watch them. Their faces were filling out, their hair was longer, and the smallest dresses she had made them now fit. While they weren't nearly old enough to sit, she was tempted to prop them up, but she didn't. Instead she scooped them up, one on each arm, and walked over to the window to show them the snow outside.

"See, everything's white and so pretty. Next year I'll bundle you up and you can go out and see it for yourself." Caroline kissed each of them. "Look, Tucker's playing in the snow." She wandered through each room of the house naming the furniture and objects. She was training herself more than teaching them, but one day they would ask her questions, and she might not know all of the answers.

Livvie and Robert fell asleep, and Caroline put each in their own cradle—those beautiful cradles. Daniel had stopped by the house for a few short visits in the last week and a half, and he accepted her invitation to dinner on Sunday. She hadn't seen Ethan since that day she had passed him on the street. Maybe I was wrong, she thought, and he hadn't been standoffish. At least she hoped if he had been that he had changed his mind about her since then.

She walked outside and chased Tucker through the snow for a few minutes. The air was cold and smelled so clean. The sun was out for a while, then more clouds moved overhead and it began snowing again. She raced Tucker to the door and went back inside. With a cup of hot tea to warm her hands and sip on, she finished hemming Mrs. Anderson's wool dress.

Late in the afternoon the bell rang out, and Mrs. Nance came inside. Caroline set aside the infant dress. "Hello, Mrs. Nance. I haven't seen you since before Thanksgiving. How have you been?"

"Fine, thank you, Mrs. Dobbs. I'm sorry it's taken me so long to settle my account. We've been so busy." She loosened the strings on her reticule. "Would you tell me exactly how much my bill is? I know it's more than ten dollars."

"Yes, I'll get your card." Caroline went back to the sewing room, pulled Mrs. Nance's account record from the file, and returned to the parlor. "You were right, Mrs. Nance. Your balance is thirteen dollars and sixty-five cents."

Mrs. Nance counted out the correct change and handed it to Caroline. "I do appreciate your patience, Mrs. Dobbs." She edged closer to the cradles. "Those are the ones, aren't they? The twins I've heard about."

"Livvie and Robert."

"Their poor mama, leaving such pretty little things behind." Mrs. Nance shook her head. "Never understood why the Lord gave such a heavy burden to women."

Caroline sighed. Everyone still had an opinion about the twins and wanted to share it with her. Be patient, she told herself.

"If you decide to split them up, I'm sure Mr. Nance wouldn't mind taking the boy."

Whatever happened to Christian charity and love? Caroline wondered. "They have a home here, together with me."

As Mrs. Nance started for the door, she said, "Well, if you change your mind, just let me know."

After the door closed behind her, Caroline muttered, "It'll be a cold day in Hades when I do."

*   *   *

Caroline changed Livvie's and Robert's dresses before Daniel and Ethan were expected for dinner. The spiced beef roll was in the oven with potatoes, creamed mushroom soup simmered in one pan, and sliced carrots in another on top of the stove. Since Ethan seemed to like pudding, Caroline made tapioca with dates for dessert.

It was midday and still freezing out. She added another log to the blaze in the fireplace and heard Daniel's wagon pull up in front of the house. Tucker ran to the door ahead of her and went out onto the stoop to wait for them. She grabbed her shawl off the peg, wrapped it around her shoulders and stood in the doorway.

Ethan stepped inside, ahead of his father, rubbing his hands together. "Hello, Mrs. Dobbs. It's cold."

She smiled at him. "It sure is. Go on in by the fire. You can leave your hat and gloves on the hearth so they'll be warm when you have to go out again."

"Thanks."

"Good weather for sledding." Daniel closed the door behind him and turned to Caroline. "You look lovely, but you always do."

"So do you," she said softly. The look he gave her was more serious than a smile. For a moment she almost felt as if they had embraced. "I hope you're hungry. Dinner will be ready soon."

"Smells wonderful."

She grinned. "When you're hungry, most anything does."

He hung his coat on a peg. "Not always." He put his hat on the shelf over the pegs and stuffed his gloves in his coat pocket.

She went into the parlor. "Ethan, would you like a warm drink? I have coffee and tea." Tucker was seated on the sofa within Ethan's reach, and he was petting him.

"Coffee, please."

"All right." She looked at Daniel. "Coffee?"

"That would be good, Caroline." He went over to the fireplace. While she went to get their drinks, he thawed out his backside and looked at the babies. Both of them were awake and looking around. "Son, did you say hello to Robert and Livvie?"

"They don't know me, but one's looking at you."

"That's Livvie. Speak to them. They'll get to know your voice. Later, they'll learn your name."

Ethan glanced at the cradles. "Which is the boy?"

"Robert is closest to you. Livvie's on this side. Use their names."

As Ethan peered into the cradle, he ran his hand down Tucker's back. "Hi, Robert." The baby turned at the sound of his voice. "He's looking at me."

Daniel chuckled. "Both of them are smart. Better watch what you say around them."

"Hi, Livvie." Livvie waved her arms, and Ethan grinned. "They aren't bad, in a funny kinda way."

Daniel hid his grin. "You were like them, thirteen years ago."

Ethan stared at his pa as if trying to picture him as a baby. "You were, too, I guess."

Daniel chuckled. "Hard to believe?"

Ethan smiled. "Yeah."

Caroline returned with the tray of steaming cups on saucers. "Sorry I took so long." She set the tray on the little table and passed out the cups. "I see the twins woke up." She looked at Ethan. "I think they like your father's voice."

Ethan glanced from the twins to his pa and Caroline. "How can they know him from some other man? Or me?"

"Oh, they know him, Ethan. When they hear you enough times, they will recognize you, too. Babies are born knowing almost nothing. Think how much you've learned."

Ethan frowned, then looked at his cup. He stepped over to the tray, spooned sugar into his coffee, and added milk from the little pitcher.

Caroline sat down in her rocker. As she spoke softly to the twins, she glanced through her lashes at Ethan. He was curious, and he seemed friendlier than the last time she had seen him. She had hoped he wouldn't resent her. "Your father said you wrote a paper for school on the issue of slave shipping."

He looked at her and nodded.

Daniel waited for him to say something, but his son remained quiet. "You never did tell me what mark you received."

"Mr. Stanton said it was very good."

Caroline exchanged a smile with Daniel. "That's wonderful, Ethan. What is your favorite subject?"

He shrugged and sipped his coffee. "Mathematics."

His other marks were likely good, too, she thought. "Do you know what kind of work you would like to do when you're grown up?"

"I want to design houses and buildings."

Daniel sat in the armchair and leaned back. She was drawing him out, and it was interesting. He hadn't expected his son to tell her about his interest in architecture. The boy had only recently told him.

Caroline smiled at Ethan. "I helped Mr. Dobbs with the plans for this house. It was fun figuring out where I wanted the rooms."

"Really?" Ethan perked up. "I didn't know ladies ever thought about those things."

She chuckled. "Women spend most of their days in their homes. Men should ask women how they want their homes, especially the kitchens."

Ethan nodded slowly.

She grinned at Daniel and stood up. "I'll have dinner on the table in a few minutes."

"Can I help?"

"Not until I call you both in to eat." She tipped her head in Ethan's direction and went to the kitchen. It wasn't long before she set the serving dishes and platter on the dining room table, filled the glasses with water, and set out the basket of hot biscuits. She called Daniel and Ethan in to eat.

As Daniel passed by Caroline, he brushed his hand across the back of her waist. He wanted to touch her, but it didn't feel right in front of his son, not until he was more confident Ethan had changed his mind about her.

She began passing the serving dishes and was happy to see Ethan putting generous helpings of food on to his plate. His father also had a healthy appetite. She buttered a biscuit and set it aside before she tasted the spicy beef roll.

Daniel met her gaze. "Very good."

"Sure is, Mrs. Dobbs. Why are your baked potatoes so creamy?"

Daniel put a spoon of butter on his potato. "She did more than bake them." He glanced at her. "What's your secret?"

"When they were tender, I scooped out the insides and mashed them through the colander. After I added a little butter, salt, and pepper, I spooned the potatoes back into the jackets and baked them a while longer."

"Oh." Ethan looked at his pa. "Do we have a colander?"

"No, I don't think so."

With all Daniel had done for her, she decided she would get a colander for him. It wasn't much, and Ethan might enjoy mashing the potatoes through the colander. They were almost finished eating when Livvie cried out. Caroline excused herself, changed the baby's clothes, and brought her back to the table.

Daniel noticed Livvie watching Caroline take each bite. It was almost funny. The next time she took a bite, the baby waved her arms. "Mind if I hold her?"

Swallowing the food, she shook her head. "Do you want to?"

"Of course." He stood up, took Livvie, and sat down with her cradled in his left arm. "Watch this," he said, putting a bite into his mouth. "See? She was staring at the fork."

"I don't think she's seen one before. You know how curious she is, Daniel."

"Mmm-hmm." He dipped his spoon into the buttery potatoes and lightly touched the spoon on Livvie's lips. She opened her mouth as if she were used to eating from the spoon, and he gave her a very small taste.

"Daniel, babies don't eat table food until they are . . . Well, at least for another year or more. Some mothers don't feed children anything but bread, honey, and milk until they are four or five."

He grinned at her. "I'm glad my ma didn't know that. Look at her, she liked it."

Caroline watched Livvie work her lips until he gave her another taste. She did like it. "She'll have a bellyache. Please, don't feed her any more. I'll fix her bottle."

"We'll wait." He didn't dip the spoon in the potatoes again, but he let Livvie suck on the tip of the spoon. He figured she must be almost two months old. Maybe he should wait a few more months to feed her from the table.

When Caroline returned with the bottle and sling, Daniel was holding the empty spoon for Livvie to suck on. He was incorrigible. Caroline slipped the sling over her head and was about to lift the baby from Daniel's arms when a knock sounded at the door. She took off the sling and went to the door.

Gilbert was standing on her stoop in front of three people she had seen around town but had never met. "Hello, Gilbert. Is there something I can do for you?"

"We want to speak with you, Caroline." Gilbert glanced over his shoulder at the others. "It is cold out. Couldn't we come inside?"

She looked at each of them and had a sinking feeling. "We have company for dinner, and we haven't finished our meal yet." Tucker walked by her and planted himself at the threshold. He never did like Gilbert.

Gilbert glared at the cat and looked back at her. "You used to have dinner—"

"Mr. Bennett," she said, cutting him off before he further embarrassed her and the others. They were backing away. "As I said, we haven't finished our meal." She could invite them to wait in the parlor, but Robert was asleep in there, and she didn't want these people near him, certainly not alone with him. Gilbert gave her an all too familiar look of contempt, but she stood firm. And silent.

"Very well, Mrs. Dobbs. We will call on you in thirty minutes."

"That would be more convenient." She stepped back, so did Tucker, and she closed the door.

"Caroline," Daniel said, walking up to her. "Is everything all right?"

His deep steady voice sounded like music, and she nodded. "It was Gilbert Bennett and three others. They will return in half an hour." She slipped one finger under Livvie's little hand and kissed it.

"You could have invited them in. I wouldn't have minded."

She tried to smile. "But I did. We haven't had dessert yet, and I made pudding for Ethan."

15

$\mathcal{L}$IVVIE WAS SO content in Daniel's arms, Caroline cleared the dining room table before she served coffee and dessert. "There's more in the kitchen, so don't be bashful about asking for seconds."

Ethan picked up the spoon. "Tapioca. Haven't had this in a long time."

She smiled at him. "Hope you like dates."

"Yes, ma'am. I sure do."

Daniel scooped a drop of pudding onto the tip of his spoon and held it up to Livvie. "You're too young for dates, but I bet you'll like pudding."

Caroline stepped over to his side. "I'll take her and you can eat the pudding."

"Maybe next time, Livvie." He handed the baby to Caroline. "What would one taste hurt?"

She shook her head, grinning. "Probably nothing, but she's happy with milk now." She slipped the sling over her head, settled the baby in it, and held the bottle while Livvie sucked on the leather nipple.

Ethan gulped down three bites before he paused for a sip of coffee. "Mrs. Dobbs, you're the best cook in town."

"Thank you, Ethan."

Daniel watched her feeding the baby and listened to his

son. It was the perfect way to spend a Sunday. "Caroline, aren't you going to have any pudding?"

"I'll have some later."

He picked up her spoon and dipped it in her bowl. "Here," he said, holding it up to her mouth. "Have a bite. It is good."

She smirked but opened her mouth. His aim was a little off. She felt pudding on her upper lip, then the spoon bumped her lower teeth. She angled her mouth, managed to draw her upper lip over the mound of pudding on the spoon and swallowed. "It isn't bad, is it?"

He chuckled and wiped her mouth with his napkin. "Want to try it again? It's bound to get easier."

"One more."

"Mrs. Dobbs, can I have some more?"

"Of course, Ethan. The bowl's on the worktable in the kitchen. Help yourself."

"I'll do better this time." Daniel raised the spoon of tapioca to her mouth. As he fed her, he held her gaze. Her lips closed over the spoon, and he slowly withdrew it. Her eyes seemed to shimmer in the lamplight. She swallowed, and then the tip of her tongue licked her upper lip. He sat back. They would have to try this again, he thought, in a couple of months, and when they were alone.

Ethan returned and set his bowl on the table. "You want more, Pa?"

"I'm fine, thanks." He ate the last bite of his pudding.

Livvie turned her head away from the bottle, and Caroline set it on the table. She took off the sling and held the baby on her shoulder. In between patting the baby's back, she finished eating her tapioca. Livvie fussed and squirmed. Caroline lay her over her lap and gently rubbed the baby's back. There was another knock on the front door, and she considered ignoring it.

"I'll answer it for you." Ethan dragged the napkin across his mouth and dashed to the door.

Gilbert's voice was unmistakable. She knew Ethan wouldn't be able to handle him and started to rise.

Daniel rested his hand on her shoulder. "Do you want me to show him in or send him away?"

She met his gaze. "I might as well find out what he wants, but I don't want him left alone with the twins." She could see the clock in the parlor. If nothing else, Gilbert was punctual.

He nodded. "I'll keep Robert company."

"Show him into the parlor in a minute." When he went to join Ethan, she hurried to the parlor by way of the kitchen and hallway. She didn't know what Gilbert wanted, but she felt she needed to protect the twins from him.

Daniel led Bennett and his friends to the parlor. "Caroline, Mr. Bennett said you were expecting him."

Daniel was so formal, she had to bite back a smile. "Yes, thank you." She looked at Gilbert. What had she ever seen in the man? It certainly wasn't his heartwarming smile.

Gilbert stepped past Daniel. "Caroline, I would like to introduce my friends. Mr. Emory, Mrs. Milton, and Reverend Newhouse, this is Mrs. Dobbs."

"Mrs. Milton, gentlemen," Caroline said, rising to meet them. Smiling at Daniel, she said, "And I would like you to meet Mr. Grey and his son, Ethan. Gilbert, you must remember Daniel. If not for you, we would not have met."

Daniel gave them a nod. "Ma'am, gentlemen."

Ethan went over to the hearth and sat down behind Caroline.

Daniel walked around Bennett and the others as he made his way to his usual chair. When Livvie burped, the look on Bennett's face was comical.

Caroline hid her grin as she kissed the baby. "Mrs.

Milton, please take a seat on the sofa. I don't have enough chairs for all of you. I don't entertain very often." She sat back down. "How can I help you?"

"Caroline, we are here . . . to tell you we have found a home for the twins. One family has agreed to take on both of the Williams infants." Gilbert looked at each of the others and back at Caroline.

"They are God-fearing people, Mrs. Dobbs," Reverend Newhouse said. "They haven't been blessed, and I am confident they would bring up the babies as their own."

Oh, Lord, Caroline thought, not again. "I can understand how they feel, but Livvie and Robert have a home."

Mrs. Milton leaned over and peered at Robert. "Mrs. Dobbs, it really would be in their best interest. These children need two parents just like other children."

Ethan frowned. "I don't—my ma's gone. You want to find me a new home, too?"

Daniel gave his son a slight smile and nodded. He was glad the boy was defending Caroline.

"Oh, no, young man. I wasn't talking about you, just the babies." Mrs. Milton glanced at Reverend Newhouse.

Ethan scooted closer to Caroline. "You don't even know her. Look how happy the babies are. She's their ma. If you could ask them, they'd say she is."

Caroline turned and smiled at him. "Thank you, Ethan." He was an unexpected ally.

"Caroline, this discussion doesn't concern the boy . . . or his father, for that matter," Gilbert said, glaring at her and Daniel.

"Gilbert, this is my home, and they are my guests." Caroline started the chair rocking. "You called on me with your friends hoping I would be alone, didn't you?"

Gilbert sputtered and pulled at his shirt collar. "Enough beating about the bush. We have come for the children."

Caroline's temper flared, and she glowered at him. "The twins *have* a home—here with me. I came as close as birthing these babies as a woman other than their mother can, and I promised her that I would raise them." She wasn't going to ask, but his overbearing attitude changed her mind. "You don't like children, so I don't understand why you want to take the twins away from me."

"Mrs. Dobbs," Mr. Emory said, and cleared his throat. "We've come on behalf of the Citizens for Decency Committee. There're many concerned citizens who believe you are not doing what is best for the infants."

"Many?" Daniel stared at Mr. Emory. "How many?"

"Well . . . several, at least," Mr. Emery said, glancing at Gilbert. "Five or six."

Caroline stared at Mrs. Milton, Reverend Newhouse, and Mr. Emory in turn before returning to Gilbert. "They have a right to their opinions, but not the right to take *my* children away from me. Did you or the other *concerned* citizens know Mrs. Williams?"

"No, but that's neither here nor there. You didn't, either," Gilbert said, rocking back on his heels.

"I spent four and a half days with her. She asked me to raise her children, and I promised—vowed—that I would. Gentlemen, do any of you think a woman's vow is less valid than a man's?"

"No, Mrs. Dobbs," Mr. Emory said.

Gilbert took a step closer to Caroline's chair. "How do we really know Mrs. Williams actually asked so much of you, a total stranger? It sounds unlikely to me."

Daniel came to his full height and faced Gilbert in one swift movement, and he said in a forceful but soft voice, "Are *you* calling Mrs. Dobbs a liar?"

Gilbert stepped back, gulped and cleared his throat, as if he were suddenly parched.

Daniel's protective stance felt like a warm cloak, and Caroline smiled at him, but she was determined to put an end to this harassment.

"If you won't take my word for it, Gilbert, I have a letter that Dr. Lindley suggested I write, and Mrs. Williams signed." She brushed her cheek against the baby's head. "You might ask Dr. Lindley, if you still believe I'm lying. He spoke with Mrs. Williams before she died." Strangely enough, she wasn't as angry with Gilbert as she had been at first. The man was a fool, a meddling, contemptible, narrow-minded prude who enjoyed stirring up trouble for other people.

She looked, hoping the disgust and pity she felt for him showed, and stepped over to the bureau. She withdrew the letter, without the notes to Livvie and Robert, and held it out to Reverend Newhouse.

Reverend Newhouse quickly read Mrs. Williams's last wishes, muttered something as he shook his head and passed the letter to Mrs. Milton.

After reading it, Mrs. Milton passed it to Mr. Emory. "I . . . we didn't know, Mrs. Dobbs." Mrs. Milton stood up. "It appears Mr. Bennett spoke out of turn."

Robert whimpered before he let out a loud wail. Caroline put Livvie down in her cradle and picked up Robert with the oilcloth. "Shh, it's all right, honey." She kissed his temple.

"I agree," Mr. Emory said with a nod.

Gilbert snatched the paper from Mr. Emory's hand, but barely glanced at it. "The circumstances haven't changed. Car— Mrs. Dobbs is—"

"Enough, Bennett." At once Daniel was on his feet and towered over Gilbert. "You'd better leave now."

"How dare you, Grey. You have no right to tell me what to do."

Reverend Newhouse put his hand on Gilbert's shoulder. "Come on. We've had our say."

"I am sorry, Mrs. Dobbs." As Mrs. Milton hurried toward the door, she paused in front of Gilbert. "You, sir, are a fool. I'll see that Mr. Milton removes our funds from your bank in the morning." She led the other two men out.

Gilbert hastened after his companions.

Daniel closed the front door behind him and returned to the parlor laughing. "Did you hear Bennett choking? I don't think he'll be back again."

Caroline smiled at Ethan and then Daniel. "Thank you both. I'm sorry you witnessed that, Ethan." And I hope the gossip is soon forgotten, she thought.

"That Mr. Bennett's a dad-gum—"

"Ethan—"

"Sorry, Pa, but he is, and that lady was a busybody, but she sure put Mr. Bennett in his place." Ethan laughed as he moved over to the sofa. "Mrs. Dobbs, don't worry about what they said."

"Thank you, Ethan. I won't." Robert cried out again, and Caroline walked over to the hall door. "We'll be right back."

The day had been so perfect before Gilbert and the others arrived, but maybe he hadn't spoiled it after all. She was proud of Ethan, and she had noticed Daniel's fierce pride reflected in his eyes.

Daniel worked on the warehouse with his men in the fog, the rain, and the freezing cold. His evenings were spent in his workshop building furniture. Mr. Peterson said he had heard about an especially nice cradle Daniel had made, and he had ordered one. There were other orders—one for a dough tray, another for a chest of drawers and a washstand—that kept him busy and left him little time to spend with Caroline.

One evening when he arrived home, Ethan had mashed the potatoes with the new colander and masher he said Caroline had given him. He'd told him that she had seen him walking down her street and had called him over to give it to him. Since then, he had stopped by her house once a week to visit her and the babies. Daniel was a little envious, especially when she seemed to grow closer to the boy at a time when he was losing patience with Ethan's constant talk about the rebellion.

Daniel had done his best to discourage Ethan's interest in the Union army and hoped he and his friends would find something else to get excited about. A few days before Valentine's Day when Daniel and his men stopped work for their midday meal, he went by Caroline's house. Her sign was out and Tucker was in the window. He tapped on the door and walked inside.

"Be right there," Caroline called out as she came down the hall.

He hung his coat on a peg as he called out, "Don't hurry," and went into the parlor. "Tucker's keeping an eye on me."

She entered the room a moment later. "Daniel, what a nice surprise." He wore his heavy, rough work clothes, his hair was creased from his hat, and his cheeks were tinged with red from the cold breeze. He looked wonderful.

"Hi. Thought I'd stop by while the men eat. Are you busy with a client?"

"No. I'll make a pot of coffee. Did you bring your dinner?"

"It's in the wagon. I'll eat later."

"Why not now? The kitchen's warm, if you don't mind eating at the worktable."

"All right." She looked so pretty, he reached out to her. Just then he heard women's voices in the distance and realized that ladies could enter any time. He settled for holding her hand. "I'll be right back."

She slowly ran her thumb up and down the length of his. "I'm glad you came by today."

He took a deep breath, hoping to waylay the sudden burst of desire she aroused. "So am I," he said, and kissed her fingers. "Be right back." He didn't bother with his coat when he went outside. He was already overheated.

She checked on the twins, picked up her cup, and hurried to the kitchen. Although she felt decidedly warm, he had been working in the cold. She added more wood to the stove and started a pot of coffee.

Daniel returned to the house and went into the kitchen. "If you have something to do, don't let me stop you."

"There's nothing that can't wait." She took a cup and saucer from the cupboard. "What did you fix for dinner?" She glanced at him as he rubbed the palm of one hand on his thigh. The cup rattled on the saucer. She quickly clamped her other hand on it and set it down on the table.

He unwrapped the plate he had brought in. "Sliced venison, bread, beans, and," he said, grinning, "mashed potatoes."

"The potatoes must be frozen."

"Probably. Ethan's so taken with the colander and masher, he makes potatoes every night so he can use them. He wants to try peas, but I told him I wouldn't eat them if he did."

"He'll get tired of it soon."

"I hope so."

She picked up his plate. "I'll heat this for you."

"Thanks. Too bad I didn't get Ethan a dog when he asked for one a while back."

She laughed. "You don't have to eat the potatoes."

He shrugged. "Might as well. They're filling."

She set a skillet on the stove top and added the meat and

beans. The potatoes were dumped into a small bowl. She chopped up a slice of onion, stirred it into the potatoes, put a dollop of lard in the skillet, and spooned the mixture into the pan. "Ethan has visited a few times in the last week."

"He has?"

"Mmm-hmm. He talks about the rebellion mostly."

Daniel nodded. "Seems to be the only thing on his mind these days."

"Has he said anything about his mother?"

"No," he said, shaking his head. "He hasn't mentioned the divorce, either." Caroline was standing in front of the stove, and as she moved, her skirts gently swayed. Suddenly the cat came from under the worktable and swiped at the bottom of her dress. "What's Tucker doing?"

She looked down and grinned. "He likes to rub fabric on his face."

"I've never seen an animal like him."

She turned the potato cake over to brown on the other side. "I got him from a neighbor back home. He reminded me of my uncle Tucker, who was a little strange, too. Anyway, Tucker came west with us and was as good as any dog or goose at warning us about danger."

"I believe you. He's a match for our old goose back home."

She dished the hot food onto his plate and set it on the table. "That should taste better."

"Thank you, Caroline. Smells good."

She poured coffee into his cup and added hot tea to hers. "How is the warehouse coming along?"

"Fine. We started putting up the roof today." He ate a bite of meat, then broke off a piece and held it down for the cat.

Caroline grinned. "You're as bad as I am, spoiling him that way."

"He earned it." Daniel took a drink of coffee and tasted

the potato cake. "This's good, but I'm not telling Ethan about it."

She watched him over the rim of her cup as she sipped her tea. He had mentioned his divorce only in passing, but he hadn't really talked about it since he brought her the newspaper with the notice. "Do you mind if I ask about the divorce?"

"Not at all."

"Have you heard from her?"

"Emmaline?" He shook his head. "I'll check the mail Friday. Mr. Johnson said we weren't likely to." He ate another bite and washed it down with coffee. "I'm not even sure where she is now."

"When do you have to go to court?"

"It was supposed to be in a couple weeks, but the judge won't be in court that week." He sat back. "Three weeks from tomorrow, the fifth of March." He picked up his cup. "Then it will be over."

"What will, Daniel?"

He frowned, staring at the cup. "The marriage—" He finished his coffee. "No more wondering if she'll come back to see Ethan." He gave a harsh laugh. "I used to think she'd remember his birthday—surprise him with a visit. Should've known better." The cat rubbed against his leg, and he idly petted him.

The woman had wounded him, and Caroline didn't know what she could say to ease his feelings. "Not all women are like that."

He gazed at her and smiled. "I know."

She shifted on the seat. "Will Ethan have to appear in court?"

"No. I won't put him through it. Besides, Mr. Johnson said it was pretty straightforward. Emmaline deserted me more than five years ago. The law says three's enough."

"What happens if she writes to you? Or returns and appears in court? Would that make any difference?"

He studied her a long moment. "You have been thinking about this, haven't you?"

"I—" She moistened her lips. "I didn't want to, but once in a while I couldn't help wondering about what was going through her mind. How could she walk out on you? And even more, on her son?" She slowly shook her head. "I don't understand how a mother would do that to her only child."

"That kept me awake many nights."

"Was . . . Was there another man?"

"Not that I knew about. But I didn't know her very well, did I?" He thought a moment. "Did you hear anything?"

"No, I didn't." She refilled his coffee cup and warmed up her tea. "I read a story in the newspaper once, a few years ago. It was about a woman who was married to two men. Neither of them knew about the other until she died in a carriage accident." She tasted her tea. "Evidently some people are good at living a lie."

"Thank you." He chuckled. "Guess I should be glad she wasn't a bigamist."

She nodded. "I didn't think of that, but you're right." She smiled at him. "I made cinnamon bread this morning. Would you like a slice?"

"One, and I'll have to get back to work."

While he ate the bread, she washed his plate and set it on the table. She cut the loaf of bread in half and placed one part on his plate. "This is for later." She wrapped the towel he had used over the plate.

"All right, if you don't want me to drop by again."

She laughed. "You might call to see what I've made another day, but I don't bake very often."

He ate the last piece of bread, finished his coffee, and

stood up. "Guess I'll have to pay my respects in a few days."

The brass bell rang. "I'll see who it is."

He picked up the plate. "Will you be embarrassed if I walk out there with you?"

"Of course not." She started walking to the door.

He caught her hand. "Soon it will be over, and I can take you out riding. You haven't seen my house, yet, or the trees I use to make furniture."

She beamed at him. "I would like that very much."

"Me, too." He brushed his lips over hers and held her for one short moment. Three weeks, and he could court her properly. "I'll see you Friday."

16

CAROLINE PICKED UP the lovely wood pansy Daniel had given her. It had been polished until it gleamed. Holding the delicate stem between her thumb and first finger, she twirled the flower. He said he would see her Friday. After he had gone, she realized that Friday was also Valentine's Day. Watching the petals reflect the sunlight, she wondered what token she could make for him. She was no poet, had no talent for drawing, and she didn't think a shirt was appropriate. Surely she could think of something in the next few days.

She heard the front door open an instant before the bell rang, and set the pansy back on the small glass tray. She turned around and saw Ethan. "Hello. Out of school already?"

"Yeah. Mr. Stanton got sick and went home early." Ethan wandered closer to the cradles and looked at the twins. "They sleep a lot, don't they?"

She nodded. "It seems like it, but they're growing and need to gain weight." Each time he paid her a visit she was surprised. He didn't stay long or seem to have any particular reason for stopping by. "Your father was here earlier. He said you had used the colander."

"It works real good. The mashed potatoes taste better."

"I'm glad." She smiled watching him study the twins. "I made cinnamon bread. Would you like a piece?"

"Yes, ma'am." He put his books down on the sofa and shed his coat. The cloth ball was lying there, and he picked it up. "This looks too big for them."

"Large toys are easier for babies to hold on to. It will be just right by the time they can sit up and play with it." She left to slice the bread and pour a glass of milk for him. When she returned, he was tossing Robert's ball in the air and catching it. She set the plate and glass on the small table near her chair. "Maybe you can teach them how to play ball next winter, when they're old enough."

"You should do that, shouldn't you? Being their mom and all." Ethan sat down in the armchair and took two swallows of milk before he picked up the bread.

"Oh, I will. I just thought you would be better at that than I am."

He gulped down some of his milk. "Do you read the *Argus* or the *Oregonian*?"

"*Argus*. Do you have to write another report for school?"

He shook his head. "Did you read 'The Peace Snivelers'?"

"I did," she said and thought she might give him something besides news of the war to think about. "Did you see the item about the importance of the coming election?"

"Yeah, but I can't vote yet." He ate the last bite of bread. "I keep thinking about people who believe the rebellion'll just go away if no one fights. How can we have peace until we free the slaves?"

He's so very serious, she thought. "Have you asked your father how he feels?"

"He won't talk about it."

"I see. Well, I believe most everyone wants peace, Ethan, but sometimes people act without thinking about the consequences. Take two boys arguing in the schoolyard. One minute they are disagreeing. That leads to shouting, and the next thing you know, one shoves the other, and they are brawling."

"That's it. You understand!" Ethan gulped down the rest of his milk. "Bullies won't listen to anyone. When Rupert picked on Herbie, he didn't want trouble so he let Rupert poke fun at him and dump his lunch pail in the mud every day. The only way we could stop him was when everyone in class threatened to beat him up."

She stared at him for a long moment. That wasn't what she had meant at all. "I didn't mean—"

He jumped to his feet. "The Union's just like the class standing up for Herbie." He looked at the twins, again, then at Caroline. "I better get home. Thanks for the bread." He grabbed his schoolbooks and started for the door.

"You're welcome." She went outside with him. "Are you meeting your father?"

"No. He'll work late." He hurried down the walkway and turned around. "Thanks, Mrs. Dobbs."

"Ethan, would you like to come for dinner Sunday with your father?"

"Don't know if he'll be working, but I'll ask him."

"All right. Bye." She went back inside and stood in front of the fire. Daniel needed to have a talk with his son, but would he welcome her interference? The only way to find out was to ask. She hoped he wouldn't forget to stop by on Friday.

The next day was Wednesday. Martha and Mrs. Penny arrived before noon and brought a can of fresh milk. Caroline showed them into the parlor and stored the milk. When she returned to the parlor, Martha and her mother were watching the twins. "Is Mr. Stanton still sick?"

Martha frowned. "Yes. How did you know?"

"Ethan Grey stopped by yesterday."

"He's nice." Martha grinned. "Does he visit you very often?"

"Once in a while." Caroline glanced at Mrs. Penny. "How have you been?"

"Just fine."

"Tell her, Mama."

Mrs. Penny loosened her shawl. "I would like you to make me a new dress."

Martha sat down on the sofa near Robert's cradle. "Papa said the petticoat you made for me was so pretty, he wanted her to have a new dress for their anniversary, one that was made just for her."

"That's very thoughtful of him."

Mrs. Penny glanced from her daughter to Caroline. "I've always made my own clothes. I don't know what you want me to do."

Caroline smiled. "First, I'll show you some pictures, and you can tell me which ones you like. You'll choose the fabric you want, and I'll take your measurements. You'll need to have one or two fittings. That's about it."

Mrs. Penny nodded. "It sounds simple."

"When do you want the dress, Mrs. Penny?"

Mrs. Penny wrapped the end of her shawl around one finger and unwound it again. "Our anniversary's March fifth. I'd like to wear it then." She dropped the end of the shawl and looked at Caroline. "Can you have it ready in three weeks?"

"What kind of dress do you want? A party dress? One for Sunday best? Or one for walking out?"

Mrs. Penny looked to her daughter. "Can we see those pictures?"

Caroline brought out her collection of fashion plates. "These are to help give you ideas. You may like the bodice on one, sleeves on another or the skirt on a different one. I can make up the dress any way you would like it." She went to her desk and withdrew a sheet of paper and a pencil.

Mrs. Penny held up a picture of a young girl. "My, isn't this girl's dress pretty? And that bonnet is beautiful."

"That is lovely, isn't it?"

Mrs. Penny glanced at the twins. "You can dress them up like that in a few years."

Caroline gazed at her twins. "Maybe once in a while. Livvie may like climbing trees too much to dress that way."

Mrs. Penny looked at a half dozen drawings. "These are far too fancy for me, Mrs. Dobbs. I guess I want a Sunday best dress." She glanced at Caroline. "These ladies don't live in Oregon—least ways not here."

Caroline grinned and thumbed through an older issue of *Godey's Lady's Book*. She had seen a dress Mrs. Penny might like. "This dress can be made of taffeta or soft wool. It has a short overskirt. What do you think of that?"

"Mmm, I don't know. . . ."

"Okay. There's one I really—" Caroline picked up another issue of the magazine from last spring. "Yes, here it is. The one on the right. It would be very nice made out of a striped muslin."

"Oh, it's real nice, and I like the plain bodice, Mrs. Dobbs, but I don't know. . . . This one's silk with velvet trim. Wherever would I wear it?"

"What would you think about this?" Caroline asked, drawing different sleeves on the blank paper. "A dark cording would be just as attractive as the velvet and more serviceable."

"Yes, that's nice." Mrs. Penny looked at her daughter. "Think your papa'll like this one?"

"It's beautiful, Mama, but the dog in that picture sure is skinny."

"Martha, really—" Mrs. Penny smiled at Caroline. "Do you want me to buy the yard goods? How much will you need?"

Caroline eyed the drawing, then Mrs. Penny. "Six yards for the skirt . . . eight and a half yards, nine to be safe. Come back to the sewing room. I'll take your measurements, and you can see if I have any fabric you like."

"Martha, you watch those babies for Mrs. Dobbs."

Mrs. Penny went back to the sewing room with Caroline, and it didn't take her long to choose a purple and black striped muslin. As they returned to the parlor, Caroline said, "That will look wonderful on you."

Mrs. Penny smiled. "I hope Mr. Penny thinks so. Will you have time to make it?"

"Yes. You'll have it for your anniversary."

"Thank you."

"Mrs. Dobbs, I'll stay with the babies. Mama drove the wagon. She can take you down to Main Street if you want." She lowered her voice and added, "Most of the stores have real nice Valentine cards."

"Thank you," Caroline said, hoping her embarrassment didn't show. Did Martha know about Daniel? Or was she teasing her? At her age Valentine's Day had seemed very romantic, as Caroline recalled. "I think I'll take a walk first. That's what I miss doing most, and walk into town afterward." Maybe she would at least look at some cards.

Mrs. Penny crossed her shawl over her chest on the way to the door. "I'll see you at home, Martha."

"Yes, Mama."

Caroline arranged to do a fitting the next week, then prepared two sucking bottles in case the twins woke up hungry while she was out. A short while later she walked in the direction of the Clackamas River. Soon it would be spring. She wanted to take Robert and Livvie on walks and show them the rivers, the trees, the beautiful green, rolling hills. To do that, Caroline realized she would need a baby carriage. When Daniel wasn't so busy, she'd talk to him about it.

She paused on a rise and stared to the hills just east of town. He had invited her to see his home, and his prized trees. That meant more to her than a compliment or endearment some men handed out so easily.

Daniel and his men stopped working at noontime. While his crew ate in the framed warehouse, he left to visit Caroline. On the way he stopped to check on his mail. He didn't expect to get a letter from Emmaline, but with the court day less than three weeks away, he didn't want any surprises.

He entered Ainsworth and Dierdorff, greeted Mr. Ainsworth, and walked over to the post office counter in the back. "Mrs. Dierdorff, how're you today?"

She smiled at him. "Just fine, Mr. Grey. What can I do for you?"

"Any mail come in for me?"

"I'll take a look. We have a stack o' letters here," she said, pointing to a pile of mail in the back corner of the counter. "Wish those people'd come in. I keep thinking about the poor friends and relatives who wrote those letters and have been waiting for messages from them."

While she searched for his mail, he saw the display of Valentine cards. Some were trimmed with lace or ribbon, a few had small mirrors on the front, others had fancy pictures with birds, hearts, and trailing vines. He stepped over to the counter and glanced inside the cards standing open. "My orb of day departs with thee. . . ." That was a bit flowery. "I fondly, truly love thee. . . ." The sentiment was right, but he wasn't free to give Caroline that one. Not this year.

"Mr. Grey—" Mrs. Dierdorff walked from behind the

postal counter and over to Daniel. "Sorry, I didn't find anything for you. Can I help you choose a card?"

"No, just looking. Thank you, Mrs. Dierdorff."

"There is a letter for Mrs. Dobbs."

Daniel glanced at her. Should he ask why she had mentioned it to him? Since he hadn't taken Caroline out riding around town, he didn't think their friendship was common knowledge.

Mrs. Dierdorff smiled and patted his arm. "She's a real lady. I would like to see her happy."

He almost whistled. Were he and Caroline whispered about all over town? Worse yet, had anyone said something to her? He had to ask. "Mrs. Dobbs and I are friends. She *is* a nice lady. What are people saying?"

"I'm sorry. I didn't mean—" Mrs. Dierdorff looked around the store. "Only a few ladies have said they've seen you at her house, and there's nothing wrong with that, Mr. Grey. How else are you going to get to know each other?" As she started back to the postal counter, she motioned for him to follow her. "I'm not supposed to do this, but with Mrs. Dobbs having the twins to watch, she doesn't get in here very often, and I know she'd want the letter from Maggie Adams." She picked out the letter. "Will you be seeing Mrs. Dobbs soon?"

"I can ride by her house."

"They were close friends before Maggie moved away with her new husband." Mrs. Dierdorff handed the letter to him. "Thank you."

He nodded and left the store. There was one more stop to make, for a silk flower, since there were no fresh blooms at this time of year. He could have purchased a silk rose from Mrs. Dierdorff, but he didn't want to give her more to gossip about. He stopped by Mr. Peterson's store for the flower and went to Caroline's house. With the small vase he had made for her in the inside pocket of his coat, he held the rose behind his back as he entered her house.

"Hello—" he called out as he walked into the parlor. She was walking toward him with one of the babies on her shoulder. Her likeness should be on a Valentine. "Happy Valentine's Day," he said, holding the flower out to her.

"It's lovely." She smiled and put her free hand on his arm. "Thank you, Daniel. It has been a long time since I've received a Valentine gift."

"You'll need something to put it in."

"I'm sure I can—"

"Try this." He handed her the vase he had made out of alder wood. "It won't hold more than a couple flowers."

The vase was heart-shaped with two hands, one reaching for the other, carved into the wood, and there was a glass vial in a hollow for a flower. "It's beautiful. I hope you aren't tired of me telling you that. It's a treasure." She ran her thumb over the glassy surface of the wood. "You've given me so many wonderful things you have created—I should feel guilty."

"Don't, Caroline, never. I made those for only you, no one else." He brushed a light kiss over her lips.

"I have something for you, too." She picked up the envelope from the glass tray and gave it to him. It hadn't been easy finding a card that didn't declare eternal love, which was an overwhelming message to give a man who had not declared his feelings for her. She had finally found one that was blank inside.

He opened the envelope with care. "The last Valentine card I received was from Ethan, one he had made for me."

"I hope you kept it." She skimmed the tips of the silk rose petals down her cheek. Maybe she shouldn't have borrowed Mr. Emerson's verse that she had found in a small volume she hadn't read in years. However, the lines reflected her feelings, though the meaning was all too clear.

He chuckled. "Yes. I have a collection of things he's done through the years."

He pulled the card out. There was no lace or ribbon, but a woman seated on a bench in a flowery garden holding a red rose. He pictured Caroline on the card with the *To My Valentine* message. He smiled at her as he opened it, then read the handwritten message. ". . . Shall not suggest a restraint, but contrariwise . . ." His stomach knotted up and his throat was suddenly tight. "Caroline . . ." He couldn't say what he was feeling, but he could show her. He shoved the card in a pocket and, framing her beautiful face with his hands, he covered her sweet mouth with his.

She had not mistaken the love in his expression or in the tenderness of his embrace. She was still holding the baby, but Daniel managed to kiss her passionately without upsetting Robert. She wanted to hold on to Daniel, to feel the strength of his body against hers. His lips moved away from hers, and he showered kisses on her cheeks, her nose, her ear, and down her neck.

He slipped one arm around her shoulders. "Thank you for the card. It means more than I can tell you."

"I'm glad. I know I can be plainspoken. I've tried not to say anything that might embarrass either of us, but Mr. Emerson's verse said what I feel."

He sighed and grinned. "I don't mind telling you, I was afraid to ask you." He gave her a gentle kiss and also kissed the baby. "I hope you know I feel the same."

She gave him a slight shake of her head. "I wasn't sure, but I needed to know."

"Two and a half weeks more—" He held her close. She rested her head on his chest, and he knew he had never known such contentment.

Robert squirmed, and she leaned back. "I'd better put him down."

Daniel took the card out of his pocket to reread the verse. Then he remembered the letter for her. "When I checked on my mail, Mrs. Dierdorff had this for you."

"Thank you for bringing it to me. I haven't thought about going by there."

He handed the letter to her. "Mrs. Dierdorff asked if I would bring it to you."

"She did?" Caroline glanced at it and smiled. Maggie hadn't forgotten to write.

"She'd heard we were seeing each other, and since it's from Maggie, she thought you'd be eager to have it."

"I am." She tapped the letter on her other hand. It felt like more than one page. "I'll have to thank Mrs. Dierdorff." She laid it down on the table by her chair to read later.

He nodded and watched her curious reaction. She didn't appear very concerned about the hearsay. "You're not worried about her spreading gossip."

"It doesn't bother me. Lord knows everyone has enough to prattle about where I'm concerned—" He looked confused, and she added, "The twins." That seemed to have died out, and she hoped would be forgotten before they started school.

"I guess it was bound to happen. Caroline, I didn't want to embarrass you." He shook his head. "The odd thing is, she acted as if there was nothing wrong with me seeing you."

"She may not know you're married. If she doesn't, why would she think there was anything wrong with you seeing me?"

He shook his head. "As long as you're not bothered, I'll forget about it."

"Good. This is your mealtime, isn't it? Have you eaten yet?"

"I will on the way back to the warehouse." He stepped up to her and wrapped his arms around her. Holding her close, he brushed his cheek over her soft hair and thought he could've held her like that forever—or at least until suppertime.

His warmth surrounded her, and she snuggled closer. "You can't stay, can you?"

He chuckled. "You know me too well."

"Not nearly, but I'm looking forward to learning."

"Me, too." He kissed her again, quickly, hungrily, as if to make up for their time apart.

When he loosened his embrace, she rested her head on his chest and caught her breath. The love she and her husband shared had been quiet and reserved. However, Daniel's embraces stormed her senses, kindled a desire that shook her very core, and held a promise she could not imagine. "Will you be able to come to supper on Sunday?"

"Mmm, that sounds nice, but I'm not sure."

"When I asked Ethan, he didn't know if you would be working or not."

He looked at her. "You asked him to tell me?"

"The other day when he stopped by after school."

"I'll have to talk to him about that."

"He probably just forgot. Would you like to have supper with me, us?"

"I sure would like to, but if it isn't pouring down rain, I'll have to work." He gazed into her eyes, and then he smiled. "We'll be here," he said softly. "What time?"

"Five-thirty? Six?" Any time, she thought.

"Okay. Nothing fancy."

"Hardtack and weevily biscuits?"

"If you cooked it, it would taste wonderful."

She laughed and held on to him. "Potluck it is." She studied him for a moment. "Are you always this happy?"

"How could I not be with you?" He swung her around once and set her on her feet. "I don't want to leave, but I better if I want to finish that warehouse."

She stood on tiptoe, gave him a quick kiss, and walked to the door with him. "I'll see you Sunday." She watched him hurry down the walkway, and as he drove away, she waved to him. She closed the door and leaned against it.

She was deliriously happy, even a bit light-headed, as if she were spinning. For the first time since she had learned that he was married, she believed there was more than a glimmer of hope. He liked her. He really liked her.

17

$\mathcal{H}$AVING WAITED TO hear from Maggie, Caroline wanted to savor the pleasure and put the letter aside to read that night. After she dressed for bed, she put another log on the fire and curled up at the end of the sofa nearest the fireplace. With her feet tucked under the skirt, and Tucker asleep at her side, she opened the envelope with care and slipped the pages out. There were three sheets of paper.

She peered over at the twins. "This's from your aunt Maggie."

She sat back and petted Tucker as she read. Maggie told her about the two-and-a-half-week trek south, from Oregon City to Sam's sheep ranch north of Sacramento City in California. They had lived in a shack until ten days ago, when their house was completed. The storm last month had caused floods, but the house was on a nice rise. She said the Sacramento River was beautiful, but it wasn't the Willamette. Jeremiah and Cap, Maggie's dog, loved the ranch, though when they went to the river, Cap had watched a riverboat, and she thought the dog missed their old sternwheeler.

Maggie confided that she had never been happier and now couldn't imagine life without Sam and Jeremiah. On the last page of the letter, she described the house and asked

Caroline a swarm of questions, including many about Daniel. At the end Maggie renewed her invitation for Caroline and the twins to visit them for a couple of months.

Caroline rubbed the downy-soft spot behind Tucker's ear. She did want to see her friend, but it would have to wait until the twins were older. Oh, and wouldn't it be grand if Daniel— Good gracious, her imagination had sprouted wings. She stared at the fire a while and pieced together the picture Maggie had painted of the ranch. She was the adventuress. After traveling the difficult trail across the country to Oregon, Caroline had had no desire to go any farther, be it north or south. But that was in the past, and she hadn't traveled anywhere in years. They could take the stagecoach, and it shouldn't take more than a week at most.

The twins woke up for their late feeding, and she told each of them about Maggie's letter while they nursed. After she had put them to bed for the night, she walked outside with Tucker. The night was clear, and she heard the first frogs of the season croaking loudly. Spring wasn't too far away. The water flowing over the waterfall was as soothing as a lullaby, but she wouldn't be able to leave her bedroom window open, so it could lull her to sleep, until the nights turned warm and the twins were older.

She looked toward the hills and said, "Good night, Daniel." Was he working on his furniture orders? As much as she wanted to visit his house, what she truly looked forward to seeing was his workshop.

A breeze ruffled her hair, and she shivered. It was almost as if Daniel had brushed his fingers over the back of her neck. So much for a peaceful night's sleep.

Caroline spent that Saturday and part of Sunday tacking the pieces of Mrs. Penny's dress together. Daniel said he wanted "nothing fancy" for supper, and she took him at his word.

No one would think her hodgepodge stew was anything more than hot and filling. She didn't even put on one of her nicer dresses but wore an everyday outfit. It was clean and comfortable, and seemed appropriate for their meal.

The weather had been warmer, but by four o'clock there was a definite chill in the house, and she lighted the fire in the fireplace. Livvie woke up, and Caroline took her in to the bedroom to change her clothes. She especially enjoyed this time with each of the twins. The baby waved her arms. Caroline spoke softly, and kissed each of her little hands and feet.

Livvie gave her a big smile and babbled happily. Caroline finished dressing her, wrapped her in a fresh blanket, and held the baby on her shoulder. "Oh, Livvie, you're getting so big." She played with her until Robert woke up, and she repeated the process with him. He didn't smile quite so easily, but when he did, he looked just like his sister.

After Livvie and Robert finished nursing from their bottles, they weren't ready to fall asleep again. They enjoyed watching Tucker as he studied them from a safe distance. Caroline was showing them the brightly colored cloth ball when Daniel arrived. Tucker jumped up to the window. She looked at the twins. "Mr. Grey and Ethan are here."

She went to the front door and greeted them. "You're early. Supper isn't quite cold, yet."

Ethan glanced from her to his father, shook his head, and went into the parlor.

Daniel chuckled. "Want us to leave and come back later?" This was a charming side of her he hadn't seen before, and he heartily approved.

She grinned. "No, but you'll have to put up with a warm meal."

"If that's the price," he said with a shrug, "guess I can

suffer through." He bent and gave her a quick kiss. "You sure are pretty tonight, kinda sassy, too."

She laughed softly. "Thank you. I suppose I should give you dessert for that compliment." She walked into the parlor ahead of him.

As he passed a side table, he saw the vase holding the rose and in front of it was the pansy. Underneath both there was a pretty white circle of cloth edged with lace. It was set apart, easily noticed, and confirmed what she had told him. She didn't mind if people knew she was seeing him. He stood a little taller and felt like dancing her around the room, the house, hell, he'd do the reel with her right down Main Street.

Ethan looked at Caroline. "I think he smiled at me. Can he do that?"

"Mmm-hmm. He must like you." She grinned at Daniel.

He stepped over to the cradles and crouched down by Livvie. "Hello. You two are as bright-eyed as your mama today." The baby waved her arms, and he couldn't resist picking her up. He shared a smile with Caroline. "We'll have to watch her. She's going to lead the boys on a merry chase in a few years."

We? Oh, if that could be true, she thought, her prayers would be answered. "I'll try to teach her a little restraint. Not too much, but some."

He nodded. If she turns out like you, he thought, she'll be just about perfect. He sat down and held the baby in a sitting position. Turning the baby to face Caroline, he said, "That's your mama."

Ethan looked over at Caroline. "Can I hold Robert?"

"I think he would like that. Why don't you sit on the sofa." She lifted the baby out of the cradle and placed him in Ethan's arms. Tucker jumped from the windowsill to the back of the sofa and studied the baby.

Daniel watched his son. "Just don't let his head wobble around."

"Can he sit up like her?"

"Here—" Caroline helped Ethan and heard him sigh when the baby appeared content.

Ethan glanced over his shoulder at the cat. "Hey, look at this, Tucker. What'd'ya think?"

Caroline left to see about supper. She put the biscuits into the oven, filled the water glasses, and set the tureen of stew on the dining room table. When she returned, father and son were talking to the twins but not to each other. However, Livvie and Robert were basking in their attention.

Ethan pointed to Caroline and raised the baby's hand. "Wave to your mama." He waved Robert's hand and glanced at the cat. "Does Tucker ever sleep with them?"

"Oh, no. They move their arms and legs too much to suit him. He's curious, but he won't get close enough for them to grab him."

Ethan eyed Tucker and grinned. "Smart cat."

"Supper is served, and these two should be tired." Caroline walked over to Ethan and picked up Robert. She spoke softly, kissed his cheek, and put him down in his cradle.

Daniel stood up and held Livvie out to Caroline. "Kiss Mama, and I'll put you to bed."

Caroline smiled at him, and then at the baby. "Sleep tight, little one."

He also kissed her before laying her in the cradle. "I'm ready. How about you, Ethan?"

"Yeah, Pa."

"This way, gentlemen." Caroline led the way into the dining room. While they took their seats, she checked the table again. "Help yourselves to the venison stew. I'll get the biscuits." She left and returned with the basket.

"Sure smells good." Daniel removed the lid from the tureen and glanced at her. "It's steaming hot."

Caroline went along with the banter and pretended to be shocked. "Gracious. How could that be? Magic?"

Daniel fought to keep a straight face. "Think it's safe to eat?"

She shrugged. "Ethan, what do you think?"

"You two're strange." He reached for the ladle and dished a generous helping of stew onto his plate.

Daniel lifted the linen covering the biscuits. "These're hot, too."

"I had to heat them up—the weevils were still wiggling around," she said with a shiver as she ladled stew onto Daniel's plate and her own.

He was chuckling as he held out the basket of biscuits. "Wanna see if they're done?"

She smirked and opened one. "Ah, all's quiet." She glanced at Ethan, but he wasn't paying them any mind. She ate a bite. "Not bad." Daniel was grinning, and she pressed the other half to his mouth.

Oh, Caroline, you're in rare form tonight. He let her feed him and drew his lips over her fingertips as he closed his mouth. "I know a few seamen who'd carry you away for stale biscuits like these."

She lowered her hand with a quick sideways glance at Ethan. Her silliness had gone on long enough, and it had put Daniel and Ethan at ease—or at least she hoped so. While they dined, they talked about the warehouse, some items in the _Argus_, and the changes in town during the last three months. Then she started a pot of coffee and cleared the table. She served dessert and brought the pie pan to the table in case they wanted another helping.

Ethan cut a bit of the pie with the side of his fork. "What kind is this?"

"Buttermilk. Have you had it before?"

"Don't think so."

"It's good," Daniel said, ready to take another bite. "Taste it."

Before Caroline finished eating her slice of pie, she poured their coffee and hoped she could encourage them to talk about Ethan's interest in joining the army. He was too young, but she had heard stories about boys lying about their age. "Ethan, have you heard from Freddy lately?" When he drew his brows together and glanced at his father, she gave him a nod of encouragement.

"Nah. His brother said his ma got a letter."

"How is he doing?"

Daniel glanced at her and wondered why she asked about him. His son hadn't mentioned the boy in weeks, and he would just as soon she didn't remind him. She met his gaze, but he had no idea what she was thinking.

"Okay."

"I believe you told me Leroy and Tim were talking about signing up with Freddy. Have they?"

Ethan shook his head and quickly shoveled a bite into his mouth.

"Would you like another slice of pie?"

"Please."

Caroline dished a piece onto his plate and looked at Daniel. He nodded, and she set one on his plate as she spoke. "Ethan asked me why there weren't any stories in the newspaper about men from here, California, or the Washington Territory going back to the States to join the Union army." As Daniel took a drink of coffee, he glanced away, but she continued. "I thought if you told him why you haven't joined, it would help him understand."

He studied her and then faced his son. "I can't very well leave you alone."

"If Ma was still here, would you?"

"No, I wouldn't." Daniel sat back, his attention fixed on his son. "I've never killed a man, and half the troops are lads, not old enough to shave yet."

"How can you say that? You said slavery was wrong—a man can't own another man. Didn't you mean it?"

"I meant it, son." Daniel knew his son had a quick temper, but he didn't know if Caroline realized it. "I—*we*—have a few cousins and an uncle, some I've never met, who live outside of Charleston. How could I live with myself if I shot one of them?"

Ethan washed down a bite with a gulp of water. "You wouldn't shoot them. At least Freddy's doing *something*."

Daniel eyed his son. "Just what is Freddy doing?"

"Well . . . he's ready to fight."

"Son, I haven't heard about any troops from here being sent to help put down the insurrection."

"Well, then anyone wanting to join the Union'd have to go back to Ohio or Illinois or—"

"That's a long trek to get into a fight. One or two boys'd have a hard time making their way across the country by themselves."

"Trackers and guides do it all the time."

"Experienced ones."

Ethan jumped to his feet, knocking his chair over. "Well, just 'cause you don't wanta fight or go 'across country' doesn't mean I can't."

Daniel shook his head. "Sit down, son. You're forgetting where you are." He fixed the boy with a hard stare until he righted the chair and sat down. "Do you want to sign up with the Union army?"

"You know I do."

"That's something each man must decide for himself."

"Yeah, you're right, and I already have."

"Okay. After your seventeenth birthday. You'll be finished with school. You can sign up then, if you still want to."

"*Seventeen!*" Ethan was on his feet in an instant and ran out of the house.

"*Eth—an! Get back in here—*" Daniel bellowed, and slammed his fist on the table.

The twins cried out, and Caroline went to the doorway and paused. "Daniel, I am so sorry," she said, and went into the parlor.

"He will be, too, when I blister his backside." He followed her. "I'm sorry for losing my temper. I didn't mean to upset the babies." She had Livvie in her arms and was trying to pick up Robert. "Here, I'll take him."

Caroline walked and patted Livvie's back to soothe her. "I hoped when he heard what you had to say, he'd be reasonable."

"He's thirteen, but acts half his age sometimes." Daniel paced the length of the room trying to calm the baby.

Next time I'll keep my thoughts to myself, Caroline decided. Livvie sobbed and quieted.

"I should've straightened him out before now." He reached out and clasped her hand on the table. "I didn't know how angry he was."

"Why don't you go after him?"

"In a while. He needs to simmer." Daniel rubbed the baby's back and kissed him. "Guess I do, too."

"Daniel, I told myself I wouldn't say any more, but I care about you and Ethan." Caroline turned and walked to his side. "I have the feeling there's more, something else you need to talk about with him." She put her hand on his arm. "Do it tonight. He looks older than his age."

He nodded. "He acted like a seven-year-old no-account. I'm sorry he ran out of here."

"It's understandable. Besides, I was the one who started it. When Ethan and I talked, I kept thinking that he should be telling you how he felt, not me." She lowered her hand and continued pacing.

He stopped and stared at her. "Is that the reason you had us over for supper tonight?"

"Only part of it. You've been working so hard, and I wanted to spend an evening with you."

"You do know how to make a man feel appreciated."

She started to laugh. Then she realized that she wasn't sure if he had complimented or insulted her—especially in light of what had just happened. She sobered at once and looked into his eyes. "Not just *any* man, Daniel." She had never felt this way before, and she didn't want him to misunderstand.

He had tried to avoid seeing the desire he felt reflected in her gaze, but he did and it sharpened his own. Her cheeks were the shade of ripe peaches, and her lips were parted as if she were about to kiss him. "So you haven't invited other men over to sample your weevily biscuits?"

She grinned. "Not everyone would appreciate them."

"I'm glad." He watched her a moment, the way she cuddled the baby and murmured softly. His dreams were filled with her, most making love with him. She seemed so real he would wake up during the night searching for her in his bed. He put the baby in his cradle. "Guess I better find Ethan and straighten him out before he does something stupid." Or I do, he thought.

She stepped over to him. "Is there anything I can do to help?"

"It's up to me now." He started walking to the front door. "I'll thrash it out with him."

Don't close your eyes to this, she thought, but wouldn't

presume to say that aloud. She went to the door with him. "We'll have to try this again sometime."

He started to reach out to her, then dropped his arm to his side. If he kissed her thoroughly, the way he wanted to, he wouldn't be able to leave, and he had to find his son. "I'll stop by tomorrow."

The expectation of his tender caress created a ripple of desire that wound through her belly and lower, but he hurried down the walkway without so much as taking her hand. She shivered. His departure was so abrupt. She had been sure he was about to kiss her, but instead he had pulled away. She covered the baby's head with the blanket and watched him leave.

Tomorrow seemed to be a long way off.

Daniel drove the wagon up and down each street in town searching for his son before checking with Jay, Tim, and Leroy. None of Ethan's friends had seen him that day. Daniel rode along the Willamette River to where the Clackamas River fed into it and headed home.

The new moon didn't shed enough light to soften the shadows at the side of the roadway. He turned onto the path leading to his house, drove on until he reached the halfway point in the stand of alders and stopped. After Emmaline left, Ethan had spent many hours wandering through these trees. Daniel listened for a rustle in the bushes, the snap of a twig, some sign that his son was nearby. Finally he continued on to the house. The boy was stubborn but not stupid.

After he stabled the horse, he went into the house and built up the fire in the fireplace. He glanced at Ethan's door. Might as well take a look. He pushed the door partway open expecting to find the room empty. Instead, he saw Ethan curled up under the covers. He was home, safe.

Their talk could wait.

Daniel stretched out in his chair by the fireplace and stared at the fire. Golden flames seared the bark and surrounded the logs. He felt almost spellbound when he imagined seeing Caroline wearing only her chemise, her hair loose over one shoulder, and his hand trailing the length of her bare leg. It was so real that he could smell her soft skin and hear her throaty gasp. The pleasure of it was nearly painful.

The day dawned bright and clear. Caroline had washed and hung the laundry outside by the time she normally was preparing breakfast. The twins woke up hungry, as usual. She fed and bathed them, and carried one in each arm as she walked around talking to them. When they became sleepy, she put them down in their cradles and mopped up the bathwater from the kitchen floor.

She mixed a batch of bread dough and set it aside to rise. Since it was so nice out and the twins probably wouldn't wake for a while, she went out for a short walk in front of the house. Tucker was sunning himself in the yard and spying on a blue jay in Mrs. Kinney's tree.

Caroline held to a vigorous pace for several lengths of the block. She was almost ready to return home, when a woman she had passed turned up the walkway to the house.

The woman stood on the doorstep, raised her hand as if to knock, then turned and looked back at the sign in the yard.

Caroline waved at her and hurried up to the door. "May I help you?"

"Hello. Do you know if Mrs. Dobbs is home?"

"I'm Caroline Dobbs. Please, come inside. I was just stretching my legs. Isn't it beautiful today?" She showed the woman into the parlor and checked on Livvie and Robert. "Please, sit down."

The woman looked around the room and smiled at Caroline. "You have a very nice home. Cozy and warm." The woman sat on the sofa and stared into the cradles. As if recalling the reason she was there, the woman glanced back at Caroline. "They are beautiful babies."

"Thank you. I think so, too, but it's no reflection on me. I'm not their natural mother." Caroline watched the woman a moment and wondered if she had just come to see the twins.

The woman glanced up from the babies. "I'm Mrs. Galvin, Irene Galvin."

"I'm happy to meet you, Mrs. Galvin. Were you interested in having a dress made?"

"No, Mrs. Dobbs. I wanted to speak to you—I believe the Reverend Mr. Newhouse told you about Mr. Galvin and myself. We are the couple who wanted to adopt Mrs. Williams's babies."

"I see." Caroline sank down on the rocker and set it in motion. Mrs. Galvin was attractive, well spoken, and probably a very nice lady, but Caroline would never change her mind about the twins. "Didn't he tell you that Livvie and Robert already had a family and home? They aren't available for adoption."

"Yes, he did explain your situation. I thought if we met, and I told you a little about us . . .well, that it might make a difference."

Caroline started to speak.

Mrs. Galvin raised her hand. "Please allow me to finish, Mrs. Dobbs. This isn't easy for me, nor I expect for you." She moistened her lips and clasped her gloved hands on her lap. "Mr. Galvin and I have been married fourteen years and have not been blessed with children. He makes a respectable income. We would be able to provide anything that the children might need—as well as a very good education and the best medical care, should they need a physician. The children would have toys, a playroom, and very good care." She drew a deep breath and gazed at Livvie and Robert. "I don't know what else I can say that may change your mind."

As Mrs. Galvin spoke, Caroline had felt her pain and well remembered the anguish of feeling barren. However, because she was a widow and not a wife, people expected her to give up her children. It was asking too much of her. "I do understand how you feel, Mrs. Galvin. Please, believe me. Mr. Dobbs and I had no children of our own, either." She stopped rocking and regarded the twins sleeping so peacefully. "I promised their mother I would raise them as my own. Their birth was difficult, and Addie, their mother, was so very proud of them. I cannot and will not go back on my word. I love them dearly. I couldn't part with them."

Mrs. Galvin nodded. "I see." She studied her gloved hands. "Two infants must be terribly difficult to care for. Especially when you were not accustomed to having children. If you ever would consider placing one with another family, *please* keep me in mind."

Caroline stared at her. "Separate the twins? I would—could—*never* do that."

"Well—" Mrs. Galvin looked at Caroline. "I am glad we met, Mrs. Dobbs. Knowing they are loved and well cared for makes it easier." She stood up and looked at the babies one last time. "I'll keep you and them in my prayers."

"Thank you. That is very kind of you." Caroline walked her to the door. "Don't give up, Mrs. Galvin. There are other children who need a loving family."

"Yes, of course there are." Mrs. Galvin stepped down to the walkway and paused. "Love them well, Mrs. Dobbs, and have fun with them."

"I assure you I will." Caroline knew she couldn't promise her twins wealth, but she most certainly would give them an abundance of love.

18

DANIEL CRAWLED OUT of bed early Monday morning. Once the fire was started, he put a pot of coffee on to boil and soon had bacon and cut-up potatoes sizzling in the skillet. If the aroma of food didn't waken his son, he would. The eggs were in a bowl ready to be cracked and fried. He poured a cup of coffee for himself and set one on the table for his son. He was refilling his cup when he heard his son's door open.

As Ethan walked into the kitchen, he buttoned up his trousers and looked at his pa. "Mornin'." He added milk to his coffee and took a drink.

Daniel wasn't feeling especially pleased or about to allow his son to think that what had happened at Caroline's had been forgotten. "You owe Mrs. Dobbs an apology."

Ethan glanced sideways at him. "Didn't you do it?"

"You ran out of her house. It's your responsibility."

"Yeah, okay," Ethan mumbled.

"You had a lot of time to think things over. What did you decide?"

Ethan shrugged. "Dunno yet."

Daniel dished the bacon and browned potatoes onto the plates and started frying the eggs as he spoke. "If you want to design buildings, you'd better finish school."

"I will." Ethan gulped down his coffee. "'Sides, I can draw plans for buildings now. You taught me how last year."

"Mmm-hmm, mostly how to illustrate what you had in mind. Do you know how to figure out what supplies you'd need for, say, a two-bedroom house?"

"I could do that."

"Estimate the cost and time it would take to build it?" Daniel turned the eggs and glanced over at his son.

"The contractor'd do that. You do."

"That's part of the architect's job so his client will have an idea how much the project will cost him. I also need to know how much time to allow for a job so I can estimate my charges."

"I guess that wouldn't be too hard."

Daniel dished the eggs onto the plates and set them on the table. "You've got a talent for designing, I'll give you that. But you have a lot to learn about stress points, bearing walls, different styles of architecture, and how to plan for the client's comfort and needs. There's a lot more to it than a few lines on a paper."

Ethan stared at his pa. "You don't think I can do it, do you?"

"You're thirteen. Do you believe you know as much as a man who went to a university and studied?"

Ethan stabbed his fork in the potatoes. "No, but I can learn. I'm not stupid."

"Just stubborn." Daniel ate breakfast in silence. Ethan could have a wonderful future, if only he didn't spoil his chances now.

Ethan shoved the last piece of bacon in his mouth and rinsed his plate in the pan of water on the stove. "Are you taking me to school?"

Daniel looked at him. "Why wouldn't I?"

"You're so dad-blamed mad, figured you might not."

"Watch what you say, boy."

Ethan clamped his mouth shut and darted out of the room.

Daniel stared after his son wondering if he had ever been that headstrong. He rinsed his dishes, grabbed his jacket, and went to the barn. He drove Ethan to school and went to the warehouse. At noontime he stopped by Caroline's house. When he walked around the wagon, he noticed her neighbor lady watching him from a side window. He waved to the woman and strode up the walk and went inside. When he entered the parlor, Caroline was talking to Livvie.

"Hello." Caroline smiled at him. "Livvie, look who's here—" She had hoped after he spoke with his son that he would be able to put aside their differences, but he appeared a bit out of sorts. Not a good sign, she decided.

"Hi there." He stepped over to her and held his finger out to the baby as he spoke to her. "How're you two today?" She was as pretty as the day in a light-colored dress with little green twigs or something on it.

"We're just fine." His voice sounded weary and he didn't even smile at the baby. Livvie fussed, and Caroline patted her back. "Did you have trouble finding Ethan last night?"

"While I looked all over town, he was asleep in his bed." He glanced around. "Smells like you've been baking."

"I was up early and decided to make bread. It should be ready to take out of the oven in half an hour. Have you eaten yet?"

He shook his head. "I have to pick up some supplies so we don't lose any time this afternoon."

She had the unsettling feeling that he was ready to bolt from the house. "Can you sit for a while and have a cup of coffee?"

"Well, I should—" *Leave*, he thought, but he didn't want to, not so soon. "Yes, I'd like that." He stepped to her side and put his arm around her waist. "Want me to hold her for you?"

"If you don't mind." She felt the warmth of his arm on her back, but his hand barely touched her. "She always enjoys your company." You must know that I do, too, she thought. She leaned into him as she put the baby in his arms. He lowered his arm, and she sighed inwardly. "I'll start the coffee."

He grinned at Livvie. "We'll have a nice visit." He sat down in the armchair and perched her on one knee. "Want to ride a horsey?" Holding her with both hands, he jostled her on his knee. She smiled and waved her arms. Such a sweetheart. He peered at her brother, who was watching them. "Hi, Robert. That's kind of a mouthful, isn't it? How about R.J.?"

Daniel looked at Livvie. "I think he likes R.J." As long as he concentrated on the babies, he could keep his feelings about Caroline at a distance. Two weeks. Certainly he could wait two weeks and a couple of days to take her in his arms.

Caroline carried the tray into the parlor and served his coffee, her tea, and a plate of warmed biscuits with a slice of sausage inside. "I see you have worked your magic with her again." She picked up Robert and sat down in the rocker.

"She just needed a little jiggling." He moved the baby to his lap and took a sip of his coffee. "Biscuits?"

"Something to keep you from starving." She helped herself to one. "How is Ethan?" When she took a bite, the baby grabbed for her hand, and she set the rest of it on the edge of her saucer.

He picked up a biscuit and met her gaze. "He got over his temper, but it's hard to tell."

"So you did talk with him?"

He swallowed the bite and nodded. "This morning."

She wondered if it really had been that simple. "I'm

pleased he agreed not to join the army until he's older. That is what you mean?"

"He sees that he can't finish his schooling and join the army now." He ate the other half of the biscuit and reached for another one. "These sure are good."

"I'm glad you like them. It won't take a minute to make more." She glanced at hers, half eaten, and took a bite. It tasted better than she had thought it would.

There was one left on the plate. He felt a twinge of guilt but helped himself. "These are plenty." He grinned. "I do have lunch in the wagon."

"Those will only whet your appetite." As she ate the last bite, she watched him play with the baby. He wasn't himself, but she didn't feel she had the right to keep prying—at least not yet.

"Look at Livvie. She wants a bite." He looked at Caroline and back to the baby. "We'll have to get your mama to make more mashed potatoes for you and Robert."

She smiled. That sounded more like him. "The next time I make them, they can have a taste."

He whispered loudly to the baby. "We'll try for two bites."

Smiling to herself, Caroline tipped the chair and started rocking. He talked as if he planned to continue seeing them, and that indeed was a heartwarming thought. "We will have to see about that."

"Livvie, I bet if you say 'Mama,' she'll agree." He drank the rest of his coffee and sat back. "Now that the weather's so nice, everybody in town seems to be out these days. How's your business been?"

"All right, but many women won't be ready to spend money on themselves until their homes are repaired and their husbands won't mind the expense." She put Robert on her shoulder and lightly rubbed his back. "Mrs. Galvin came in this morning. Do you know her or Mr. Galvin?"

Daniel thought a moment. "I don't know the name. Who are they?"

"Evidently the couple that Reverend Newhouse told me about. The ones that wanted to adopt the twins."

He sat up. "Why did she come by here? Didn't he tell her the babies had a home? They never were up for adoption."

"She knew, but she seemed to believe, or had hoped, that if she spoke to me, I might change my mind." Caroline kissed Robert and rested her cheek against his head. "The Galvins don't have any children. I understand how she feels. Hopeless. I can't believe Gilbert and the reverend would raise her hopes that way. That would've been very cruel."

"Did they send her over to change your mind?"

"No, I'm sure they didn't. I know how it feels . . . and I saw it in her eyes. She even offered to take one of them—"

He interrupted her. "*One?* How could she possibly even suggest splitting them up?"

"Desperation can make people do unreasonable things. I feel sorry for her."

"You're sure Bennett and his friends didn't send her to see you?"

"Very." She glanced at his cup. "I'll get more coffee."

"Caroline—" He reached out and gently took hold of her hand. "I can't stay." Her fingers were icy, and he hoped her affection for him hadn't cooled as well.

"I'm glad you stopped by. I was worried about you." She still didn't believe that whatever was bothering him had been settled, but it was clear he did not want to discuss it. "You look tired. Try not to work too hard."

Work was the one thing that helped pass the time, but that was his business, and he didn't want to burden her. "I won't." He moved the baby to his shoulder and stood up. "Want me to put her in the cradle?"

"Please. I can manage very well one-handed but not holding both of them." After he put the baby down, she walked to the door with him. "Take care, and please tell Ethan hello for me."

"He's supposed to come by after school and apologize. Let me know if he doesn't. He wants to be a man, so he'd better act like one." Daniel started down the walkway, smiled at her over his shoulder, and kept putting one foot in front of the other. If her neighbor lady was watching, he didn't want to give her any more to gossip about.

As he walked around the wagon, he glanced back at Caroline's house. The north corner needed something to add a little character and block the neighbor's view. A fir tree would help and a trellis—from the ground to the eve of the roof—would look real nice with blackberry vines filling in the spaces.

Later that afternoon, Caroline pressed the bodice and skirt of Mrs. Penny's basted dress. It was ready for the fitting the next day. Caroline stirred the pot of chicken soup simmering on top of the stove and set aside a pan with two boiled potatoes to cool. The bell rang softly, as if someone had eased the door open, and she went out to see who had entered. Ethan was looking into the parlor. "Hello. I'm glad you stopped by."

"You are?" He shifted his weight from one foot to the other. "Uh . . . I'm sorry about yesterday. I shouldn't'a hollered and run outta here."

"Thank you for apologizing." She smiled and put her hand on his shoulder. "How would you like some fresh bread, jam, and a glass of milk?" He was so skittish, she wasn't sure if he would bolt or relax, but he gave her a shy smile.

"It smells good. Okay."

"You can leave your books on the table and hang your jacket on one of the pegs." She recalled a comment Daniel had made about Ethan being a boy one minute and a man the next and agreed. At the moment he was a little of both. She went into the kitchen and sliced the bread. Ethan came in and walked over to the stove.

"You can sit here at the table and keep me company while I make dumplings." She set the jam in front of him along with the plate of bread and a knife.

He hesitated a moment and picked up the knife. "Are Robert and Livvie sleeping?"

"Finally. They were awake most of the day." She poured his milk and handed the glass to him. "How was school?"

As he spread jam on the second slice of bread, he shrugged one shoulder. "The same."

"Mmm—" She set the colander in a large bowl and dumped the potatoes into it. "Did you settle your differences with your father?"

"He wants me to stay in school . . . but how can I forget about the insurrection? It's in the newspaper every week." He ate a bite of bread and looked at her.

"The editor's job is to tell the reader what is happening. Have you studied the American Revolution?"

"Yeah. Everybody knows about that."

"Well, instead of learning about something that happened some seventy or so years ago, you're reading history in the making." She started pushing the potatoes through the colander with the masher. "I doubt many mothers living in the East, North, or South want to send their young sons off to fight."

Ethan chewed the bread, swallowed and took a gulp of milk. "All men have mothers, so they are sons."

"Indeed," she said, and smiled. "The difference is age. Before a boy becomes a man he should learn from his parents. You are a bright young man, but, Ethan, you're still learning. No one your age is expected to have the experience and knowledge of an adult."

He was about to take another bite but lowered the bread. "I'm taller than you. I could help do something—"

She started scraping the colander. "What if you were shot? Or, Heaven forbid, lost your arm or were wounded in the head. Could you be an architect? That's an important position. Once the rebellion is settled, people will get back to living and building up the towns. Wouldn't you rather be part of that?" She set the colander aside.

He chewed slowly and looked at his arms. "I didn't think about that. . . ."

She looked at him and softly said, "I hope you will." She seasoned the potatoes and added an egg to the mix. "If you were grown up and had a little brother, who was your age and told you he wanted to join the army, what would you tell him?"

Ethan frowned at her. "You know I'd tell him he's too . . . young."

"Yes, he would be." She turned to the stove with her back to him and smiled. After she stirred the soup, she returned to the table. "Would you like more bread or milk?"

"No, thanks."

She took a large spoon out of the drawer and started working the egg into the potatoes.

He watched her and glanced at the stove. "You like my pa a lot, don't you?"

She hadn't expected that particular question, but she suspected that he already knew the answer. "Yes, I do. He's an easy man to like." She looked at him and added, "Do you mind?"

"Nah, not anymore." He finished drinking his milk. "You kinda reminded me of my ma, but I was little when she went away." He met Caroline's gaze. "Oh, you don't look anything like her, and you sure cook better'n her."

She opened the flour bin under the table, scooped out a small amount, and added it to the potato mixture. "You must miss her very much."

"Yeah, I guess. . . . But you're nice, and you make Pa happier than he's been in a long time."

"Thank you. I like you, too." His compliment was so sweet she almost felt a girlish blush heat her cheeks, and quickly began working the flour into the mixture. "He's a very nice man, Ethan, and a good man. One day you'll understand what a fine father you have."

He peered into the bowl. "What're you making?"

"Potato dumplings."

"Pa likes the babies, too. He always wanted a bunch of younguns. Said I'd have at least five brothers and sisters. 'Course I don't."

That was quite a change of topics, but she had the feeling he wasn't paying close attention to her answers. "Would you mind being a big brother?"

"I don't know. What would I have to do?"

She grinned, wondering if he would recognize the likeness. "Answer questions about anything and everything. Teach your brother or sister how to do all sorts of things. He, or she, would probably tease you, follow you around, and get into your belongings."

"Jay has a little brother. Milt has a sister, but she's almost his age. They're pests—sometimes."

"They might be, but I'm sure there are times that they're

kind of nice." She set the spoon aside and put a dipper of water in a small bowl. "I always wanted a big brother."

He looked at her. "You did? Really?"

"Oh, yes. My best friend had a brother, and none of the boys teased her more than once because her brother threatened to beat them up." She stuck her hands into the mix and glanced at him. "I shouldn't have told you that."

He grinned. "I won't tell anybody." He stared at her hands. "Are those balls ready to eat?"

"Not yet. They have to boil in broth first. Would you like to try one?"

"Can I?"

"Do you think two would spoil your supper?"

"Oh, no. Two'd be fine."

She thought she saw him lick his lips as she turned to drop two of the dumplings into the simmering chicken soup. She enjoyed his visits and could almost imagine what it would be like to be his—

Her imagination had taken flight, again. Daniel cared for her, how much she wasn't sure, but it was certainly premature to consider being Ethan's— No, she refused to allow herself even to think the word. She was so very grateful to have the twins that it seemed greedy to want more.

When the dumplings rose to the surface, she scooped them out onto a plate and set it in front of him with a fork. "Let them cool off a bit or you'll burn your mouth."

He leaned over the plate and smelled the steam.

She finished forming the dumplings and covered them with a towel. "They'll cool faster if you break them open with the fork." While she rinsed off her hands, it occurred to her that he did not actually say he had changed his mind about the army. However, they were getting along so well, she didn't want to bring it up again.

He blew on the half dumpling and popped it in his mouth and smiled as he chewed it. "Mmm, these're good."

"I'm glad you like them. They're easy to make. You watched me."

"Mashed potatoes, an egg, and flour. How much flour?"

"Enough to make the mix stick together so you can form balls." She poured a dipper of water into the bowl and washed it out.

He ate the other half. "I made the pudding, but it didn't taste as good as yours."

She smiled at him. "It just takes practice, as with most things."

After he had eaten the second dumpling, he stood up and pushed the chair under the table. "Thanks for the food. I better go now."

"All right." She walked to the door with him.

He pulled on his jacket and picked up his books. "I'll see ya."

"Call any time." She closed the door and hoped he would tell his father about his visit. Daniel should be proud of him. His son was very much like him. She arched her back and sighed. With Daniel's court date set, the days seemed to pass so slowly. At this rate, sixteen days would feel as long as that many weeks.

The strangest part was that she had the feeling he was looking forward to something important, other than his divorce. He had been so serious lately, she couldn't help wondering if it was something he would rather not face.

Robert and Livvie watched Caroline when she passed their cradles. The poor little dears, she thought. She carried them around the house frequently, but they spent most of their days staring up at things. She didn't have a carriage to take them on walks, but she didn't see any reason they couldn't lie on the floor and look around.

She spread a blanket on the floor, covered it with a sheet and anchored the corners with pieces of furniture. She put Livvie and Robert down facing each other and set the ball between them. Tucker jumped on the small table between the chairs and watched them in the same manner he would have studied a beetle making its way through the grass.

It didn't take Robert very long to hold himself up on his outstretched arms. He wobbled a bit but stared around with new interest. As if Livvie were determined not to be outdone, she soon stiffened her little arms and held herself up, too.

A swell of happiness nearly brought tears to Caroline's eyes. She glanced at Tucker and looked back just in time to see Robert roll over onto his back. He waved his arms at the ball. She waited, then she put him back on his belly. Sure enough, he tried to grab the ball but lost his balance and had to start over. He was a stubborn one, or maybe just persistent. She watched as he tried over and over to grab the ball while leaning on only one arm. His sister, however, discovered she could make the ball move by bumping it with her head.

The brass bell rang. Tucker went to the window and Mrs. Penny came inside. Caroline quickly got to her feet. "Hello, Mrs. Penny."

Mrs. Penny set the milk can down and stepped over to the sheet. "That's good for them to move around. I brought the wagon I used to carry mine about. Thought you might need it."

"I do indeed. Thank you, but I want to pay you for it. The weather has been so nice, I've been thinking about getting one."

"I'll lend it to you, but I won't sell it," Mrs. Penny said, shaking her head. "No, ma'am. I don't need any more babies."

"All right, Mrs. Penny, I will be happy to return it."

Caroline put the twins in their cradles and folded up the floor covering. "Your dress is ready to try on. Let's go back to the sewing room."

While Mrs. Penny undressed, Caroline put away the fresh milk and set the empty can by the front door. Tucker scratched at the door. After she let him out, she returned to the sewing room and helped Mrs. Penny into her new dress. Caroline marked the places that were too loose, too snug, and pinned the hem of the skirt.

Mrs. Penny looked in the mirror again. "Mrs. Dobbs, this is the nicest dress. I know Mr. Penny will like it." She ran her hand down one sleeve. "This'll be my Sunday-best dress."

"I'm glad you like it. It will be ready for you on the fourth, Tuesday."

Mrs. Penny unbuttoned the first two buttons and glanced back at the mirror. "It feels so good, I don't want to take it off."

Caroline chuckled. "That will make it harder to finish."

When Mrs. Penny had changed her dress, Caroline carried the milk can out to her wagon. "I can't tell you how much I appreciate the fresh milk." She put the can in the back of the wagon and paid Mrs. Penny. "The wagon is perfect."

Mrs. Penny helped her lift it down to the ground. "It isn't fancy, but Mr. Penny put good springs on it so the babies won't get jostled too much."

"I can take Livvie and Robert for an outing. Now Martha won't have to spend her Wednesday afternoons here. I'll tell her when she comes later."

Mrs. Penny left, and Caroline pulled the wagon into the house. The twins had fallen asleep. She fashioned a cover and padded the bottom of the wagon. Later she would take down her sign, close up shop, and take her first stroll with the twins, *her* babies.

They could go by the warehouse and say hello to Daniel. She was almost giddy.

19

LIVVIE AND ROBERT had enjoyed their fill of sweet milk, and were wearing their pale yellow dresses with pin tucks across the bodices. Caroline, too, had freshened up before she settled the twins in the wagon with a nice blanket over them and set off on their first constitutional. Mr. Noyle was in his front yard, and she greeted him.

He went over to her. "Hello, Mrs. Dobbs. Lovely day, isn't it?"

"It certainly is. The new buds and leaves are so cheery. Your rosebushes have a good start this year."

He brushed a pine needle off one rose leaf. "How have you been, Mrs. Dobbs?"

"Very well."

"These are your young charges, are they not?"

She couldn't help grinning. "Livvie and Robert. She's closest to you." She glanced at the twins and felt inordinately proud that they were looking at him.

He studied them a moment. "Beautiful infants, Mrs. Dobbs, and very bright-eyed. That's a good sign of intelligence."

"Thank you." She wished they would grow up happy and healthy. "We will see you again."

"We're due for a good rain. Enjoy this fair weather."

"We will." She proceeded down the street and managed to avoid the deepest ruts and clumps of grass and weeds.

The twins were bundled at the back of the wagon facing forward. She glanced at them frequently and stopped to point out birds, trees, and various buildings or houses. She had noticed people watching them; some had called out or waved. She smiled and returned the greetings, and continued on to the south end of town. The street became a roadway.

She paused on the rise where the road curved toward the river. The sun glistened on the Willamette and sparkled through the bright new branches and leaves on the trees lining the river. She crouched by the wagon, checked to make sure the twins were secure, and kissed them. Before they neared the warehouse, she heard the hammers and saw the new roof in the distance.

Pushing, rather than pulling the wagon, she went down the incline slowly. They had reached the bottom, and she heard her name. Shielding her eyes and squinting into the glare coming from the river, she saw Daniel waving and walking to meet them. She waved to him and felt the breathless flutter of anticipation skitter through her insides.

This was the first time she had met him out in public, and she was very much aware of his crew watching from the warehouse. "Hello. We thought we would pay our respects while we were out."

He hadn't trusted his vision when he first spotted her coming down the hill. She wasn't wearing a bonnet and her hair stirred, gently framing her face. "What a wonderful surprise. When did you get the wagon?" He hunkered down and kissed each of the babies. The sides of the wagon weren't very high. In another month or so they could tumble out. He needed to make them a proper buggy.

"Mrs. Penny brought it to me when she came for her

fitting. Wasn't it nice of her? Now we can take walks together." His sleeves were rolled up above his elbows and his shirt was unbuttoned halfway down. Goodness, she had had no idea how very appealing he looked when he was working.

He stood up and took her hand in his. "It's sure nice to see you. It seems like it's been a week." The tip of her tongue darted across her lower lip, and he drew her hand to his chest. "Would you like to see the warehouse?"

"Yes, I would, if you have time."

"Mind if I introduce my crew?"

She stepped back, shook the dust out of her skirts, and smiled at him. "Not at all."

"Good. The ground's pretty rough. I'll carry the wagon."

"Want me to take the twins?"

"I won't drop them." He lifted the wagon. "What do you think of this, R.J.?"

"R.J.?"

"Robert's a junior, isn't he?"

"You have a good memory."

"That I do," he said softly. "I thought R.J. would be easier for them to say. Robert's kind of a mouthful for a little tyke."

Oh, Daniel, she thought, you have become an important part of my life—our lives. Is that what you honestly want? Or has that even occurred to you? she wondered. Ethan was right. Daniel was taken with the twins, almost as if they were his own, but a small part of her prayed that wasn't his only reason for spending time with her.

He pinned the wagon against his right side with that arm and balanced the end with the babies with the other hand. "Watch your step."

She raised her skirt a little and managed to keep up with

his long stride. She followed him to a wide opening that she guessed would be a doorway.

"I'll help you up." He raised the wagon and set it down on the floor, then he stepped up into the building and turned to Caroline. He reached out to her, grasped both of her wrists and swung her up to him. For one brief moment, they stood toe to toe. Her lips parted and were so close to his. But they weren't alone. He stepped back and reluctantly released one of her hands. "That trench will be filled in later."

"With dirt or water?"

"A moat. That's an idea." He moved her hand to his arm, grabbed hold of the wagon handle, and walked over to his men. "Mrs. Dobbs, I would like you to meet Mr. Brook, Mr. Roby, and Mr. Vale. Men, this is Mrs. Dobbs."

She acknowledged each man and was relieved to see nothing untoward in their expressions. "I am happy to meet you."

Mr. Vale motioned to the wagon. "Daniel's told us all about those little tykes. Sure are cute."

Mr. Brook nodded and grinned. "Glad to see they're real. To hear him tell it, they're talkin' and walkin'."

She glanced at Daniel. "As you can see, they aren't able to sit up yet, but Robert rolled over for the first time today."

Daniel eyed Robert. "R.J., is that true?"

She struggled to keep a straight face while Daniel posed as if he were the proud papa. It was funny, and flattering, she realized. "If he answers you, I'll . . . dance up High Street."

He chuckled. "We've been working on it."

"I'm not surprised," she said, brushing her arm against his. She looked around at the cavernous building. "This is enormous. You've accomplished a lot in the last few weeks."

"We still have a ways to go." Daniel glanced overhead. "Long as we don't get a late freeze, we'll be okay."

Her hand was still on his arm, and she pressed her fingers just enough for him to feel it. "We better start back before it gets cool." She smiled at Mr. Brook, Mr. Roby, and Mr. Vale. "Thank you for allowing me to interrupt your work."

"Come back anytime, Mrs. Dobbs," Mr. Vale said with a glance at Mr. Brook and Mr. Roby.

"Thank you. I just might."

Daniel walked her back to the road and set the wagon down. "Ethan told me he apologized to you."

"He's a good boy, Daniel. Sometimes he needs to talk things out the way he probably did with his mother. He wasn't angry, but he didn't say he wouldn't join the army, either. I did give him a couple of ideas to think about."

He lowered his arm and held her hand in the fold of her skirt. "For a while he thought if he liked you he was betraying his mother. I think he knows better now."

"I hope he does. No woman could take her place in his affections." She leaned into him ever so slightly. "Will you be working evenings?"

"'Fraid so. Either here or in the shop, but I'll see you in a couple of days."

"Good. I have a store of coffee." She gave him an offhanded smile and stroked his thumb with hers. "If you don't drink it, I'll have to learn to like it."

"We can't have that, can we?" He raised her hand and pressed a kiss to the back of her wrist. "This won't last forever. Fourteen more days and it will be better."

He said it again and this time she had to ask. "Why? You keep counting the days. What will happen in two weeks?"

"With a little luck, my divorce. You didn't forget, did you?"

She slowly shook her head. "I have the feeling there's

more to it than that. Lately there have been times when you've been . . . distant or maybe you've had a lot on your mind." She took a deep breath. "I— Or have you grown bored with me?" He was being attentive now, but there had been times when she had wondered, and she didn't think she could wait two weeks to find out.

"No—never." He held her hand in both of his. "I have the *highest* regard for you. Please believe me, Caroline." He hadn't the right to say more, not until he was completely free. Hell, it was difficult doing the right thing, but she was special, so very special.

"I do." It wasn't exactly what she had hoped to hear, but it was much better than *we'll always be friends*. She glanced down at her hand in his. "I have to get the twins home." She slipped her hand from his and took hold of the wagon handle.

"Be patient a little longer." *Don't give up on me yet,* he thought. "I'll see you soon." He walked back to the warehouse.

She walked up the road and looked back when she started around the corner. The warehouse was a good sturdy building, and it reflected its builder. If he would only take her into his confidence, but maybe that was asking too much. He had seemed to blow hot and cold, and now he asked her to be patient. She would—until after his divorce.

If he didn't tell her what was wrong, she would have to accept that she had wanted his love so much that she had convinced herself that he returned her affection.

The next week passed for Daniel with long hours at the warehouse and late nights in his workshop. He worked until he was too tired to do anything but fall into bed. He had seen Caroline twice but for only a few minutes each time. Up until the last month, he had believed he was a patient man.

Now he knew differently. Each day he thought about and planned the moment he could tell her how he really felt.

He continued checking at the post office for letters from Emmaline. When there were none, he didn't know if he should be glad or worried. What if she had decided to appear at the hearing? Worse than that, what if she returned for Ethan? God help him, Daniel thought, she would have one helluva fight on her hands.

Six days before the hearing, he sent Ethan to meet the steamer *Rival* at the Fourth Street wharf to pick up supplies and hardware he had ordered from San Francisco. After Caroline had talked with him, Daniel had decided to have him work after school. The boy appeared to have lost interest in the Rebellion. It seemed to be working out, and he had her to thank.

He was nailing up wall boards when Ethan returned and went out to help him unload the wagon. "You made good time. Did you have any trouble?"

"No—" Ethan didn't look at his pa but picked up a crate and carried it into the warehouse.

Daniel started moving the supplies inside, also. On his third trip, he realized his son wasn't there. After the barrels and crates had been stacked and covered with canvas, he told his men to leave for the day and walked around the area looking for Ethan. It wasn't like him to take off without saying a word. Daniel hadn't seen any other boys around, but his son could have gone to a friend's house.

He put his tools away and had his foot on the wagon wheel in the process of stepping up, when he noticed a crumpled piece of paper on the ground. There were scraps of wood and other materials lying around, but no other paper. He picked it up and flattened the page. It was a letter, and it was addressed to him. He looked around again, but there was still so sign of his son. Turning his attention to the letter, he glanced at the bottom of the page. It was from a woman in San Francisco, but not from his wife.

Mr. Grey,
I saw yor notis in the paper taday and thot ya'd wanna no bout Emmaline. I was a good friend a hers but she nevr tole me she was marryed. Gess sum one shood giv ya the sad news. She got the fever 'n passed mor'n a year ago, so ya got no need to divorce her now.
                    Emmi's friend, Estel Otis

Emmaline dead . . . for more than a year. Could it be true? He stared at the handwriting. The penmanship was poor, and it didn't look anything like his son's. He didn't see an envelope and dropped to his knees to search under the wagon. Nothing. Staring at the letter and trying to make sense of it, his hand began to shake. If it was true, he was no longer married. He was a widower. He was single, free to . . .

Then he realized that Ethan must have read the letter. What a terrible way to learn that his mother had died. He shoved the letter in his pocket, climbed to the bench seat, and headed home. Staying to the less-traveled back streets, he drove the horses as fast as he dared. When he arrived home, he started calling his son and continued as he ran through the house, barn, and finally his shop. There was no sign he had been there.

He rode to where Ethan used to go to work out his problems. The woods, Ethan's childhood hiding place. Daniel hiked through the area and back to the wagon, but it was obvious to him that no one had been through there recently. He returned to Oregon City and went by each of his son's friends' homes to no avail. Feeling desperate and hoping Caroline might be able to help, he drove to her house.

It was late and her sign had been taken down. He knocked on her door and came close to barreling inside just as the door opened a crack. "Caroline—is Ethan here?!"

A moment after the pounding on the front door, the twins' shrill cries rang out. She peered around the partially opened door and sighed. "Daniel? What on earth—! Come in." She had almost decided to bar it rather than see who was there. He charged past her and into the parlor. She had never seen him in such a state. "What's happened?" She hurried over to the cradles and attempted to quiet the bawling twins.

"I've got to find Ethan. Has he been here?"

She was on her knees, bent over between the two cradles, patting Livvie and Robert. "I haven't seen him in the last week. Daniel, *tell me* what is going on."

He pulled the rumpled letter out of his pocket and waved it in her direction. "I found this by the wagon. He must've gotten it when he picked up the supplies from the steamer and read it. I've got to talk to him. God, what he must be thinking." He paced the length of the room, his long stride quickly covering the distance.

Caroline was ready to scream. "What—"

His wife. It must be, she realized, and her heart seemed to drop to the pit of her stomach. "Daniel, is it your wife? Is she coming back for the hearing?" She stared at him, waiting for an answer, her throat tight, each breath a painful reminder that he was married.

"No . . ." He laughed, a harsh release, and handed the letter to her. "I must find him, Caroline."

She kissed each of the twins and sat back on her heels to read the letter. His wife wouldn't return, not ever. Now she understood his dismay, and his panic to locate Ethan. She folded the page and handed it back to Daniel. "If Ethan read this, he must be devastated. Have you asked his friends?"

"Yes," he said without pausing. "I've looked everywhere I can think of. I'd hoped he might've come here to talk to you." He shook his head. "I don't know what else to do."

He looked lost and frightened. She met him in the middle of the room. "Come in the kitchen with me." The twins had quieted, and she hoped she could calm him down, also. She took him by the hand and walked through the dining room into the kitchen. Questions suddenly came to mind. His wife had died. He had been prepared to divorce her, but how did he feel about her death?

He dropped onto one of the chairs at the worktable and raked his fingers through his hair. "Why did he run away from me? Didn't he know I'd care?" God, his head felt like it was in a vise. Thoughts streamed through his mind, but he couldn't quite grasp on to any one of them.

She filled the coffeepot with water. "He probably wasn't thinking straight. He'd just learned that his mother died over a year ago." As she measured out the coffee, she watched him. "I'd say you're stunned, too. It's natural. That news is quite a shock."

While the coffee brewed, she heated the beef soup and sliced bread as she spoke. "How do you feel about her death?"

"Dumbfounded . . . confused." He shook his head. "Numb. But what I can't forget is that her friends in San Francisco didn't know she was—or had been—married. Or knew she had a wonderful son. God, how that must hurt him."

She stepped behind Daniel, put her arm around his shoulders, and rested her cheek on his. "Wounded creatures hide to heal their injuries. I don't think he went too far." Tucker darted into the room and jumped into the kitchen window. A moment later he sat on his haunches, pawed at the window, and yowled.

Daniel glanced at the cat. "What's wrong with him? I've never seen him do that."

"There must be something outside." She wiped her hands on the towel. Tucker sprang from the windowsill and ran down the hall to the back door. "I'll just let him out." The door was barely open before Tucker pushed his way out. He only acted that way when he was chasing after something or some*one*—

She slipped outside and closed the door. The bushes at the far edge of the small shed rustled. Holding her skirts up and stepping carefully, she made her way to the near side of the shelter and listened. Tucker meowed, and Ethan whispered to him. Thank the Lord. She glanced at the house. Should she tell Daniel and let him discover his son or should she try to speak to the boy? Then it dawned on her that of all of the places where he could have taken refuge, he had chosen her yard. He hadn't run away or joined the army. He must feel safe here, she thought.

She stepped around the corner and crouched down. "Tucker, please tell Ethan I would like to talk to him. That is, if he trusts me . . ." A branch shook, and Tucker's loud motor answered her, but Ethan didn't. She sat down on the ground by the bush. "Your father let me read the letter. That was a terrible way to hear about your mother's passing." There was a long silence, and she wondered if he was going to answer.

"Ye—" he croaked, then cleared his throat. "How . . . how come she didn't tell her friends about us? Did she hate us *that* much?"

"No, oh, no, Ethan. I have the feeling she was searching for something and didn't know how to find it."

"That don't make sense. She was ashamed of us, of me." He choked and sobbed.

She peered through the branches. He was crying his heart out and petting the cat. He was a boy who had lost his mother, and she couldn't leave him there. She crawled between the bushes, sat down at his side, and put her arms around him. "It's all right. This has been a long time coming, I think."

He rubbed his shirtsleeve over his eyes and stared at her. "What're you doin' here?"

"Sitting with my friend." She smiled at him. "We are friends, aren't we?"

He hesitated a moment, then wrapped his arms around her. The tears kept coming, and he nestled his head on her shoulder much like a little boy. "I . . . I'll n-never see her again."

A tremor shook him, and she held him tighter. "No, you won't, but you have her in your memories. Those will always be with you." Tucker crept up on Ethan's leg and lay down across both of them. "I'm glad you came here, but I wish you had come inside. Your father is desperate. He's searched all over for you."

"H-he won't miss her. He was divorcing her."

"Yes, he was, but he's worried about you. And I know he would never wish for this to have happened. He and your mother weren't happy living together, but he wouldn't've wished her any harm."

Inside, the soup started boiling, and Daniel wondered where Caroline had gone. He went to the back door and stared at the yard. "Caroline—are you out here?"

She didn't move but spoke softly. "I can't let your father think I've run off, too. Will you answer him?"

Tucker came out from the far side of the shed and walked up to Daniel. He crouched down and held out his hand.

"What's going on?" The cat rubbed against his hand and returned to the bushes. As if he were coming out of a dense fog, it started to make sense. Daniel walked over to the shed. "Ethan? Caroline? Are you out here?"

Ethan let go of Caroline and sat back. "Yeah, Pa. We're here."

"Thank God. I thought— Never mind." The cat darted out. Ethan appeared next. Daniel took his son's arm and helped him to his feet, then embraced him heartily. "You scared the hell out of me."

Ethan hugged his pa. "I . . . I didn't mean to. I—"

Caroline watched Daniel with his son and felt tears well up in her eyes. He was a strong man and yet he didn't hesitate to show his affection for his son. She bent over and crawled out from under the bushes. Suddenly Daniel's large hands circled her upper arms and lifted her to her feet. She gazed into his eyes and smiled. "Thank you."

He cleared his throat and shook his head. "Look at you two, sitting in the bushes like a couple of younguns."

She grinned and brushed off her skirt. "Let's go inside and have a warm drink." She linked arms with Daniel and with Ethan. It was a beginning.

20

$\mathcal{T}$HE NEXT MORNING Daniel woke with a jolt. The sun was bright. He should have been up long ago, then he remembered it was Saturday, the latest supplies had arrived, and he didn't have to be at the warehouse early. Besides, he still needed to speak with Ethan, and that was more important than work. Daniel washed up, dressed, and set to work making breakfast.

While he cooked, he kept seeing Caroline with his son. She understood him and saw him in a different light. He was sure she liked him and really cared about him, but would she want to be part of their family? Or want them to be part of hers? At some time during the night he realized that he needed to see Mr. Johnson and withdraw his petition for divorce. He wasn't married. The date of the hearing was so fixed in his mind that he had to keep reminding himself that he was single.

He could tell Caroline how he felt about her and ask her the question he had been holding back for the last six weeks. But first, he wanted to tell Ethan. They were a family, and he shouldn't feel left out.

Ethan came into the kitchen and walked over to the stove. "Someone coming for breakfast?"

Daniel looked at the skillet with pan eggs and fried

potatoes, a smaller one with sausage, and the plate of flapjacks to the side of the heat. "Aren't you hungry? I'm starved."

"You won't be after you eat all that." Ethan poured himself a cup of coffee and added milk.

"Grab a plate and help yourself." Daniel filled a plate and sat down at the table. "You and Caroline seem to be good friends."

"She's real nice and a good ma to Robert and Livvie. They're lucky." He joined his pa at the table and scooped a large bite of potatoes onto his fork.

Daniel took a drink of coffee and cut a piece of sausage. "Would you like to have her as a second mother?" He felt his heart lurch and didn't realize until then how anxious he was about asking his son.

Ethan's fork clanged on his plate. "You asked her already?"

"No, oh, no. I wanted to talk it over with you first."

"She likes you a lot and everyone knows you like her."

"*Everyone?*"

Ethan lowered the fork brimming with sausage and eggs. "She's the only lady you've called on in years."

"Guess you're right." Daniel took a deep breath. "But how do *you* feel about it?" Sometimes the boy knew more about what was going on than he realized.

"I like her."

"Are you saying you wouldn't mind if I ask her to marry me?"

"Yeah, if you want to."

"But would you be happy living with her? And with the babies? You'd be their big brother."

"We talked about that. That'd be okay."

Daniel was beginning to wish he had asked more questions before. "You did?"

"Yeah, when we were . . ." Ethan shrugged and filled his mouth.

Daniel sat back and pushed a bite of flapjack around the plate. "She actually talked about being married to me with you?"

"Oh, no. It wasn't like that. She asked me what I'd tell my little brother, if I had one, an' he wanted to sign up with the army."

"I see." Daniel smiled and ate a bite. Maybe it wouldn't be as difficult as he had imagined. Maybe.

Ethan picked up his cup and paused. "When're you gonna ask her?"

"Think tonight's too soon?"

"Nah. You got her a pin or something special yet? I heard ladies like that."

"Where did you 'hear' that?"

"Around." Ethan gulped down some of his eggs. "Can I stay at Jay's tonight? We wanted to hunt frogs, and I don't wanna watch you and Mrs. Dobbs."

Daniel managed to swallow his coffee before he choked. "Sure. That sounds good." It also solved one problem he hadn't figured out—how to be alone with Caroline. "Did you and Jay already talk this over?"

"Yeah. Before I read the letter, I forgot to ask you."

Caroline was washing the sucking bottles when Daniel arrived. He came into the kitchen before she had dried her hands. "Good morning. You're looking much better than I expected."

"It's a very good morning." He put his hands on her waist, lifted her off the floor, and swung her around until she braced her arms on his shoulders.

She was beginning to feel dizzy and couldn't imagine what had brought on this merry spirit of his. She had never seen him smile the way he was, then the expression in his eyes changed, grew serious. He lowered her, gave her a quick tender kiss, and set her on the floor.

"Would you mind if I invite myself over tonight? Ethan will be staying with Jay."

Her heart pounded, and she tried to tell herself not to start weaving dreams now. "Can you come for supper?"

He held her close and the realization that he was unmarried struck him anew. Now the only boundaries he had to be concerned with were the ones they set. "Afterward would be better." He knew he wouldn't be able to eat a bite sitting with her, not until he had finally taken a step he had longed to take for weeks.

His breath caressed her cheek and a tingle went down her back. "All right, if that's what you want to do." His excitement was catching, but she wished she knew the reason for it.

"Would you like some coffee?"

"Can't now. Ethan's waiting for me."

"How is he doing?"

"Fine. Just fine." He kissed her once more and grinned. "I'll see you tonight."

Before she could answer, he dashed out of the front door. He had gone through there like a whirlwind, and she was reeling from it. He had been as excited as if he had won a grand prize. After last night she was glad he was feeling so very good.

She made sure she didn't have much time to think about that evening. In between caring and feeding the twins, they went for a long walk, she sewed, and when her mind started to wander, she cleaned the house.

By suppertime she had bathed, washed and dried her hair, and was so anxious she didn't want more than a few spoons of soup. The twins were hungry as usual around half past five. She changed their clothes, fed them, and put them down on their blanket to play, while she put on her forest green dress with the cream undersleeves. After she had tried different hairstyles, she gave in and tied a dark green ribbon around her hair to keep it back from her face.

Livvie and Robert fell asleep in her arms within a few minutes of each other. Even though Caroline wanted them to distract her from repeatedly glancing at the clock, she put them down in their cradles. Tucker went outside. A horse and rider went up the street. So did a buggy and a group of young boys. It was almost eight o'clock before she heard Daniel's wagon stop in front of the house.

She brushed a few specks of lint from her bodice and greeted him at the door. He had shaved and changed clothes, too. His trousers had a crease and his white shirt had been pressed, but she was glad he hadn't put on the collar or a cravat. "Hello. You look very nice. Even more handsome than usual."

He bowed and smiled at her as he took off his hat. "You're especially lovely tonight, too. I wish we were going to a dance." He wasn't feeling half as sure of himself as he had that morning. "Are Robert and Livvie still awake?" He shrugged out of his coat.

"They fell asleep a little while ago." She hung up his coat, put his hat on the shelf and walked into the parlor. "But they'll wake up later for the last feeding of the day."

He rubbed his palms on his trousers and reached out for her hand. "Caroline," he said, gently pulling her into his arms. "You feel so good." He wound a few strands of her reddish-brown hair around one finger and watched it slip off in a ringlet.

A delicious prickling sensation tickled the back of her neck. She wrapped her arms around him and snuggled closer to him. "I'm glad you wanted to come over tonight. It's been so long."

"I know, but it's so hard to be near you and not take you in my arms like this." He rested his cheek on the top of her head. "You haven't said anything about the carving on the cradle rocker. Didn't you like it?"

She leaned back. "Carving? I haven't turned the cradles over."

"When you have a chance, look under Robert's cradle." He bent his head and kissed her slowly, tasting, exploring, trying to make up for all of the times he hadn't allowed himself the pleasure. She didn't just submit to him, she matched his ardor. He drew her lower lip between his and traced it with his tongue. She murmured, and he knew there had never been a sweeter sound in all the world.

She clung to him, breathing hard, and stared at him in wonder. His eyes seemed to shimmer with an inner glow of longing. Not ever had she imagined a kiss could be so powerful. Before he had aroused her body and nourished her expectations, but this time he also seduced her mind. She lightly fingered his shirt and the firm muscles beneath. Her thoughts were all confused. It hardly made sense to offer him coffee, and she didn't believe her legs would support her much longer. "Do you mind if we sit down? You've quite taken my breath away."

He chuckled and picked her up, cradling her in his arms. "We have sat in separate chairs for months. Tonight we're going to try out the sofa." He brushed his lips over hers. "I don't want to stop touching you."

"Oh, Daniel, I don't want you to."

He sat down with her on his lap and skimmed the back of his fingers down her cheek. "I'm sure Ethan would say I should get down on one knee, but I like where I am just fine." He felt short of breath and as terrified as any man about to declare himself. "I love you, Caroline. I have for such a very long time, but I didn't have the right to tell you."

"Ohh—" She had wanted to hear those sweet words, and she prayed she had heard him correctly. "I—"

If he didn't tell her now what he had rehearsed every night for the last six weeks, he might never say it. "Let me finish. . . ." He cleared his parched throat. "Catherine, will you do me the honor of being my wife?" Good God, what had he said?

To say she was shocked couldn't begin to describe what she felt, but the horror she saw in his expression surpassed her own, and his face was almost as white as his shirt. He was as nervous as she was. She burst out laughing.

He felt as if he had been kicked in the gut, and she was laughing so hard her whole body shook. "*Caroline*, how could I have made such a mistake? I've asked you a thousand times in my mind. Never have I forgotten your name. It's branded in my soul. Please, believe me."

She pressed her forehead on his chest until she had composed herself. He wanted to marry her. "I do, Daniel." She tipped his chin down with her finger and kissed him. "I would be proud to be your wife."

"You would?" He eyed her. He didn't think she would tease him about such an important question, and he hadn't expected her to turn him down, but— She said yes . . . He smiled, inhaled deeply, and held her close.

"Very much." She snuggled on his lap and rested her head on his chest. "Who's Catherine?"

He stared at the top of her head and felt her smile. "Which one?"

She sat up grinning at him. "We're even. But if you make that mistake again, I'll not let you off so easily."

"Then I think we should spend much more time together."

"When will your work be done on the warehouse?"

"In a couple of months." He buried his hand in her long hair. "How do feel about short engagements?"

"Maggie's was only a day or two." She looked up at him. "You mentioned Ethan. What has he said about your marrying me?"

He held her tighter. "He liked the idea, but I think he was worried that I might not ask you the right way."

She chuckled. "I'm not complaining." He really wanted to marry her. She had been putting off finishing Maggie's letter until his divorce had been granted, but now she had the best news of all. "We should celebrate. How about a glass of wine?"

"Definitely."

The front door rattled. "Tucker wants in." She kissed Daniel and stood up. "I'll get the wine." After she let the cat in the house, she went to the kitchen and set out two of her best glasses. She poured a generous amount in each and carried them into the parlor.

He accepted the glass and held it up to hers. "To a lifetime together."

"At least the next eighty years." She sipped her wine. To think that the other day she had asked him if he was bored with her. "I am so happy, but I have to ask. What have you been worried about these last weeks? There were times when you had been here all of five minutes, and it seemed like you couldn't leave fast enough."

"It was the waiting for the hearing. That was the worst part. I didn't feel I had the right to offer you my love and devotion while I was still married." He held her free hand. "I thought of you so much, it was hard to keep my hands off of you when we were together."

"Thank goodness. I did my best to think of you as only a friend." She grinned at him. "But I wasn't very successful."

"I'm sorry. I didn't realize I was making it more difficult for you."

"You're forgiven." She curled up at his side. Tucker was sleeping in Daniel's chair, and the twins were showing signs of waking. They were going to be married and live together. There would be many more evenings like this. No more hoping and wondering if he would stop by. "What's your idea of a short engagement?"

"No more than a few days. What do you think? How soon can you be ready?" He couldn't stop touching her hair, her hands, her cheek.

"I have a good dress in my wardrobe. We could be married here in the parlor with Ethan."

"I'll find a preacher tomorrow." He set down his glass and took her into his arms. "I'll be a faithful husband, I swear."

She had no doubts about him, not now. "Until I loved you, I didn't believe I would ever want any man the way I want you." She set her glass near his and noticed Robert staring at him. "Look who's awake."

Daniel leaned over the cradle and held a finger out for the baby to grab.

"You can hold him. I want to see what that carving is." She put the oilcloth over Daniel's leg and handed him the baby. "I wish I'd known before. . . ." She lifted the bedding out and turned the cradle on its side. There, on the inside of the front rocker, were the words, "Crafted with love, D.G." Tears immediately blurred her vision, and she wiped them away with the corner of the baby's blanket. "Daniel, that is beautiful." She stepped around the cradle and hugged him. "Do you sign each piece of furniture?"

"I put my mark and initials on everything I make." He moved the baby over and put his arm around her. "When I made it, that was the only way I could tell you how I felt."

"I'm sorry I didn't find it." She kissed him and settled at his side. There was something she needed to ask him. "You know I want the twins to keep their father's name. Will you mind if they don't take yours?"

"Not at all. They have every right to their parentage. I won't take that from them." He looked at Robert, who was in turn watching them. "Loving them is easy. Their name won't make any difference."

"You're a very special man, Daniel Grey." She kissed him on the cheek and rested her head on his shoulder.

Daniel refilled their glasses with wine and took them into the parlor. He had the pleasure of feeding Livvie, while Caroline fed Robert and of course Tucker supervised. Daniel glanced around at his new family. Life couldn't be any better. "You're sure you won't regret having a small ceremony?" He drank some of his wine and set the glass down.

"Oh, no. I don't want all the fuss a formal wedding would bring on." Caroline put Robert to bed and joined Daniel on the sofa. When he put his arm around her with his hand resting on her shoulder, she rubbed her cheek on the back of his hand.

Slowly he ran his fingers down the length of the satin hair ribbon binding her hair and gave a gentle tug, releasing the bow. "I like your hair down." He slid the ribbon all of the way off and combed his hand through her hair. It felt the way he imagined liquid silk would feel running between his fingers. He kissed her forehead, her temple, the soft spot under her ear.

She tipped her head back and turned to him. It amazed her how his touch caused such a stir of emotions and desires within her. His mouth covered hers, and she tasted the wine as he deepened the kiss. She felt his hands on her neck, cupping one breast, and she rubbed his hand against her, wanting more than tender caresses. Her arousal was swift, though in truth he had begun seducing her before Christmas.

He pressed kisses along her jaw and down her neck, and rested his head on her shoulder. He playfully nipped at her ear. A tremor shook her and his body responded. "I want to carry you in to your bed, strip off that pretty dress, and show you how very much I adore you."

She slid her arms around his neck and smiled at him. "Why don't you?" They had waited so long already.

Her husky voice was all the encouragement he needed. He crushed her to him for one heated kiss, then scooped her up in his arms and carried her down the hall and into her room. The minute he set her on her feet, he started unbuttoning the row of buttons down the front of her dress. She quickly had his shirt open, pulled the tails free, and began working on his trousers. There was just enough light from the hallway to see her creamy soft skin when he slid the top of her dress down. He trailed kisses across the edge of her chemise as he fumbled with the satin ribbon.

She reached up to help him. "I can do that."

"I'll figure it out," he said, grinning. "I think most of women's clothes were designed to protect their purity or drive men mad."

Each brush of his lips sent a new wave of yearning fluttering down through her belly. "I've heard that half of the fun in finding a treasure is in seeking it." She felt his large hands almost circle her ribs as he pushed up her shimmy. "Mmm . . . I would have . . . to . . . ohh . . . agree." She clung to his shoulders as he peeled it away.

He slipped the soft beribboned sleeves to the chemise down her arms. It slid down to her waist. A half dozen ties later, layers of petticoats and the chemise pooled around her legs. He quickly stepped out of his trousers and drawers, and lay down on the bed with her. "You are beautiful." He loved looking at her, the feel of her skin, the way she gazed up at him with half open eyes and parted lips. He lifted her heavy breasts and buried his face in their warmth.

She moaned and arched her back and ran her hands over his smooth taut back. He enfolded her in a world of heavenly sensations, closing out the rest of the world. There were only the sounds of rapid breathing and the rustle of the comforter each time they moved, the feel of his hot skin straining against hers, and the faint scent of musk. A weakness spread through her with an overwhelming need for completion. He caressed and fondled her body with his hands, his mouth bringing her to a fever pitch. She wanted to feel his weight on her. She twisted and parted her legs, urging him to nestle there.

Each brush of her silky skin increased his desire for her. He thought he could spend hours exploring the curves and crevices of her body, but his own would not wait. He moved over her, covering her body with his, and she felt good, so damn good. She rolled her hips and drew him into her moist warmth. He knew she had filled an emptiness he hadn't realized had been there. He withdrew and entered her again, and again, prolonging the pleasure, yet seeking to satisfy their consuming need.

She trembled and felt a deep moan rise and blend with his. Merciful Heaven, she had never experienced such passion. When his chest expanded, waves of pure pleasure surged below her lower belly and spread through her limbs. She rocked her hips and met each thrust. Suddenly she was shaken with the most exquisite sensations flooding her body and mind, and she tightened her embrace.

She made love to him with a passion he had dreamed about. He was weak, and had never known such peace and fulfillment. He felt as if he could fell a stand of trees, run the length of Clackamas River, and love this woman till his dying day. He kissed her shoulder and her chin, and brushed her hair back from her face. "Are you okay?"

"You underestimate yourself. I feel unbelievably wonderful. And you?"

"Better than all of my dreams rolled into one." He moved to her side and held her close. "Eighty years won't be nearly long enough."

She giggled and kissed his chest. "Do you realize we have one problem we haven't discussed?"

He tipped his chin down and looked at her. "What's that?"

"Where will we live? Many of my ladies walk here. They wouldn't be able to get out to your house. And you need to be near your shop and your special trees."

"Mmm . . ." Thank God that's all it was, he thought. "Why don't we live at my place—our house—and you can use this one for your shop. I'll drive you here, or we can get you a buggy. Think that'll work?"

She raised herself on one elbow. "I haven't even seen your house yet. Is there room for all of us—me, the twins, and Tucker?"

"It wouldn't be home without Tucker." He grinned and kissed the tip of her nose. "We'll make room. After the ceremony, we'll go home. If you don't like it, we can make changes."

She lay down again in the circle of his arms and kissed him. "I'll like it." Heaven had smiled on them, and she had kept her promise to Addie in a way she had not known was possible. "I love you, Daniel Grey."

Dear Reader:

Caroline and Daniel's story was a pleasure to write. I hope you enjoyed their romance. When I was shopping the other day, I saw a couple pushing a double stroller with adorable twins and immediately thought of Robert and Livvie. My sons are grown now, but I have fond memories of their childhood, which may be why I have enjoyed writing Homespun stories.

This is my favorite time of year. The weather here in the northwest is turning cool, and I am looking forward to the first winter storm blowing in from the ocean. The trees bend, the windows may rattle, and the surf surges to the shore. It's a good excuse to build a nice fire and make a cup of hot cocoa.

Now I am working on a new story about two childhood friends. One is rather traditional, the other is headstrong and outspoken; together they are a force to be reckoned with. The setting is the western foothills of Mt. Hood, Oregon. I hope you will watch for my new book next year.

Sarah Wood

P.S. If you are online, please visit my homepage: http://www.tlt.com/authors/dwood.htm

ROMANCE FROM THE HEART OF AMERICA
Homespun Romance

___TOWN SOCIAL		0-515-11971-7/$5.99
	by Trana Mae Simmons	
___LADY'S CHOICE		0-515-11959-8/$5.99
	by Karen Lockwood	
___HOME TO STAY		0-515-11986-5/$5.99
	by Linda Shertzer	
___MEG'S GARDEN		0-515-12004-9/$5.99
	by Teresa Warfield	
___COUNTY FAIR		0-515-12021-9/$5.99
	by Ginny Aiken	
___HEARTBOUND		0-515-12034-0/$5.99
	by Rachelle Nelson	
___COURTING KATE		0-515-12048-0/$5.99
	by Mary Lou Rich	
___SPRING DREAMS		0-515-12068-5/$5.99
	by Lydia Browne	
___TENNESSE WALTZ		0-515-12135-5/$5.99
	by Trana Mae Simmons	
___FARM GIRL		0-515-12106-1/$5.99
	by Linda Shertzer	
___SWEET CHARITY		0-515-12134-7/$5.99
	by Rachel Wilson	
___BLACKBERRY WINTER		0-515-12146-0/$5.99
	by Sherrie Eddington	
___WINTER DREAMS		0-515-12164-9/$5.99
	by Trana Mae Simmons	
___SNOWFLAKE WISHES		0-515-12181-9/$5.99
	by Lydia Browne	
___CAROLINE'S PROMISE		0-515-12193-2/$5.99
	by Deborah Wood	

Payable in U.S. funds. No cash accepted. Postage & handling: $1.75 for one book, 75¢ for each additional. Maximum postage $5.50. Prices, postage and handling charges may change without notice. Visa, Amex, MasterCard call 1-800-788-6262, ext. 1, or fax 1-201-933-2316; refer to ad #411

Or, check above books Bill my: ☐ Visa   ☐ MasterCard   ☐ Amex _____ (expires)
and send this order form to: Card#_____
The Berkley Publishing Group
P.O. Box 12289, Dept. B   Daytime Phone #_____ ($10 minimum)
Newark, NJ 07101-5289   Signature_____
Please allow 4-6 weeks for delivery.   Or enclosed is my: ☐ check   ☐ money order
Foreign and Canadian delivery 8-12 weeks.

Ship to:

Name_____   Book Total $_____
Address_____   Applicable Sales Tax $_____
                                           (NY, NJ, PA, CA, GST Can.)
City_____   Postage & Handling $_____
State/ZIP_____   Total Amount Due $_____

Bill to: Name_____

Address_____   City_____
State/ZIP_____